Jean & Co., Unlimited

HELEN PERRY CURTIS

Jean & Co., Unlimited

10,000 Miles in Europe

ILLUSTRATIONS BY GRACE PAULL

ISBN: 978-1-950843-50-3

Parafine Press
5322 Fleet Avenue
Cleveland, Ohio 44105
www.parafinepress.com
Cover and book design by Meredith Pangrace

Dedicated to
All Jeans the world over
and especially to
the Jean nearest home

AGAINST THE SHINING SNOW, THE PROCESSION WAS A
NEVER-TO-BE-FORGOTTEN SIGHT.

(See page 198)

Contents

Preface to the Revised Edition

WHAT A DELIGHT it is to bring to new generations the story of Jean and her mother's Grand Tour of Europe.

In November, 1937, Helen Perry Curtis published *Jean & Company, Unlimited.* Favorably reviewed, and chosen as a Junior Literary Guild Selection of the Month, the first printing of 10,000 copies of *Jean & Company* quickly sold out. Many copies went directly to libraries, which had standing orders for books receiving the Junior Literary Guild designation. But some lucky young girls found a copy of their own under the tree on Christmas morning. One such girl was my mother.

Twenty-five years later, my mother handed her beloved copy of *Jean & Company, Unlimited* to me. I too eagerly followed the story of Jean's journey to Europe aboard a glamorous ocean liner. While Jean's mother travels the Continent gathering material for a book on folk costumes and customs, Jean attends a Dominican convent boarding school in the south of France. There she meets girls from all over Europe who share her name: Jeannette from France, Giovanna from Italy, Hannah from Austria, Janesika from Czechoslovakia, Jenny from Norway, and so on. The girls form a club with the businesslike name of Jean & Company, Limited. Jean subsequently, often in the company of her mother, visits her new friends in their own countries, and, as she continues to meet other Jeans, decides that the name of the club should be Jean & Company, *Unlimited.*

Jean & Company sent me on my own journey. The interest that it sparked in European history and travel led to a Ph.D., a long college teaching career, and many trips to Europe. In 2015 the adventure took another turn. Through a fortunate series of events, I located Helen Perry Curtis's granddaughters. Excited to know that someone knew of their grandmother and her book, the three invited me to come to New Jersey and meet them. That first afternoon, Martha, Pat, and Susie brought down box after box from the attic and closets, from under beds and from bookshelves. Letters, photos travel diaries, magazine articles: a wealth of material documenting a life more fascinating, more historically significant, than I had imagined. I knew that Helen's life demanded a proper biography. The result was the publication, in October of 2020, of *Helen Perry Curtis and the European Trip of a Lifetime.*

And the adventure continues. Numerous people who read Helen's biography contacted me asking how they could get a copy of *Jean & Company*, a book long out of print. The renewed interest in Helen Perry Curtis sent the price of the increasingly rare copies available on Amazon or eBay soaring, and convinced the publisher and editors at Parafine Press that a reprint of *Jean & Company* was in order.

Although Helen Perry Curtis published *Jean & Company, Unlimited* at the midpoint of her long life, I came to see the book as the culmination of her life's interest and work. In writing *Jean,* Helen drew on a lifelong fascination with folk costume and culture first encountered in the immigrant communities of her native Nebraska, fostered in her work at a settlement house in an industrializing New Jersey, and developed in the course of her career as a museum curator and director in Newark and Trenton. Helen's interest in European handicrafts was shaped by her education in the art and design program at Columbia Teachers College, where she was introduced to the international Arts and Crafts movement. Helen incorporated into *Jean & Company* experiences from her initial European trip, taken in company with *her* mother, on the eve of World War I. And the beautifully rendered descriptions of European cities and countryside are the work of a woman who honed her craft over two decades of freelance writing for magazines throughout the 1920s and the 1930s.

Now *Jean & Company* is available to a new audience: whether the young adult readers for whom it was first intended or older readers discovering— or revisiting—the charming story of an American girl's first encounter with Europe. For all readers, the underlying message is a timeless one. Not only is *Jean & Company* an affirming story of the bond between mothers and daughters, but, in the words of the long-ago *New York Times* book reviewer, "a tempting invitation to travel which stresses the most essential of travelers' requirements: good-will and a readiness for experience."

In the end, Helen Perry Curtis created in *Jean & Company, Unlimited* a story that has outlived the lives of its protagonists and characters. Ninety years after Helen's trips to Europe with her daughters, we enter again, through the pages of a book, a world in which Jean is forever a young girl, standing beside her mother in the bow of the ocean liner, turning her face "towards the palm-shaded shore which was Cannes," and exclaiming with joy: 'O Mother, here comes our adventure!'"

I hope you enjoy the journey.

—Laura Gellott
September, 2021

Foreword

SUSIE WAS BOTH surprised and delighted one cold winter's day in January, 2015, to receive a letter from a complete stranger, asking if she'd be willing to share any information about her beloved grandmother, who had passed away thirty-five years earlier. A quick phone call to her cousins in New Jersey started the ball rolling.

That unexpected request resulted in five years of the three of us, Susie, Pat, and Martha, helping Laura Gellott research our grandmother's life from a treasure trove of family photographs, letters, travel journals, and diaries from our ancestors that had been saved through the generations. As the icing on the cake, we've also been blessed with a very special friendship with Laura, who wove the life story of our grandmother from the family archives along with her own original research. We are so thrilled with Laura's book, and grateful that she has honored our grandmother's life with such an insightful and understanding narrative of who she was, and the full life she lived.

Laura's book has rekindled an interest in *Jean & Company, Unlimited,* which, written by our grandmother and published in 1937, propelled Laura into her lifelong love of European history, and her career as a college professor.

With so few copies of *Jean & Company* currently available, the time has come for this reprint. It is sure to delight readers, as they discover the Europe our grandmother and her Jean discovered nearly ninety years ago, and which led Laura to her own "European trip of a lifetime."

Happy reading!
— *Margery (Susie) Fauteux and Pat and Martha Wells, Helen Perry Curtis's granddaughters*

NOTE ON THE REVISED EDITION

CERTAIN WORDS and phrases commonly accepted in 1937 are considered offensive by modern readers. With the permission of Helen Perry Curtis's descendants, this manuscript has been lightly edited in a few places to remove anachronistic language.

The Book that Wrote Itself

THIS BOOK was never really written. It wrote itself. Jean made a journey, and for her Europe suddenly came to life. Together she and her mother visited every country mentioned in this book, with the exception of Iceland. Only Jean's father saw that, but by the time he had finished the telling, the others felt that they had been there, too.

All the people in the book are real people. Little Sister Irmengarde still unlocks the convent gates with her giant keys. Jenny's doctor-grandfather annually visits the hospitals for fishermen along the bleak Norwegian coast. Tante Hildegarde, under a different name, of course, continues to model exquisite little figures for a multitude of Christmas crèches, and Jeffrey, believe it or not, still hopefully looks forward to finding America practically filled with buffaloes and Indians. Even Jani, who frightened the girls into arming themselves against burglars with a pair of brass candlesticks, was a real dog.

Jean actually attended a convent in southern France where she met girls from all over Europe, whom she later visited. She spent weekends in the villa in Provence and lived for two months in a tiny Venetian palace overhanging a canal. She studied dancing at the Duncan School in Salzburg, visited a Lapp village at the top of the world, and fed the stately swans on the river Thames. The climb to the crow's nest really happened, and so, alack and alas, did the measles.

It was Jean who made the book, because she lived it. Her mother merely jotted it down from time to time. The *American Girl*, a girls' magazine in America, asked for the jottings and published them and to this magazine Jean's mother makes grateful acknowledgment. After a while there were enough of them to make a book, but they were still separate stories. So Jean's mother started at the beginning and told how they came to plan the trip and what happened to them on the way over. She added connecting links to make the separate stories into consecutive chapters. By this time Jean had "discovered" America, and that made another chapter.

Now that it is finished, it is not a proper book at all, written respectably at a desk with dictionary, atlas, and grammar close at hand and a deep and logical plot to lure the reader on. It is the simple chronicle of Jean's journey, written down here, there, and everywhere, gathered into a single packet, and placed with affection between two book covers–a journey come to life!

—Helen Perry Curtis
November, 1937

CHAPTER 1:
SHIP AHOY!

Jean sat disconsolately on her steamer trunk, elbows on her knees and chin in her hands. From one end of the trunk hung a red sweater sleeve and two pink ribbons, and from the other hung the blue taffeta ruffles of her new evening dress. She was exhausted after a brave but hopeless struggle. First she had knelt on the trunk from behind, trying to poke in the ruffles and ribbons and leap upon the lock before they could pop out again. Next she had attacked it from the front, carefully tucking in, as she thought, all the unruly odds and ends, and then turning suddenly to sit down hard on the edge of the lid and pull the clasps shut.

Finally, after removing two pairs of shoes and a half-dozen tennis balls and jumping on the top with both feet, it had closed at last and she had turned the key triumphantly in the lock—only to find the aforesaid ribbons and ruffles still exposed. Now, limp and exhausted, she had collapsed in a disconsolate heap on the impossible trunk, and was wondering if it was really worth the effort, after all.

Going to Europe made life so difficult. For days she and her mother and old Lucinda had been rolling up rugs with moth balls, covering the chairs with slip covers, taking down curtains, putting away silver. All around her in the twilight were suitcases, hat boxes, umbrellas, cameras, odds and ends of absolutely unpackable sizes and shapes. Jean groaned as her eye fell on her tennis racket, riding boots, and skates. She couldn't possibly get them in, but she wouldn't leave them behind for anything.

It was a little late now for regrets. After all, she had decided herself that she wanted to go to Europe for a whole adventurous year with her mother. She might have gone to boarding school in Connecticut, spending weekends and holidays with her grandmother. She might have lived with her aunt in Virginia and gone to high school. But she and her mother had been talking about this trip for months, and even this morning Jean had been thrilled about it. Her father had already gone to Russia as an engineering expert, to be there one or possibly two years, and Russia was dreadfully far away from America.

Her mother, who had always been interested in European folklore, had decided this was a good time to travel and collect material for the book she was writing. And while her mother was studying folk music and folk costume, Jean would go to an enchanting school in southern France, a convent kept by Dominican sisters. Her mother had told her all about it. She herself, although not a Roman Catholic, had attended this school many years ago. Besides that, she had traveled and lived in Europe for some time as a young girl and had many friends there. Jean had often heard her speak of rosy-cheeked baby Jan and his mother in Holland, of Tante Hildegarde in Germany, of Madame Cekic and the little daughter whom she had never seen, but who was just Jean's age. Her name was Jovanka, and she lived in faraway Zagreb, which Jean's mother had pointed out to her on a queer, outlandish part of the map. Wouldn't it be fun if she could come to know all these exciting people, too? She might even learn to speak their languages. Her mother knew French and German and a little Italian, so why shouldn't she?

Already she was looking forward to living in a great convent dormitory with dozens of other girls, to reading in the walled garden where white-robed sisters walked, to playing tennis and riding horseback all winter long in the warm sunshine, and to bathing on the sandy shores of the Mediterranean. It was here that she would learn French and German. She would make friends not only among French girls but among girls from other countries as well. Her mother had told her that to this school came girls of all nationalities. She had imagined so many things that might happen. For some week ends she would be invited to visit her new friends. She could spend her longer holidays traveling with her mother, and perhaps sometimes her father could join them. It had seemed just too good to be true!

But now at the end of a long day of putting away familiar treasures which she must leave behind, of saying goodbye to intimate friends, especially Peggy and Betsy Jane, of trying to make lumpy objects fit into flat trunks and suitcases, she wondered wearily if it was worth the backache and heartache. Sitting there on her trunk in the deepening twilight with the rain beating dismally against the windowpane, she was afraid she was making a terrible mistake. Wouldn't her friends forget her? Wouldn't she have to drop back a grade in school when she came home again? Wouldn't she find foreign girls very queer and very different? Wouldn't she die of homesickness if she couldn't spend Christmas with Grandmother?

She was so miserable that she didn't hear the door open. Suddenly she was struck amidships by a small, yapping catapult, a white, woolly whirlwind that almost knocked her off the trunk, dashed about dragging her new traveling dress by the belt, overturned hat boxes, scattered umbrella and tennis balls, and finally sat down in a far corner to chew rapturously at a riding boot. Jean chased the dodging puppy, rescued her beloved frock, stumbled over her best hat, and sat down flushed and breathless in an open suitcase.

"Napoleon," she gasped, "Napoleon Bonaparte Jones, you ought to be ashamed of yourself. Just wait till I catch you!"

She heard a low chuckle and there was John in the doorway, his hands in his pockets, his red hair standing up on end, and his freckled face one enormous grin.

"Such undignified conduct on the part of a lady grieves and surprises me," he said with sudden solemnity. "Allow me to assist Madame," and he politely pulled her out of the suitcase, straightened the feather on her somewhat battered hat, and rescued her boot from Napoleon, who immediately sat up on his hind legs and begged for something else to chew.

"O John!" wailed Jean, "I'm so glad you've come. I'm so homesick already I don't know what to do," and she sank down again on her steamer trunk.

"Seems to me you're acting as if you were sick of home, going off like this to heathen lands. Better watch out for cannibals! You'd make a nice fat, juicy steak for somebody."

"Silly," laughed Jean. "I'm going to countries so civilized that they will make America look positively primitive. I am going," she declaimed with oratorical gestures, "to see cathedrals five hundred years old, Roman ruins twenty-five hundred years old, skeletons of prehistoric man millions of years old, and— and— But I don't want to go the least bit," she wailed. "I want to stay at home!" And much to John's embarrassment down went her head on her arms, and her shoulders began to heave suspiciously.

"Oh, I say, Jean, I'll—," and John looked around for something to comfort her. There was Napoleon standing on his hind legs right in front of them now, with his bright beady little eyes looking from one to the other. John swallowed hard. "I'll give you Napoleon to take along, if that will make you feel any better." Then cheerfully, "Did I ever tell you why I called him Napoleon? Because he's so good at pulling a bone apart!"

Jean struggled bravely with herself and finally managed to smile through her tears. "A nice, restful companion he'd make! He'd probably bite the captain and chew up the life preservers and fight all the dogs in France. Wouldn't you, Napoleon?" and she gave the puppy a hug. "But you're nice to think of it," she added softly to John.

John changed the subject suddenly. "I say, where do you put all these tennis rackets and whatnots? Carry them in your vest pocket, I suppose!"

"I wish I knew," groaned Jean. "I can't even get my trunk shut, and just look at all the things that are left out." She waved her hands dramatically at the surrounding confusion and looked as if she might burst into tears again.

John rolled up his sleeves and felt of his muscle, bending his arms experimentally at the elbows. "Come on, I'll help you get your stuff packed," he said. "The Augean stables had nothing on this. Observe the mighty Hercules at work!"

It seemed no time at all until the trunks and suitcases were closed and all the lumpy odds and ends packed into a convenient wicker hamper that Jean had forgotten about, just made for the things that wouldn't fit anywhere else.

Before Jean could thank him, John was whistling to Napoleon. "Hi, Napoleon, we must think of our beauty sleep. Don't forget we've got to get up early to see that this weeping willow doesn't swamp the boat tomorrow morning. So long!" and he was gone.

Jean giggled. Then she looked around proudly at all the neatly piled baggage. Strange how much better she felt. Going to Europe wasn't so bad after all.

When her mother came in a few minutes later, she found Jean dancing gayly around the room, with a golf bag for a partner, singing, "Then blow ye winds, heigh-ho! A-roving I will go!" She dropped the golf bag and, clutching her mother, wet mackintosh, umbrella, and all, whirled her about dizzily. "I'm off for the morning train!" she sang at the top of her lungs. "I'll cross the raging main! I'm off to my love with a boxing glove, ten thousand miles away!"

They both dropped breathless onto the wicker hamper. "Mums, will it really be ten thousand miles? I do hope so. Half an hour ago I didn't want to stir a step. Now I just can't wait to say 'Bonjour' to the maharaja of Timbuktu!"

Jean could remember nothing about the next morning except a dreadful confusion of baggage, taxis, porters, passports, tickets, gangplanks, tearful relations, ship's officers in uniform, and a great many people rushing distractedly in every direction. With her arms full of last-minute bundles, she squeezed through the crowd behind her mother and finally landed in the stateroom, which was heaped with even more baggage, bundles, books, boxes of flowers, and baskets of fruit.

"Queer, they all begin with b's," thought Jean, her mind going around and around in a confused circle. "Baggage, bundles, baskets, books, boxes." In a daze of excitement she pounced upon the first box that came to hand, a small, square, silver one tied with a blue ribbon. With a squeal of joy she lifted out a tiny, old-fashioned bouquet, a rose in the middle and forget-me-nots and violets around the edge, all set in a lace-paper frill. Underneath was a much chewed bone and attached to it by a wide, red ribbon a card, "Goodbye from N. B."

"O Mums," cried Jean, "I haven't seen John and Napoleon, and they said they were coming to the boat."

Off she dashed through long corridors, bumping into hurrying people on the stairs, squeezing through the milling crowd until she finally came out on the upper deck. Already, the great, white ship was moving. Streamers of colored paper and clouds of confetti were floating through the air, and the band was playing.

Upturned faces on the pier were shouting unintelligible farewells, and people on deck were shouting them back again through cupped hands. Some were laughing; others were crying. But all through the waving and laughing and weeping and general confusion Jean's eyes searched for John and Napoleon. Perhaps they hadn't come after all or perhaps she had missed them in the crowd on the pier, and her heart sank.

But what was that! Away out at the end of the dock on the highest wooden pile was a bouncing, barking ball. It was Napoleon Bonaparte himself. Beside him, holding on to the dog with one hand and throwing up his cap with the other, was John. Jean almost fell overboard in her excitement, waving the bone and the bouquet both at once.

"Look out for cannibals!" shouted John.

"Yap, yap," barked Napoleon. And until they were out in the middle of the Hudson River, Jean could see John's red hair and the white ball that was Napoleon Bonaparte.

"If they are truly patriotic," thought Jean, "perhaps they are just a little bit blue over my leaving. Three cheers for the red, white, and blue!"

She looked up to find her mother beside her, and together they watched the noisy tugs chugging importantly about, pushing and pulling the big boat till it headed straight out toward the great Atlantic and Europe beyond. All around them were other boats. A slim, gray one bound for Bermuda, a squat, red one sunk almost to the water line under her load of coal, a long string of yellow sand barges, here and there a pert little motor boat, and one tiny sailboat dainty as

AWAY OUT ON THE END OF THE DOCK WERE
NAPOLEON BONAPARTE AND JOHN

a butterfly. They passed Battery Park with its green carpet and the round-roofed Aquarium. They passed Ellis Island, the Statue of Liberty, Fort Wadsworth, and away off in the distance, Coney Island. And then they were on the broad Atlantic.

Jean pinched herself to see if she were really awake. She suddenly felt as if she were sailing straight into a story-book. Here she was on an ocean liner, next best thing to a magic carpet, headed for who-knew-what adventures among lands and people she had only read about. She was sure, too, that there would be illustrations on every page, story-book children in vivid costumes, quaint thatched cottages, castles on hilltops, snowy mountain peaks, and unbelievable color. Almost anything might happen before she came home again, even meeting cannibals. She giggled at the thought.

And now there was a tremendous din behind her. "The lunch bell," said her mother, as a waiter went by banging a great gong.

Jean suddenly realized that she had been much too excited to eat any breakfast. But when she got down to the dining room, it was so hard to choose what to eat. It gave her the fidgets to have the efficient waiter standing ready with his pencil while she read down the menu which seemed a yard long, and up again and down again. Near her was a huge table loaded with dozens of delicacies, turkey in aspic, hams dressed up with cloves and celery, great trays of appetizers, spun-glass baskets full of little cakes, architectural puddings, bouquets of ices. Going around the dining room was one waiter wheeling a tableful of steaming hot dishes, and another who made paper-thin pancakes while you watched, deftly rolling them up with jelly inside and dropping them on your plate. "Crêpes Suzettes," whispered her mother.

Jean thought and puzzled and frowned, put her head on this side and then on that, and finally in a very matter-of-fact voice ordered roast beef, mashed potato, and vanilla ice cream.

"What a girl," laughed her mother, as she herself ordered all kinds of things with unpronounceable names.

"But I have two weeks to make up my mind about the other things," said Jean, "and I think I'd rather stay American for one meal."

It was fun now to be able to look around quietly at the other people, all of whom were busily eating. She and her mother made a game of guessing who the other passengers were. There was a beautiful pale blonde in tight black satin who must be a movie star. There was a plump, black-haired matron who was undoubtedly an opera singer, and that was obviously her manager with the smartly trimmed goatee. There was a cheerful family of five assorted children, a sweet, young bride with her handsome and devoted husband, and a spinster schoolteacher with a long, sharp nose and tortoise-shell rimmed spectacles. There was, too, a very fat man with a big mustache, "Just like a walrus," murmured Jean, and "Oh, joy!" the jolliest-looking boy and girl about her own age. Jean almost bumped into them as they went out of the dining room, and they smiled shyly at each other.

"How can we make friends with them, Mums?" whispered Jean. "They look awfully nice."

"That's easy," said her mother. Turning to them with her friendliest smile, she asked, "How would you like to play a game of deck tennis this afternoon?" and it was done.

Jean loved deck tennis, a game which was played by tossing a rope ring over a high net. During the game she found out that Paul and Polly were twins on their way over to meet their father and mother who were already in Switzerland. They were traveling alone in the Captain's care (he was a friend of their father), and they thought it a glorious adventure.

"We sit at the Captain's table," said Paul.

"We are going to stay up late for the concert and costume ball and everything," added Polly.

In less than half an hour they were fast friends, and Jean's mother, smiling contentedly, knew now that she would have plenty of time to herself to sit in a steamer chair and read and rest. With Polly and Paul, Jean explored the ship. They found the gymnasium and swung on the rings and rode the electric horses. They discovered the swimming pool and nothing would do but that they should take a dip immediately.

"Why, it's salt water!" called Jean, as she came up gurgling and choking after her first dive. "And look at the waves!"

Sure enough, as the big boat dipped and rolled on its way, the water swept to one side of the pool and back, making an exciting, big wave to ride on. The pool was lined with blue tile and was clear and cool, and the tile floors all about it were slippery with splashed water. One could sit on the edge and slide in.

"I suppose we'll just about live down here," said Paul.

"I'll say we will," echoed Polly.

When they came up on deck, they saw all the steamer chairs stretched out in long rows, with hundreds of people bundled up in steamer rugs sitting in them. Some of the passengers were reading, some were watching the horizon rise and fall beyond the ship's rail. The bride and groom were openly holding hands. The spinster, her spectacles halfway down her nose, was sleeping peacefully, and the "Walrus" was snoring with his mouth wide open, his stomach heaving up and down. Paul and Polly and Jean nudged each other and dashed around the nearest corner to laugh. They almost ran into the deck steward, who was wheeling out a table with a great samovar of tea and a lower shelf full of sandwiches and little cakes.

"Oo-oo," cried all three and followed him until he had stopped. "No tea, thanks, but may we please have some sandwiches and cakes?"

With their hands full they clambered up the steep stairs to the upper deck and settled themselves comfortably in a lifeboat to eat at their leisure.

"Wouldn't it be exciting if we really had to use these boats!" exclaimed Jean. "I've tried on my life belt already, and it fits beautifully and is very becoming. I think a wreck would be thrilling."

"My father was in a wreck once," said Paul.

"So was Mother," said Polly.

Jean tried in vain to think quickly of some near relative who had gained dangerous distinction. "Well, anyway," she mumbled at last through a sandwich, "my favorite uncle was in a plane crash, and that makes us even."

A steward came along looking for Polly and Paul. "The Captain wants to take you down to the engine room. Would the other young lady like to come, too?"

Off they went, first to the bridge where the Captain showed them all his maps and instruments, and then down, down, down queer, steep stairs into the throbbing heart of the great ship. Shiny brass pistons as big as cannons pushed backward and forward; great wheels revolved. The noise was deafening, and there was a strong smell of oil and grease. The girls held tightly to each other and backed away as far as possible from the terrifying machine, but the Captain took Paul down a ladder into the midst of the engine room.

From there they visited the kitchen, and the Captain obligingly turned his back and talked to the head steward while the white-capped chef, with a sly wink, passed his guests some sticky little cakes, which they took at a single gulp, and were innocently examining a saucepan when the Captain turned around again. "No musta feed ze passengair," whispered the chef to Jean, confidentially, with another wink and a shrug.

When Jean and her mother went to their staterooms to dress for dinner, there was a note asking if they would honor the Captain by sitting at his table during the voyage.

"Whoopee!" squealed Jean. "Now won't we have fun. He's fat and jolly, and has crossed the ocean three hundred and twenty-seven times, and he tells the best stories. And he speaks English, too, even though he's captain of an Italian boat!"

Her mother laughed, "Silly! Of course he speaks English, and probably French and German, and possibly Spanish and Portuguese and Greek. Every captain who sails the seas must speak the languages of the ports where he touches."

"I'm going to ask him right away how many languages he speaks," cried Jean. "And then I'm going to try and learn just as many. A little competition is all I need," and she turned a back somersault on the bunk, almost wrecking the stateroom with her long legs.

"Will you never grow up!" groaned her mother. "Hurry and get ready for dinner. If we are going to sit at the Captain's table, we must put on our prettiest frocks so he'll be proud of us."

Jean sat between Polly and Paul. The head steward told them the best things to order, and the Captain lit his pipe when the coffee came and spun delightful yarns about his first trip on a sailing vessel when he was twelve years old.

That day was only the beginning of all the fun. There were games every morning and movies in the afternoon. There was a daily Punch and Judy show at which they almost burst their sides laughing, and horse racing with tiny wooden horses in the salon after dinner. There were ridiculous sporting contests on deck, three-legged races, jousting matches on a spar above a canvas tank of water, pushing a penny down a board with one's nose. There were deck tennis and shuffleboard tournaments, and a concert with all sorts of professional and amateur talent atrociously punctuated by the foghorn. Best of all there was a costume ball with balloons and confetti and bright colored streamers, and absurd prizes for the best costume. Paul and Polly won a rubber loving cup as the Siamese twins, dressed up together in the Walrus' swallow-tailed coat and two top hats which they borrowed. Jean was a quaintly picturesque figure in a Kate Greenaway frock and poke bonnet. Her old-fashioned bouquet from Napoleon Bonaparte was still fresh enough to carry, and she did a much practiced minuet with the Captain.

The last day but one, as the Captain was having his after-dinner pipe, Paul and Polly both nudged Jean. "You ask him," they whispered.

The boat had been doing very strange things for the last two or three hours, not dipping steadily on her way with an occasional roll as usual, but with considerable sidestepping and pitching and tossing in between.

"You ask him," whispered Paul again.

"Yes, you ask him," echoed Polly on the other side.

Jean started bravely. "There is just one thing we haven't done, Captain, that we're dying to do."

"What's that?" asked the Captain.

"We'd like to climb to the crow's nest."

Just at this moment, a porthole flew open with a bang, and there were surprised shrieks and much jumping on the part of the family with five children, as a great green wave splashed over them. The stewards rushed forward and fastened the porthole shut again while the children shook themselves like puppy dogs and dashed out of the dining room.

The Captain tried to look very grave, but his eyes twinkled. "Getting rougher," he said. "I hope you are all good sailors." He thought a moment. "I will tell you! Usually it is against ship's rules to allow passengers to climb to the crow's nest, but the Captain may make exceptions. If any one of you weathers this storm without missing a meal, we will break all rules and take the winner up!"

The ship rolled and lurched as they ran up the stairs, and the three supported themselves by walking arm in arm, as the deck rose and fell beneath them. They tried to play shuffleboard, but the deck had a way of tipping up unexpectedly and sliding the blocks around. Suddenly Polly turned pale green, leaned a minute against a cabin, and then disappeared hurriedly.

"One down," laughed Paul. "Let's walk fast around the deck. That will keep us feeling fine."

They started walking briskly, stumbling and laughing as the floor left them unexpectedly or came up and hit their feet. There were canvases along the rails now, and once in a while fine spray hit their faces. There was almost no one on deck and only an occasional steamer chair was occupied. The movie actress had a tray on her knees which slid off with a crash, and a steward hurried to pick up the pieces. The Walrus was slightly green. The schoolteacher lay with closed eyes and an expression of acute despair on her face. The opera singer, supported by her manager on one side, clutched the banister rail and staggered down the stairs.

"We are lost, the Captain shouted, as he staggered down the stairs," quoted Paul oratorically. Suddenly he made a dash for the rail and hung over it limply. Jean fled.

"If I keep out in the air, I'll be all right," she decided, and stood in the pitching bow, where the cold, salt spray stung her cheeks. Presently she too began to feel very queer. She hurried back, groped along the wall, felt her way with her eyes shut, and sank into the first steamer chair.

"Oh, dear," she thought, "I do hope I am not sitting in anyone's lap, but I just can't go a step farther."

Whenever she opened her eyes, the horizon rose and fell sickeningly, so she kept them shut. "I mustn't be sick," she murmured. "I must climb the crow's nest."

She was cold and wanted the steamer rug over her, but could she possibly reach that far? Cautiously she lifted one hand but dropped it, exhausted. If she moved, she would be overcome, she knew. Very slowly, slowly, she slid down into the chair until she could reach the rug without moving her hand. "Crow's nest," she moaned, "must—climb—crow's nest." Inch by inch and after what seemed like hours, she finally pulled the steamer rug about her. She fell into a half stupor. Even to open her eyes was the greatest possible effort, and there was the dreadful horizon heaving up and down. She remembered faintly the story of the seasick man who was first afraid that he would die and then afraid he wouldn't. The ship lurched and quivered and leaped from the top of one mountainous wave to the top of the next, then sank sickeningly down and down into a deep valley of water. Jean heard her mother's voice in her ear and waved her feebly away. "Crow's nest," she murmured.

After what might have been hours or days she slowly revived. She felt the cold wind blowing in her face and began vaguely to realize that the ship was no longer pitching and tossing, but rolling gently in quiet waters. She opened one eye painstakingly. The horizon was moving, to be sure, but much more sedately. She felt herself carefully. Yes, she was all there. What was it she had just been thinking? Oh, yes, the crow's nest. She sat up and looked around. There was her mother smiling in the next chair.

"Well, young lady, how goes it?" she asked.

Jean hesitated, opened her eyes wide, slid carefully out of her chair, stood up and stretched. "Fine! Wait until I tell the Captain." Off she went, a little unsteadily at first, stopping a minute to brace herself at the rail and then clambering up the ladder to the bridge. Her mother smiled understandingly.

At dinner that night the Captain asked, "Where's Polly?"

"She didn't feel very well," answered Paul. "And I'm not a bit hungry myself, either. Guess I'll go up on deck!"

The Captain leaned over and patted Jean on the back. "You win the crow's nest," he laughed. "Meet me on the bridge at ten o'clock tomorrow morning!"

At ten o'clock Jean was there, Paul and Polly looking on rather forlornly as the Captain fastened a rope beneath Jean's arms and explained to her how to climb the rope ladder. Down she went with one of the sailors to the deck below. She had put on her slacks so that her skirts might not catch in the rigging. One sailor went up ahead of her holding the rope, and one behind her lest she fall. It was the proudest moment of her life as she stood beside the lookout in the crow's nest. All about her was the limitless ocean. Beneath her the great ship swung from side to side.

She threw her arms wide to the wind and breathed the tangy, salty air. "Now I know why my ancestors

all went to sea," she shouted to the lookout, the wind almost blowing the words back into her throat. She stood there a long time watching the gulls as they followed the ship, the shining wake of foam, the dolphins leaping through the sparkling waves away off at one side. Once the lookout pointed to the long, green, undulating body of a shark, swimming beside the bow. Jean shivered a little.

Suddenly on the horizon appeared a speck. The lookout handed her a telescope. There, framed in the circle of the glass, was the most beautiful ship Jean had ever seen, a great, square-rigged vessel, all sails set.

"That's like me," she thought. "She's bound for faraway ports, and who knows what treasure will be in her hold when she comes back again? Perhaps sandalwood, ivory, cloth of gold, and—and—" But she couldn't think of anything else poetic enough. "My ship will be full of friends and languages and Roman ruins." She giggled a little at the thought of Roman ruins in her hold. Where was her hold, anyway?

Here the lookout interrupted her and pointed in the other direction. "Land," he shouted, and Jean felt as if she were sailing with Christopher Columbus. She leveled her glass again and saw a slender lighthouse, a distant walled town on a hillside, and boats in a faraway harbor.

She leaned out of the crow's nest toward the bridge and waved to the Captain. "Land!" she shouted. "Land!" as if she herself had discovered it.

When she had clambered down again, Paul and Polly and the Captain gathered eagerly around her. "Can't they go up, too?" asked Jean, her hand on the Captain's sleeve.

"What was it like?" asked Paul.

"Did the ship rock much?" asked Polly.

"Oh, it swung just like a hammock beneath me," cried Jean enthusiastically. "It was marvelous, swinging and swaying with nothing around me but the sea and the sky."

"Do you still want to go up, you two?" asked the Captain, with a twinkle in his eye.

"Perhaps we had better pack now," said Paul hastily.

"I think so too," echoed Polly, disappearing in his wake.

The Captain slapped Jean on the back. "Well, shipmate, when do we have our next voyage together? These landlubbers are all right in fair weather," winking after the departing twins, "but you are a real hurricane sailor!"

Jean dashed off to find her mother, who was just closing up the trunks, and it seemed no time at all until they were bobbing away on a little boat toward land, Jean standing stiffly in the bow and saluting the Captain on the bridge.

Then she turned her face toward the palm-shaded shore which was Cannes, with shining white houses climbing up a green hill and purple mountains in the distance.

"O Mother," she cried. "Here comes our adventure!"

CHAPTER 2:

THE CONVENT

It was a difficult moment for Jean when her mother finally left her in the outer courtyard, with little Sister Irmengarde waiting to take her in charge. Somehow Jean hadn't thought about this part of it before. She had talked for months about going to the convent in France, and now, at last, she was there. From the moment she had first seen the gray pile of buildings against the green hillside of Provence, she had wished the car might go faster, so that she could get there sooner. And she had immediately liked the grave and stately Mother Superior who welcomed them so graciously.

But there was her mother disappearing through the iron gate, and she was being left behind. Tears sprang to her eyes. She brushed them hastily away, hoping that Sister Irmengarde hadn't seen. After all, she was fourteen years old and perfectly able to take care of herself. Even if she did like to turn cartwheels and stand on her head sometimes, she realized that she was no longer young. The gate clanged shut, and her mother stopped for a moment to look back through the vine-covered iron grill of the outer garden.

"I'll be here again on Tuesday," she called out encouragingly.

Jean swallowed an enormous lump in her throat as she waved goodbye then she turned resolutely toward the convent again. Sister Irmengarde was dressed in the long, white robe and black cape of the Dominican nuns. A starched white hood framed her rosy face, and a black veil covered her head. She was so tiny that Jean seemed to tower above her. At her belt she carried a bunch of keys, such keys as Jean had never seen, great, clanking ones seven or eight inches long. She wondered why anyone so small should be made mistress of the gates of this citadel that was the convent. She couldn't help thinking that perhaps it was the weight of the keys that for so many years had pulled her down and made her so little.

Sister Irmengarde first unlocked the outer door and let Jean into a cool, damp hallway, bare of all furniture save one hard bench, where mothers sometimes waited for their daughters. She locked the door again behind her, leaning for a moment with her back against it. Then she unlocked another door, and they came out into the sunshine of the inner garden. This door she also fastened behind her.

On one side the garden was enclosed by the convent building, mossy and old, on the other by a high plaster wall covered with heliotrope and climbing roses. Stone benches stood under ancient trees, and the shadows were black and cool and moist in contrast to the hot, golden sunlight that poured through every opening in the leaves.

In the far end of the garden Jean caught glimpses of other nuns. From the back they looked all black, with their long capes flowing around them. But when they turned toward her, she saw the folds of white which framed their faces and caught a glimpse of the white of their under-robes. They all seemed beautiful to Jean, beautiful and serene as angels, as they lifted their downcast eyes to smile at her as she passed. Other women passed to and fro also, in plain black, badly fitting dresses, their hair arranged in high pompadours. They were the teachers, Sister Irmengarde explained, and Jean did not think them beautiful at all.

Was it the simple, flowing robes that made the nuns seem so gracious and serene, or was it some deep, inner beauty shining in their quiet eyes? Jean did not know, but she wished that sometime she might have eyes like that. It was not until she knew the nuns much better that she realized they were just like other people, after all—some plump and pleasant, some thin and crotchety, some gentle and wise. The one she finally grew to like best of all was a peppery little sister who scolded the girls until they wept, but later slipped cakes of chocolate into their pinafore pockets and saw to it that they had extra tidbits for lunch.

As they passed a little chapel, they heard children's voices murmuring the service. The sounds came out in meaningless waves, soft rhythms of warm, childish voices. As they crossed the open courtyard in the brilliant sunshine, Jean saw the tennis and basketball field below and the market garden stretching off down the hill, with its borders of fruit trees and berry bushes. They met a troop of little tots in blue and white checked pinafores coming out of a classroom, two by two, children who looked curiously at Jean in her dainty dress, whispering in soft French and ducking their heads shyly as they passed her.

Sister Irmengarde led her through a cool archway into a great auditorium and gymnasium. Here Jean saw a stage, with some older girls busily at work on a setting. Sister Irmengarde introduced her, and they all began to chatter in French. Jean understood a little of what they said, but it sounded quite different from the French she had learned so painfully at school in America. The words were there, but the way they pronounced them made it seem like another language. Would she ever be able to speak it like that?

Back in the cool hallway again, they climbed a long flight of steep, stone stairs, coming suddenly into the dazzling sunlight of a great dormitory as big as the gymnasium beneath it. Here were two long rows of iron beds, set head to head down the center of the room, each with a chest of drawers and a chair beside it.

"Pour les chères petites," said Sister Irmengarde.

But she led Jean to one of the larger beds in a row of curtained alcoves along the side of the dormitory. By drawing the curtains on both sides and at the foot of the bed, Jean could shut off a diminutive room, with its own bureau and chair. At the far end of the dormitory was a row of basins and alcoves for shower baths. About as much privacy as a goldfish, thought Jean. But she was to learn that modesty was one of the cardinal virtues in the convent, and that even the babies undressed inside their night-gowns.

Meanwhile Sister Irmengarde laid out her uniform, a simple, blue serge dress with a pleated skirt, long sleeves, a white collar and cuffs, a blue jacket, and a beret. There was a black pinafore that buttoned in the back, to wear over it during school hours. Jean sighed a little as she took off her dainty, flowered dimity with the short puff sleeves and her straw hat with the smart feather on it, wondering whimsically, as she watched Sister Irmengarde take them away, whether she would ever see them again. So many doors had been unlocked before her and locked again behind her; there were such thick, stone walls and high, iron gates about her that she had a queer feeling she might be there for the rest of her life.

By the time she was dressed, Sister Irmengarde came back again with a girl about her own age. "Jean, voilà Jeannette," she said and left them.

"Bonjour, Jean. Shall we go to, how-you-say déjeuner, lunch?" Jeannette spoke English with a soft, musical accent.

She took Jean down to the big, basement lunch room, smiling and speaking a comical jargon of French and English that Jean understood much better than Sister Irmengarde's precise French. There each girl had her own knife, fork, spoon, and napkin in a little bag, and each stood in line, behind her own chair, at a long refectory table, until a sister gave the signal to sit down. Aside from the scraping of the chairs and the clattering of the dishes, there was not a sound. Jean started to speak, but Jeannette nudged her and put her finger to her lips.

The soup was full of lentils and bits of floating sausage. Jean tasted it experimentally and decided she liked it. She liked, too, the thick, slanting slices of bread from the long French loaf and the crisp, green salad. It was rather fun trying out all these new kinds of food, but how dreadful not to be able to say a word!

"Pour les Chères Petites," said Sister Irmengarde.

How would she ever learn to speak French, if she could never say anything? As she sat in silence, waiting until everyone should be finished, she grew more and more depressed. She hadn't realized how different this was going to be from an American school. However, she didn't have to stay if she didn't like it, she thought with a wave of homesickness. Her mother had said so, and she would be back again on Tuesday.

But after luncheon everyone rushed joyously out into the sunshine, and then such a chattering and laughing as began, like so many magpies suddenly let loose. The older girls gathered around Jeannette's new friend, while she introduced them one by one. Some answered politely in English, some in French, some in German, and one or two in strange languages that Jean had never heard before. Some of them had been at the school for several years. Others had only come at the beginning of the term a week before, but as Jean was the newest, they took her all around, to the basketball field, the tennis courts, the vegetable garden, the classrooms, and the library. After they had shown Jean everything, they sat down in a little arbor.

One of the girls asked her again what her name was. "Jean," she answered.

"Gin," they repeated after her.

Jean laughed and tried to spell it for them in French, but it was too difficult. Jeannette came to her rescue, however, explaining that it was the same as Jeanne in French.

"And Giovanna in Italian," exclaimed a slender, dark-haired girl, excitedly.

"Viva l'Italia!" laughed the others, jumping to their

feet and giving a salute.

Then a plump blond, older than Jean, was pushed forward. "Ich bin Hannah von Austria," she said blushing, and bobbed an embarrassed curtsy.

Jeannette disappeared suddenly, coming back a few minutes later with two younger girls, one of them very lame and frail looking.

"Voilà Janesika from Prague," she said, "and Jane from England."

"Jane is only my middle name. Does that matter?" asked the frail little English girl, shyly.

"And I have seven other names, too," explained Janesika apologetically.

At this moment there was a shout of joy, and the whole group fell upon another girl who came up from the tennis court, her racket in her hand.

"O Jenny, how could we have forgotten you?" and Jenny was unceremoniously dragged up to Jean. "This is another Jean, from Norway."

Jean was now all excitement. "What a lot of Jeans!" she exclaimed. "Mother told me that I would find them in every country, but I never dreamed they would be here, all together. We ought to start a club, a Jean-club, this minute."

Jeannette translated this idea, and they all laughed and nodded. It was Giovanna's turn now to rush off. Everyone waited eagerly for her to come back. When she did, she was leading a tiny toddler with blond hair and a checked pinafore by the hand.

"A club must have a mascot. See, Ioannochka shall be our mascot. She will bring us luck," and they danced around this littlest Jean of all. Giovanna picked her up and ran back with her again to the nursery, her pale hair shining like a halo in the sunshine.

"Ioannochka is a Russian orphan whom the sisters have adopted," explained Jeannette. "She is the pet of the whole convent."

Just then a bell rang, and off they trooped to classes, the Mother Superior herself, all in white, coming to find Jean and take her to her first class. She spoke a few words of English and she seemed gentle and sweet.

"You will find everything a little difficult at first," she said, "but everyone will help you, and soon it will be easy."

Jean went with the other girls to afternoon benediction, and with the help of Jeannette, found her place in the little book. The Mother Superior had told her it was not necessary for her to go always, but Jean decided she wished to learn what other people believe, as well as how they live and dress and behave in other countries.

When night finally came, it was a very tired and bewildered Jean who crept into bed. She had had so many new sensations all at once that she hardly knew what to think about anything. She disliked intensely being locked into this convent, with bolts and bars and high walls and she didn't enjoy being told when she could speak and when she couldn't. She had been able to understand scarcely a word of French in the classes, neither was she sure that she liked sharing her bedroom with sixty or seventy girls.

On the other hand, she knew that Sister Irmengarde was watching her tenderly to see she had no lonely moments, and already all the other Jeans in school were her friends. Everyone seemed eager to make her comfortable and happy. She wondered where her mother was at this moment, and she smothered a sob, just the smallest sob, of homesickness. After all, this was only the beginning of their great adventure. If she did not do her part, her mother would not be free to travel and write. And what would her father say about her sportsmanship? She certainly must not fail them!

In the dim light her curtains were parted, and Sister Irmengarde rustled softly in, standing for a moment by her bed. "Tu vas bien, chérie?" she whispered as she smoothed Jean's pillows lightly. Almost before she had gone, Jean was asleep.

When she awoke the next morning, the dormitory was flooded with sunlight and as full of twitterings as a great nest of birds. The younger children were in all stages of shoes and stockings and underwear, dressing on their beds, trotting back and forth to wash. The older girls were popping in and out of the curtains along the sides, while several sisters moved quietly here and there, helping with shoestrings and buttons. Jean loved the soft, foreign voices, the low laughter, the peace and happiness of this sunny place. She could imagine the bedlam if sixty hilarious American girls awoke in the same room at home. She could see pillows flying through the air, could hear the bedsprings groan as the girls leaped from bed to bed, could feel her eardrums splitting with the noise of sixty unrestrained throats. Perhaps the convent had its advantages after all.

Work now started in earnest. It was queer that, in spite of having studied French for several years in

America, it should be so difficult to understand what was going on in classes. Jean's head ached with her attempt to concentrate, and she was sure that she would never be able to master this impossible language. Even her own words sounded strange, and the girls who listened so politely often had no idea what she was talking about.

"Doucement, doucement, do not hurry too much," said the Mother Superior gently, when she found Jean strained and tired. "It will come in time," but Jean was not so sure.

The girls sat two by two in double seats in the classroom, Jean sharing hers with Swedish Greta, blond and fair-skinned, a real daughter of the Northland. Fortunately she spoke English, so their cautious whisperings were intelligible to each other. Ahead of them sat plump Madeleine, taking up much more than her half of the seat, and thin little Yvonne, who sat precariously on the edge and wept whenever the teacher said, "Un point," sternly after her recitations. Jean learned that "un point" meant "one point," and that practically everything that happened, from a poor recitation to a mere whisper, counted a point against someone. Everyone seemed very vague about how many points there were from which the teachers might keep on subtracting before the fatal moment which meant a letter home.

The geography teacher wore a pompadour slicked tightly back over a large "rat," or pad. Jean had seen her arriving one morning, with a surprised-looking hat perched uncertainly on top of her head. The girls thought she must wear a bustle, too, as her figure looked rather queer from the rear. The history teacher was fat and jolly, and almost never said, "Un point." The long-faced catechism teacher always came in rubbing her hands gloatingly, as if to say, "I'll get you this time," and she always did. Jean *couldn't* remember her catechism. For special tutoring in French, Jean and Hannah and little Jane went to a rosy-cheeked young sister who waited smilingly for them in the grape arbor. There, in the sunny garden, she patiently helped them with their unruly pronunciation, her soft laughter rippling out joyously. She was so young and so gay that her name, Sister Maria Dolorosa, did not seem to fit her. It was she who helped Jean over the first hard days and made her believe that sometime she would really be able to master French.

By the time her mother came back again on Tuesday, she had made enough progress to feel hopeful of the future. "I'll be a French mademoiselle in no time at all, Mums, dear, and you needn't worry about my being homesick any more. Sister Maria Dolorosa helps me every day; Sister Irmengarde always comes and tucks me in if she thinks I'm lonesome, and all the Jeans are so kind to me."

Consequently, it was with a quiet heart that her mother went off to Italy on the trail of folk songs, with the promise to come back whenever Jean might want her.

Jean quickly fell into the routine of the convent. Every morning the girls went to Mass, filing into chapel in long double rows. Jean did not understand much of the service, but she loved the statue of the Madonna that looked down on them, the flickering candles on the altar, and the long rays of colored light which filtered in through the stained-glass windows. The orphans, in their blue and white checked pinafores, sat on one side of the chapel, and the schoolgirls, in black pinafores, on the other side. The priest who read the Mass was the only man allowed within the high walls of the convent. Once the head of the order himself came, all in white robes, with a white cloak and hood, and the girls spoke in awed whispers the whole day long.

One day a week they had a singing class, the girls sitting in rows on long benches in the auditorium, while little Sister Irmengarde played the organ and Sister Cecilia waved her arms and sang so energetically that her face grew purple, and Jean was afraid she might burst her stiffly starched white underbonnet.

Twice a week there were sewing classes. The new girls first learned to darn, in meticulous basket-weave stitches, so that they might keep their own stockings and clothing in order. Then they were taught to make neat little square patches and smoothly felled seams. Buttonholes were the hardest, but Hannah sat beside Jean and helped her with the troublesome stitches. Later on, they would embroider samplers. Hannah said that would be loads of fun, but Jean wasn't so sure.

Sometimes the schoolgirls were allowed to help in the orphans' classes. Since the convent was also an orphanage, these children were each taught a trade, so that they might eventually earn their own living. Some of them were taught to be seamstresses; some of them expert laundresses; some helped with the cooking and gardening. They all learned to read and write, but they did not have as much regular schooling as the other girls.

When Jean and her friends went for walks, they took off their pinafores and put on their jackets and blue berets. They marched two and two, in a long procession, with two sisters ahead and two behind. When they came to an open field, they were allowed to scatter and pick flowers and play games, but in the city they must walk sedately. The orphans wore their checked pinafores even on the street, and stiff black-straw sailor hats, with ribbons hanging down behind. Their dresses were usually too big and too long, and Jean was always wanting to make them fit. It was hard for little Ioannochka to stay in her own line if she happened to see any of her especial friends in the other line. At first Jean loved walking up the hill to the old town, entering it through an ancient arched gate and wandering about the quaint and narrow streets. But it was so tantalizing never to be able to stop before any of the shop windows or buy cakes and candies where the delicious odors came wafting out or have tea at the little tables under gay awnings, that she finally preferred to stay at the convent and play tennis and basketball.

On Sundays, however, she liked to march up to the great cathedral at the top of the town, while the bells rang loudly, and the tile roofs of the old city shone in the sunshine. When the others took Communion, she sat quietly in the back of the church, dreaming dreams of the time when this quaint town was young, when pennants waved from its walls and towers and knights on horseback rode clankingly over its steep cobblestones. She shut her eyes and saw at the windows of the old town stately ladies in rich brocades and heard peasant lassies in wide straw hats and bright petticoats crying their wares in the market place. She knew how they looked, for she had seen the collection of old gowns in the Fragonard Museum.

Jean was afraid she was going to grow up to be romantic, even though she preferred turning handsprings and standing on her head, and she made no end of fun of the older girls and their silly ideas. But turning handsprings was not encouraged at the convent, and the only place she could find to stand on her head was behind her own bed curtains. She finally had to give that up, for one night she crashed through the curtains feet first, right into the dormitory. Even Sister Maria Dolorosa, who was tucking in the little ones, had looked shocked. Perhaps she would end up by writing novels, like Aunt Sally, or be an actress and play Romeo and Juliet.

Already she and Greta had experimented with Pyramus and Thisbe, each sitting on the floor of her tiny bedroom and whispering through the curtain. But they had giggled so much that Sister Cecilia discovered them, and they had had to learn three Latin verbs the next day. It was worth it, though. And that was not all. There had been the night when Hannah had had trouble with her bed. She got in, but her feet would not go to the bottom properly, and Sister Irmengarde had sputtered a good deal as she helped her remake it. She looked suspiciously at Jean as she went by her bed afterward, but Jean was already sound asleep.

Sometimes they had midnight feasts behind the curtains, when Jeannette smuggled in almond cakes after a week end at home or somebody's mother brought a box of chocolates. It was easy to pass things along next the wall, and if a pillowcase got too sticky, it could always be turned over.

Meanwhile, the Jean-club met every afternoon in free time, while those less fortunately named strolled arm in arm, just out of hearing distance and wondered what it was all about. The Jeans hardly knew themselves, but it was fun having discovered one another.

"But the club must have a purpose," said serious little Jane, after several weeks of this pleasant trifling.

"To help Jean parler français," suggested Jeannette, frivolously.

"Aber ja, a purpose," agreed plump Hannah, "perhaps a singing club," while black-haired Giovanna chimed in vaguely, "Or something about art."

"I know," cried Jean, "let's have a club for peace—peace among all nations." Just then the schoolbell rang, as it always did when something really important was being discussed.

When they next met, they decided that even before they settled on the purpose of the club, they must give it a name. That was essential. It should be called after some famous Jean, but there were so many of them, both male and female.

"We might call ourselves the Société de St. Jean," suggested Jeannette, "because all the Jeans come from John anyway."

"Oh, but we ought to have a woman's name for a girls' club," argued Jean. "How about Jeanne d'Arc? She has always been my favorite Jean. If only she wasn't all mixed up with war; we want a name that stands for friendliness.... Perhaps Jane Addams would be better. She did so much for the poor people of America and for the cause of peace, too."

"Or Lady Jane Grey, who was so lonely and sad," contributed little Jane. "I've just been reading about her, and she was a lovely lady." She sighed romantically.

"Or Jenny Lind, the Swedish songbird," cried Jenny.

"Or Jan Huss. He was the greatest John that ever lived; he even died for his people," piped Janesika.

But it was Jane who came back again to the name, Jeanne d'Arc. Of course Jeanne d'Arc went to war, explained Jane, because she had to follow the voices. But she didn't want to go in the first place, and she kept hoping all the time that she could go home again and live in peace. "So we could carry on where she left off, and work for peace," concluded Jane.

Jeannette and Giovanna shook their heads dubiously over the peace question. "Our fathers are both in the army," said Jeannette, "and it would be unpatriotic for us to talk against war."

"But peace means the same thing as friendship," said Jean. "We needn't talk about it, but we can be working for it all the time, by being friends ourselves and helping girls in all countries to be friendly. If we can't decide on any Jean in particular to name the club for, why not just name it for Jeans in general?" She thought a moment. "I know; let's call it Jean and Company, Limited. That sounds nice and businesslike." And so it was settled.

They decided to keep the name a secret and meet only once a week, so that other girls shouldn't feel badly about not belonging. But they also decided they must begin work—being friendly—right away. They would all help Jean and Hannah with their class work, because French was still hard for these two to understand. Jean would teach Janesika to play tennis, her greatest ambition in life. Hannah would do Giovanna's darning, a job she hated, and in exchange, Giovanna would teach her to play on the guitar. All of them secretly planned to save steps for little lame Jane, who had been sent to southern France to see if the warm sunshine and sea bathing would make her stronger. Then, of course, they must help the sisters take care of tiny Ioannochka. One was to give her her bath; another was scheduled to sit with her at mealtimes; another to take her for a walk at recess. Being friendly would keep them tremendously busy!

"After we leave school, we can visit each other," proposed Jean practically. "Perhaps I can visit some of you this coming summer, and you will all have to come to America to see me. Besides that, we can have a Round Robin for the rest of our lives, wherever we are."

"What is a Round Robin?" asked little Jane wistfully. "Is it something that I can do, too?"

Jean hugged her quickly. "It's something that every one of us can do, always. It's a fat letter that goes from one to the other, and keeps going all the time. I write a letter, and it goes to all of you. When it comes back to me again, I take out my old one and put in a new one. Each of you does the same, so that each time the letter comes, we all hear from everybody else." She paused a moment, quite breathless, while the girls still looked puzzled. "If we add our letters quickly enough, and send them on, we would receive a Round Robin every few weeks. My mother still hears from her school friends after twenty years, and in the letter now there are always pictures of the husbands and children. It's such fun!"

"Could we please start it right away?" piped little Janesika. They all laughed.

"Silly," said Giovanna, tickling her, "we can't write to one another when we are all together."

Janesika sighed. "It will be so hard to wait. I just love getting letters."

"Well, anyway, it will give us something to look forward to in the holidays," said Jane brightly, knowing that she would miss these new friends more than she could say, when they were separated in the summer.

Jeannette was thinking very hard. "Voilà, I have an idea. Every club must have a president, and I know who would make the grandest one of all. Jane!"

Jane ducked her head shyly. "But I don't know how to do anything much. Besides, you have to vote for a president with a ballot, and nobody else might want me. I won't mind if you'd rather have someone else—much," and she sighed a little wistfully.

"This is a unanimous vote," they all cried, forming a circle and dancing around her. "Hurrah for Madame President!"

Hannah picked Jane up like a kitten and put her on her shoulder. Jean put her shoulder under from the other side, and off they all marched, around the big tree, down the hill to the meadow, across the tennis courts, and back again through the cabbages and currant bushes of the vegetable garden, singing lustily to the tune of the *Marseillaise*. Jeannette had made up the words, and even though they didn't fit the tune exactly, the girls had all learned them.

"Allons, la Jeanne et Compagnie,

Le jour de paix est arrivé,"

"They're all right if we just wiggle our tongues a little," declared Jean, so they all wiggled their tongues and sang with a will.

It was a tired but happy little Jane whom they tucked in that night. After everyone else was asleep, Jean tiptoed out quietly to see if she was all right. A strip of moonlight shone straight across her bed, and Jean could see that she was still awake, her eyes shining with the glory of being president.

"O Jane, I'm so glad they chose you," whispered Jean.

Jane smiled in the dark. "You know, I thought I was going to be dreadfully lonely at a strange school, so far away from home, and not doing everything that other girls do. But you've all been so good to me and I haven't been homesick the least bit."

Both girls were quiet for a moment.

"Jean, do you think I ought to do it? The other girls are all so much cleverer. Jeannette writes beautiful poetry and Giovanna plays the guitar and your tennis is wonderful, and Hannah," hesitating, "well, Hannah yodels. I just sit and look on while other people do things. I thought perhaps it wouldn't be fair for me to be president."

"But you have more time than anybody else to think of other people and make plans for being friendly. That's why you'll make the very best president of all," whispered Jean, tucking Jane's arms in again and kissing her tenderly.

Even little Sister Irmengarde, coming quietly down the room to see who was still awake, went on as if she hadn't seen anyone.

CHAPTER 3:
OLD PROVENCE

Jean stretched luxuriously, but without making the slightest effort to open her sleepy eyes. In the back of her mind she knew vaguely that this was an especially important day in her life, but she was much too comfortable even to try to remember why. Instead she rolled over to her other side and curled up cozily again for another forty winks. Suddenly, very close at hand, she heard the tinkle of dishes, and her eyes opened with a snap as she sat up in bed and looked around her. There before the fire was the crispest, perkiest little maid she had ever seen, arranging a breakfast tray on a low table. Another moment and the door across the room burst open, and in popped a dark little head, with sparkling black eyes.

"Bonjour, chérie. Have you slept well?" cried a merry voice.

It was Jeannette, of course, and here was Jean spending a week end at Jeannette's home. Now she remembered all about it. For two months they had slept in adjoining beds in the big dormitory, and even though they could speak to each other only in a strange mixture of French and English, they understood each other perfectly and were the best friends imaginable. They often whispered together about important things through the curtains of their queer little separate rooms long after everyone else was settled for the night. Just the week before, Jeannette had asked Jean if she would come and stay with her. That was how Jean happened to be visiting in a real Provençal home for the first time. Was there ever another girl as lucky as she?

"Hurrah for Jean and Company, Limited!" she cried as she hopped out of bed.

By this time the little maid had built a cozy fire on the hearth and brought in another tray for Jeannette. The two girls curled up in low armchairs in their kimonos, to enjoy the luxury of a lazy breakfast. Nothing like that in the convent, where they had to jump out of bed with the rising bell and eat breakfast all together at a long table in the refectory.

Such a breakfast as this was! There was not a great deal of it—because the French think it a most unfortunate custom to eat heavy cereal and bacon and eggs at the beginning of the day—but a big bowl of steaming, fragrant chocolate, a pile of croissants, which were flaky, crescent-shaped rolls that melted in the mouth, and apricot marmalade in a yellow dish. Jean was surprised when Jeannette told her that in France one always had breakfast upstairs, each member of the family having a tray to himself, and a crackling fire in each bedroom to dress by. They drank their chocolate from the bowls, and it was not until the last drop of it was gone and not a crumb of croissant left, that Jean really had time to look around her. It had been too dark the night before, and the girls had been too sleepy to do anything but tumble into bed.

So this was the house Jeannette had told her about, a house that had belonged to the family for over two hundred years and which they had tried to keep in its original form. Aside from adding a bathroom or two and a kitchen stove, no changes had been made in it.

Jean's room was finished in rough plaster, whitewashed, with a big hood over the fireplace, and a raised hearth. Her bed was set in an alcove with curtains of red and blue checked cotton, to shut it off from the rest of the room during the day. It was almost like sleeping in a cupboard, Jean thought. The bureau was big and sturdy, with heavy carving and beautiful brass handles, and there was a huge walnut chest in which to keep blankets. In one corner there was a triangular shaped washstand, with a pitcher and a bowl of yellow pottery sprinkled with tiny flowers. On the red tile floor beside the washstand was a tall copper jug, steaming with hot water, which the maid had brought in. There were sturdy chairs and tables of dark walnut and two low, comfortable armchairs covered with a blue hand-woven stuff—woven in their own family, Jeannette explained.

The walls were plain, but in one of them was a little arched niche, painted blue, where stood an exquisite old ivory Madonna. There were lovely pewter candlesticks on the narrow mantelpiece, and some bowls in which floated tiny wicks to burn olive oil. How much more thrilling it was to use candles than pushing a button and getting a glare of electric light, thought Jean.

Jeannette opened the long, arched French windows, and Jean looked out on a most enchanting garden, with terrace after terrace of lawn and flowers, olive trees and vineyards, and far below in the distance the blue Mediterranean.

The girls looked and squeezed each other rapturously. "Oh, do let's get out in the sunshine,

Jeannette, and promise to show me everything, absolutely everything," cried Jean.

They slipped quickly into their clothes and flew down the stairs, not even stopping to look at the great hall as they ran through it. Along the loggia where the sunshine streamed in and out into the garden they raced. In the middle of the first terrace was a fountain, and on the terrace below another one. Around the velvet lawns, which were laid out in rectangles, were low borders of boxwood, trimmed as neatly as a pin. Against the old stone walls were hollyhocks and lavender flowers and pink geranium, all of them seeming to have grown there for as long as the house had stood. Straight flagstone walks led through arches at both ends of the upper lawn, one of them into the neatest of vegetable gardens, the rich, black earth dug in deep furrows between the rows of cabbage and celery and artichoke. The other led down a lane of tall, black-green cypresses to a cluster of low, pink buildings with red tile roofs.

"The peasants' houses," explained Jeannette. "Would you like to see their animals?" Off they went again, galloping down the path like two young colts, for sheer joy of being alive on such a day.

"We can walk sedately again when we get back to the convent," laughed Jean. "I don't know when I've felt so skittish. I suppose being proper so much of the time is what does it."

Jeannette was quite breathless. "These are the oldest houses on the place," she explained, "built by my great-great-great-grandfather. The peasants who take care of our olive groves and vineyards live here now."

They had to stoop under the overhanging geranium vines, as they pulled aside the striped curtain and went in the door. The peasant's wife greeted the two girls with delight, chattering in a strange kind of French which Jean, in spite of her two months in a French school, found difficult to understand at all. At one side of the room was a fireplace with a hood and a raised hearth, and hanging on an iron crane, steaming away, was a big copper kettle full of soup. Brightly polished copper pots hung around the walls. On a high walnut dresser stood rows of gayly colored bowls and plates of pottery. The table was spread with a checked cloth in red and yellow. In the high windows were pots of red geraniums. The walls were mellow with many years of smoke, and the great beams of the ceiling were so low as almost to touch one's head. This was the kitchen, dining room, living room, all in one, to Cecile and Pierre and old Fifi. Cecile, for it was she who had greeted them, gave them each a hot, sweet cake freshly baked in her stone oven, and then took them to see the animals.

From the next room in the cottage had come various grunts and squeaks. Here the girls found a litter of pink pigs in a pen in the corner, and a row of rabbit hutches in which rabbits of all sizes and colors hopped about. The French love to eat rabbit even better than they do chicken. Jean was surprised to find animals under the same roof with human beings, but she said nothing, as Jeannette seemed to take it as a matter of course. In the next shed was a plump little donkey, one ear up and one ear down, that just fitted the blue cart outside. As the girls entered the shed, a

BELOW THE HOUSE WAS THE GREAT STONE POOL.

whole flock of chickens rushed out squawking. Above in the loft were piles of fragrant hay and freshly cut grass for the rabbits and the donkey. As the girls stood there, old Fifi came in with a great sack of newly cut hay balanced on her head and a sickle in her hand. Jean felt very sorry for her, but Jeannette explained that when the peasant women grew too old to work in the fields or do the washing, they still liked to be busy with something out-of-doors. So they watched the sheep or cut hay a little at a time for the animals.

Below the house was a great stone pool at which three or four women were washing clothes, slapping them on the tile edge of the tank, rubbing them with soap, or beating them with sticks. Their hands were red with the cold water from the mountain springs, but their cheeks were red, too, and they were chattering briskly in their curious patois. Jeannette told Jean that these washing places were the newspapers of the peasant women, for it was here that they exchanged all the gossip of their neighbors, finding out whose cow had died, whose baby was born, whose cabbages were planted, and whose olives were gathered. They laughed and chattered incessantly as they splashed and pounded away in the sunshine.

At this moment Pierre came around the corner with the little donkey hitched to the cart. Without waiting to be asked, the girls scrambled into the cart, much to the surprise of the donkey, who turned his head inquiringly, then trotted off with them down the hill. It was a bumpy ride, and the girls had to hold on tightly, but that made it all the more fun. They passed fragrant fields of jasmine, orange and olive groves, and terrace after terrace of vineyards. Jeannette told Jean that all these fields and vineyards belonged to her father.

The jasmine, gathered in the early morning with the dew still on the blossoms, was taken each day to the perfume factory near by. The vineyards supplied grapes and wine for everyone on the farm. The olives were shaken down each autumn, the best of them saved to pickle and eat, and the rest taken to the olive press where oil was made, enough for salads and cooking the year round. Then there were the great vegetable gardens, with many of the vegetables bearing three or four times a year in this warm and sunny climate. Practically everything that they needed or wanted, including meat from chickens, pigs, and lambs, grew on the place, and what was left over, the peasants sold at market.

At the bottom of the hill the girls scrambled out again, so that the cart could be filled with neatly tied-up fagots made from the dried twigs of olive, trimmed off during the winter. Jean could see that not even the smallest thing was wasted in this wonderful country, the leaves and twigs which would have been burned up in America being saved for fertilizer and firewood. Even the vineyards and jasmine fields were as beautifully kept as the lawns and gardens around the house.

From below Jean had a splendid view of the house itself. It stood high above them, its soft pink walls and green shutters half hidden in a grove of tall, black cypresses. Behind it were the far, blue mountains, and around it, falling away in terraced steps supported by gray stone walls, were shiny, green, orange groves, purple vineyards, and silvery olive trees. Above was the bluest of blue skies. Jean felt as if she were looking at a painting. It couldn't be real.

They had to climb the long hill again on foot, stopping a moment to watch a pair of cream-colored oxen plowing in the upper field. And they were quite ready to hear the luncheon bell tinkling as they breathlessly clambered up the last steps to the garden. There was a jolly little table set for two in the shade of a plantain tree, and here the girls had lunch, looking out over the sea in the distance. Not meat and vegetables and potatoes all served at once, no indeed! Dainty hors d'oeuvres first—little side dishes of ripe olives and radishes and stuffed eggs and artichoke hearts—then an omelet, after that chicken with a green salad. Last of all came cheese and fruit. There was plenty of food for two starving young ladies, aged fourteen, and all daintily served, one dish at a time. Jean liked everything about that outdoor luncheon, with flowers around her, the fountain singing in her ears, and the sun shining warmly through the plantain leaves.

After lunch they stretched out in comfortable chairs under the grape arbor, and how their tongues wagged! Jean wanted to know everything about the farm, and of course Jeannette asked dozens of questions about America. In a queer mixture of French and English, giggling over their mistakes, they chattered away as if they had always known each other.

It was here that Jeannette's father found them later in the afternoon and took them off for a long tramp across country. They zigzagged up another hill to a quaint, walled village with medieval towers. "Just like another painting," thought Jean. Through the old gate of the town they went, with the grooves still showing where once the ancient portcullis let down, up steep little streets flanked by gray stone houses, to an open square where there was music. Here they had tea and cakes under a gayly striped awning. Across the way were the brilliant booths of a traveling fair, where children clustered like flies about honey. Farther down the street was a tinkling merry-go-round. On the way home they stopped at a tiny chapel half hidden among tall, old cypresses, watching the sun set over the sea in pink and silver glory from the stone bench before its door.

They got home in time to dress for dinner, and Jean tried to look very dignified and grown up in her flowered silk dress. There was another charming meal by candlelight and firelight, at a long table set in a big room with green curtains drawn at the tall French windows. Afterwards they went through the wide-arched doorway into the great salon for coffee before a fireplace as high as the ceiling itself.

Jean loved the quiet evening best, when she talked in French to Jeannette's father and mother, who helped her along when she was hopelessly puzzled and laughed merrily with her over her mistakes. She had been so homesick for her own father and mother that it warmed her heart to be taken into this lovely home. Then Jeannette played softly at the old spinet and taught Jean some of the songs that she had heard the children singing in the street. Her father added his hearty bass, so that it was great fun. When they were all tired of singing, Jeannette played Mozart's *Minuet*, written for just such a tinkly spinet. Jean sat with her eyes half closed and tried to imagine the stately figures of two, three, four generations ago, moving about the dusky corners of the candlelit room. The mellow walls, the rare old tapestries, the great carved chests made a perfect setting for such a picture. If these rooms could speak, what tales they might tell of love and high adventure!

It was from such waking dreams as these that the girls at last tumbled sleepily into bed, to dream more dreams until morning came, and with it the time to go back to school again. But Jean had had something which she would never forget, a glimpse into the real life of old France and the new France as well. For the new France carries with it much of the romance and gentle beauty, the sturdy industry and high courage of those older, more adventurous times. Surely, Jean thought, she had learned to love and understand France and the French, as well as Jeannette herself, more than she ever could have in any other way.

CHAPTER 4:

CHRISTMAS IN SWITZERLAND

Every Christmas of her life Jean had spent with her grandmother in her quaint old house in Connecticut. There was always the welcoming wreath on the front door and green garlands twined around the columns of the little porch. Visions of the Christmas tree, the fireplace where she hung up her stocking, the turkey and cranberry sauce and mince pies, enough of them for all the children and grandchildren, came before her eyes. She could see every single thing, even to the mistletoe hung in the hallway where everyone had to pass. She couldn't even imagine any other kind of Christmas.

But here was a letter from her mother suggesting winter sports in Switzerland for the holidays. In the next mail came a letter from Paul, with the usual postscript from Polly, begging her and her mother to join their family at a little inn up in the mountains, where there would be tobogganing and skating and skiing and all the things that go with winter in the Alps. Of course, she did not know Polly and Paul very well, but being together on a ship for two weeks had been a great help. It wasn't so difficult to get acquainted with twins, anyway, as it was with two separate people. After all, Christmas wouldn't be so bad if she could spend it with her mother and Polly and Paul on the top of an Alp, thought Jean.

When she and her mother stepped from the train which had carried them through pitch-black tunnels, around hairpin curves, and over lofty mountain passes, she could hardly believe her eyes. This was certainly the top of the world. All around them were shining white peaks, dark pine trees flashing with crystals, quaint little chalets half smothered in snow, and a whole troop of boys and girls in gay ski suits who had come down to meet the train. Jean looked eagerly about for Paul and Polly, but they were nowhere in sight. Suddenly she heard sleigh-bells, and around the corner of the picturesque little station dashed the jolliest sort of sleigh, bright red, with pictures painted all over it. Paul was driving and he drew the horse up with a flourish beside the platform. Out hopped Polly to hug first Jean and then her mother. The horse jumped and stamped impatiently, and Paul had to shout, "M'lord, the carriage waits," several times before anyone paid any attention to him. Then Jean scrambled into the front seat and washed Paul's face with a mitten full of snow, by way of friendly greeting, while her mother and Polly tucked themselves cozily in behind.

"Oh, it's so exciting to see snow again," cried Jean, reaching for another handful.

"No, you don't, young lady," cried Paul, ducking just in time and poking Jean in the ribs with his whipstock. "I'll dump you right out in a snowdrift if you don't behave," and he almost did as they went around a sharp curve.

There were many exclamations of delight as they skimmed along over the well-packed snow, first through the little village that looked exactly like a

Christmas card, then back and forth up hairpin turns until they came to a chalet bigger than the rest, with a wide, overhanging roof covered with snow and with long icicles reaching almost to the ground. A boy in short trousers and a green vest ran out to take their bags, while Paul and Polly and Jean began to pelt one another with snowballs.

Meanwhile Polly's father and mother appeared, and there were greetings all around. The chalet was an inn where only about twenty-five people could stay, and was a perfect place for the holiday, they all agreed. Jean looked around. Above the chalet stretched a long ski-run with a jump at the bottom. Below in the valley nestled a lake where they might skate, and a bobsled track zigzagged down the mountain. Other inns and hotels were scattered about and a few chalets seemed to be almost hidden in snow. Here and there she saw little knots of people in bright sport clothes or caught flashing glimpses of skiers and coasters speeding down the slopes. Everywhere was the background of shining mountain peaks.

Twilight came on as they talked, and they watched the sun set in golden glory over the snowy peaks, leaving behind it deep blue and purple shadows in the valleys. The pine trees stood like black sentinels in the snow. Gradually tiny lights shone out here and there in mountain chalets, and an occasional lantern followed the sound of a tinkling sleigh. Voices called back and forth, but fewer and more faintly, as toboggans and skates and skis took their owners home for the night.

"Oh, dear, how can I ever wait till morning," groaned Jean. "Sleeping is such a waste of time."

"Isn't it though," said Paul.

"I'll say it is," echoed Polly, and they all sighed heavily.

After supper everybody gathered around the fireplace in the big main room. Besides the Americans, there was an English family, a French family, a group of German boys and girls, and several Italian children with their governess. One of the Swiss boys played an accordion, while the others yodeled and sang Tyrolean songs. Later in the evening he played Viennese waltzes, and the couples whirled and whirled in the fast German dance. Paul pulled Jean up and they whirled too, round and round till Jean was quite dizzy and breathless.

Then one of the German boys, in leather shorts and embroidered suspenders, took off his jacket of quilted blue and white print, and danced the *Schuh-plattler*, while the accordion wheezed merrily. Jean did not see how he could possibly do it, clumping up and down as he danced, alternately slapping his leather trousers and the soles of his shoes, besides leaping into the air and whirling around between times. He received wild applause and had to do it again and again, while everybody kept time by clapping. Hans asked Jean to teach them an American song. So she and Paul and Polly sang "Jingle Bells" for them until Hans was able to play it on his accordion, and the others could join in. Late in the evening their host brought out bowls of steaming chocolate and dark bread and cheese with big holes in it, which everybody fell upon with a will.

When Jean reached her room, she opened the little window and looked out. The thin crescent of the moon was just rising over the mountain's edge, faintly illuminating the dim, blue slopes and the pointed roofs of the chalets that peeped up out of the snow. In the distance she heard a song, a lovely, eerie sound away down in the valley. From her side of the mountain came a yodel, another mountain picked it up, and still another yodel came from across the vale, like so many echoes of a vagrant voice. Up from below, in a wandering zigzag, wound the red glow of a lantern, and with it came the tinkling of sleighbells. How beautiful it all was!

The next morning the boys and girls were swarming around the bobsled run, laughing and chattering and making up teams.

"Hans is a marvelous steerer," shouted Paul above the din. "Let's ask if we may go down with him."

Jean and Polly and Paul piled on to the big bobsled behind Hans, and he explained just how they must lean going around corners, how Paul must manage the brakes when he shouted at him, and how they must all hold on for dear life. Hans himself sat behind a steering wheel like that of an automobile.

"Now," he shouted, and off they went, whizzing down the zigzag slide, leaning dangerously to one side as they rounded the hairpin curves, sliding up the bank at the slanting corners, and easing down again for the straight runway. Jean scarcely caught her breath all the way down. When she did, it was only to squeal with excitement. In no time at all they were at the bottom, skimming out over the ice at the end of the lake and into a big snowdrift where they all rolled off. There they hitched a donkey to the sled and he plodded up the hill with it, taking a short cut back to the chalet, while the young people trudged along beside him, pelting each other with snowballs.

Once when Jean jumped on to the sled, the donkey stopped and looked around in great surprise, refusing to move until she got off again. Other whizzing, shrieking, waving bobsleds on the way down passed them. One sled ran up over the bank on a curve, spilling off all its riders in the soft snow, where they rolled and struggled, but finally managed to scramble up and dash off after their sled, which was sailing merrily down the mountain by itself.

The slide was so long and the climb up again so arduous, that after four or five coasts it was time for lunch. What appetites they all had! Jean ate a great bowl of soup as well as quantities of bread and cheese, sausage and fried potatoes, and ended up with a fluffy, golden jelly omelet. She was sure she had never been so hungry in her life. There was something about this mountain air—clear and crisp and invigorating—that she could not quite understand. It was so cold that the snow was dry and soft, and the lake was frozen to a great thickness. But it was so warm, too, that when they exercised, Jean first had to take off her coat and then her sweater. Everyone gradually emerged in thin shirts and blouses. The pine trees were festooned like Christmas trees with discarded scarfs and sweaters and caps and mittens.

Polly told Jean that there was a sanitarium for tubercular children on the next mountain, where the children played in the sunshine with nothing on but boots to keep their toes from freezing in the snow. Jean could hardly believe it, but her mother later told her that it was true, and that many children were cured by the sunshine and clear air and rich milk of these wonderful mountains.

In the afternoon Jean tried her hand, or rather her feet, at skiing. She had skied some at home, when there was snow enough, but she had never seen anything like the way these Swiss and German and Italian boys and girls sped down the snowy slopes, swooping like birds, deftly lifting their skis into the air at curves and putting them down again around the corner with a quick little leap, balancing themselves skilfully with their poles, and spreading their skis wedgewise to come to a sudden stop. Some of them even went down the professional ski jump, rising to the jump, soaring out into the air, and landing unbelievably on their feet on the lower slope. Jean always shut her eyes at the crucial moment; she was so afraid they would fall.

She herself only experimented cautiously on the gentler slopes, falling now and then to be almost smothered in the deep, powdery snow, or standing still to watch the others do hair-raising stunts of jumping, turning, and stopping. She was stiff and tired that first night, quite ready to crawl into bed long before the others had finished singing and dancing.

"But tomorrow I'm going to try everything that anybody else does," she murmured, as she dropped off to sleep to the tune of a Viennese waltz.

The next day she did try everything, with many bumps, smotherings, and entanglements of her legs with sleds and skis. But by the end of the day she could go down a short slope without falling, and she had steered the bobsled once down the run, with only Paul on it to work the brake.

That evening there was an ice carnival on the lake. Jean wore her old red, velveteen dress with the full skirt, borrowed a white ermine jacket of her mother's, made herself a high headdress with a cascade of bright ribbons streaming down the back, and went as a Russian. Paul borrowed an old French uniform from the landlady. Her father had had it in the days when the French army still wore red trousers and long blue coats. Polly was dressed as a boy, in Hans's leather shorts, embroidered suspenders, quilted jacket, and a pointed felt hat with a long pheasant feather sticking straight up in the air. All the others begged, borrowed, exchanged, or invented jolly costumes, and it was a gay party that went coasting off down the hill to the lake.

A noisy band from the neighboring village welcomed them as they slid across the lake on their sleds, the skaters scattering with shrieks of alarm. Then began something that Jean had never seen before. As the band played a waltz, couples all over the lake began dancing on skates, swinging and whirling in perfect rhythm. Jean thought it the most graceful skating she had ever seen. Paul and Polly had already done some practicing, and Paul tried to show Jean, but somehow or other they tripped each other up and fell in a heap. When Fritz saw her plight, he dashed over and helped to disentangle her. He was so big and waltzed so well that he succeeded in holding her up until she learned the steps. After that it was fairly easy. One waltz followed another, the fat bandmaster with purple cheeks blowing on a big horn that looped itself all the way around him, the other players puffing and fiddling and drumming. They seemed to keep warm, in spite of the snow and ice.

While the band rested, Hans got out his accordion, and a Swiss couple started performing marvelous feats to music, whirling together, swinging away from each other, skating together again, leaping into the air, and landing lightly as birds. Jean had never seen figure skating before, either, and could scarcely believe her eyes. Fritz jumped up and tried to do the *Schuh-plattler* on skates, but that was too much for his balance, and he skated straight into Paul and Jean and Polly, upsetting them all completely, amid wild applause.

Before the evening was over, Jean was dancing successfully with anyone who was strong enough to hold her up, and who did not try to do too many fancy steps. Such fun as it was! Jean decided she must learn to do it perfectly. Then she would give a skating party the next Christmas at Grandmother's, and teach everybody else how to dance on skates. The musicians would freeze in New England though, so she would have to end up by using a phonograph, which would take all the poetry out of it.

Hot chocolate and thick slices of bread and cheese were served in a gay little booth, and they all ate as if they had never eaten before and never expected to again. It was long after midnight when they trudged up the mountain side, singing as they went, to warm themselves by the roaring fire in the chalet.

The next day was Christmas Eve, and everyone was full of plans for celebrating it. In the morning they trooped out on the mountain—the whole crowd of young people—to cut down a tall fir tree. They dragged this home on the sled, singing "O Tannenbaum, O Tannenbaum," at the top of their lungs as they came. They set the tree up in the corner of the big hall, and the landlord brought out candleholders and Christmas candles and jolly little figures of fat cherubs to hang all over the tree. The boys climbed up on stepladders, while the girls handed the trimmings to them and made clever suggestions or stood off to admire the boys' handiwork.

Fat Herr Schmidt, the landlord, almost as round as he was tall, burst into unusual enthusiasm. "Ach, how beaudiful," he cried, folding his hands over his fat stomach and cocking his head on one side. "Das ist fur Germans, und meine Frau vill some little cookies make, auch, birds und animals und anchels for alles. Now fur die English, must ve for dis efening a surprise alzo haf." Thereupon he beamed.

"A Yule log," they all shouted, and off they trudged again, this time with the big wood sledge in tow. They hunted for a dead tree, and, finding the very one, the boys took turns chopping at it and trimming off the smaller boughs. Meanwhile the girls were gathering green fir branches here and there, cutting them carefully with hatchets so as not to spoil the trees, and weaving them into garlands with long pieces of fine wire which they had brought with them. They all marched home triumphantly, the garlands looped from shoulder to shoulder, everyone pulling on the long ropes that dragged the sledge. They hid the Yule log behind the chalet, hung the garlands about the paneled wooden walls, and made a huge wreath to go over the fireplace.

"But what about France?" cried Jean and Polly. "We'll go ask Frau Schmidt," and off they went to find her.

The big room was then closed. No one was allowed in, except Jean and Polly who went back and forth mysteriously for most of the afternoon. Their elders took the red sleigh and drove off in the direction of the village. Everyone else rushed around busily, too, for Herr Schmidt had said that everybody must do something for Christmas Eve, sing or play or entertain the others in some way. The whole chalet was buzzing with excitement. There were snatches of music here and there, furtive parents sneaking down the corridors with mysterious packages, giggling young things dashing in and out of doors in strange costumes. Such fun as it was! Jean thought it almost as thrilling as Christmas at Grandmother's.

It was nearly time for dinner. Jean had just slipped into her most Christmasy red dress, when she heard a yodel in the distance and then another from the opposite direction. She popped her head out of the window, and from every side, or so it seemed, came bobbing lanterns and echoing yodels. Gradually the lanterns and voices gathered in a group and came marching up the hill singing old German and French and Italian carols.

"Sie sind die Kinder von all die chalets," said Herr Schmidt, "und dey efery Christmas come." He gave these youngsters cookies and candies, and then they went on to the other hotels across the valley, the lanterns bobbing and the yodels dying away faintly in the distance.

Tinkling bells called them down to dinner, a whole string of little cow bells from the size of a thimble to a coffee cup. Jean's mother had told her that she had heard these tiny cow bells in the summer, wandering herds of cows tinkling gay tunes as they went up the valleys to pasture in the early mornings.

Herr Schmidt threw open the doors of the hall with a flourish and what was meant to be a courtly bow, his hand on his heart. But as his arm was too short to reach farther than his stomach, and as it was impossible for him to bend very far, the gesture was more hospitable than graceful. A long table, made up of many little ones placed end to end, stretched down the center of the room. Its red and white plaid cover was dotted with red candles set in low holders, their bases hidden by long garlands that twined from one end of the table to the other. In one corner of the room stood the Christmas tree that the boys and girls had decorated that morning, all a-twinkle with little candles. Their festoons and wreaths hung against the mellow walls.

At one side of the room was a smaller table on which were grouped exquisite figures of the Madonna and Child, Joseph, the shepherds, and the Wise Men. It was this that Frau Schmidt had let Jean and Polly arrange. She told them that every family in Provence had such a crèche handed down from one generation to the next. Each year they add something to it, perhaps a hand-carved manger, perhaps a tiny figure modeled from clay, perhaps a new house for the village, or another tiny lamb. All the traditions of Christmas cluster about it, and the children of France love it dearly. Jean and Polly had arranged it beautifully. There was a tiny manger with miniature fir trees about it, a little lake made of a bit of broken mirror, a green pasture covered with velvety moss, and diminutive rocks and shrubs and flowers. There were oxen and a donkey in the stable and lambs on the green hillside. There were the Wise Men bearing gifts.

Coming up from the toy houses in the miniature village below were other figures bringing their gifts to the Christ child, the spinner with her flax, the farmer with his sheaf of grain, the milkmaid with her pails of foaming milk, the vineyard keeper with his basket of grapes—all of them bearing the fruits of their daily toil. Not only did the French children love this exquisite portrayal of the first Christmas, but all the others exclaimed over it, too.

As they sat down to dinner at the long table, the boys dragged in the Yule log, caroling as they came. Now it was the turn of the English family to be surprised and delighted, and they all joined lustily in singing, "Deck the hall with boughs of holly," while the Yule log was set ablaze. Then the father, who had a tremendous bass voice, rose at his end of the table and sang, "God rest you merry, gentlemen, Let nothing you dismay, Remember Christ our Saviour was born on Christmas day," and all who knew it joined in the chorus.

The door from the kitchen burst open, and in marched the waiters, each in a bright red vest, and each bearing aloft a great platter. On one was a whole pig, plump and brown and savory, with an apple in his mouth. On another a goose, and on still another a fat and golden turkey all garlanded in green. There was something to please everyone, a great yellow cheese, a quaking, red mound of jelly, a huge bowl of crisp salad, and one after another special delicacies followed, French, German, American. But the grand climax was a flaming English plum pudding.

Between courses everybody sang carols. Herr Schmidt toasted the French, and they responded with, "Bring a torch, Jeannette, Isabella, Bring a torch, to the cradle run," but sung in French, of course.

Jean and Polly and Paul and the other Americans sang, "Away in a manger, no crib for His bed." Then all together, some in English and some in German sang, "Silent night, Holy night, All is calm, all is bright."

Jean had scarcely noticed that the little Italian children had slipped away, but now a curtain was drawn back in one of the doorways, and there was a tableau. Tiny five-year-old Angela, with a soft white veil over her head, was the Madonna. In her arms she cradled a doll wrapped in swaddling clothes, rocking it gently to and fro. Behind her stood Beppo as Joseph, with his staff and lantern and long cloak. Two shepherds came in, kneeling before her to sing the familiar Bagpiper's Carol, "While shepherds watched their flocks by night." Then Mary gently crooned, "Far la nanna, bambin." The children were so small and had acted so sweetly and reverently, that there were tears in Jean's eyes, which she brushed hastily away. These were all songs that she had learned at school. It was fine to hear them sung now, each in its own language, by people who loved them, caressing the words as they sang.

Suddenly there was a great commotion of sleighbells outside, and in dashed Santa Claus himself, his familiar red sleigh pulled by half a dozen waiters, all of them singing "Jingle Bells" at the top of their lungs, but with a German accent that made it sound like "Jinkle Pells, Jinkle Pells." Everybody else joined in lustily. Santa Claus leaped from his sleigh and began dancing the *Schuh-plattler* in full Santa Claus regalia, while Hans played his accordion with a vim. The crowd roared with laughter as it recognized big Fritz beneath the false whiskers. There was great excitement as he began pulling packages out of his pack, gifts for everyone, some beautiful, some ridiculous, but all of them thrilling. And there were red apples, animal cookies, and paper cones full of Christmas candies for all the children. It was time now for the youngsters to go to bed, but first they hung up stockings on the mantle and set out shoes on the hearth, just in case Santa Claus had anything left over for the morning!

Jean's mother began thinking out loud and counting on her fingers. "We've had American turkey, English plum pudding, and German roast pig; a French crèche, an Italian presepio, an English Yule log, and a German tree; American stockings, French shoes, and carols in all three languages. Aren't there any Christmas traditions that are just Swiss and nothing else?"

"Ach, ja," cried Herr Schmidt, "I vill tell to you," and in a queer mixture of German, English, and French, so that everyone could understand, he told them of quaint Christmas customs which still persist in some of the more isolated parts of Switzerland.

First of all, he sent for an onion and some salt. Cutting the onion in half, he carefully peeled off twelve layers, one for each month of the year, and filled them with salt. In the morning, he said, the farmers could prepare a calendar for the coming year, depending on whether the salt in each cut should be wet or dry.

He then called for the family Bible, and asked Jean if she wanted to know how many more years she had to live. Opening it at the book of Psalms, he told her to count the stanzas in the first Psalm that her eye fell upon. The number of verses in that Psalm would tell how long she was to live.

He also told them that the animals talk to each other on Christmas Eve, between eleven and midnight.

"Let's go and listen," cried Polly, hurrying to the door that led to the barn.

But Herr Schmidt stopped her. "For anyvon who listens, it iss bat luck," he said solemnly.

He amused them all by telling of the romantic tradition that if unmarried girls go out alone on Christmas Eve and drink in nine fountains, they will meet their future husbands in the church door at

Santa Claus Began Dancing the *Schuh-plattler*.

midnight Mass.

"Does it ever come true?" asked Jean, so seriously that Herr Schmidt laughed.

"Vell, ass almost eferybody goes to Mass on Christmas Efe, it iss almost impossible to miss."

At that moment bells began to ring in the valley. "Here iss de chance to dry. Who vishes to go?"

"Oh, we all do," cried everybody at once, dashing off for his coat.

"Mustn't miss this opportunity," laughed Paul, as he buttoned himself into his big reefer. "I know Polly has her mind on that nice fat butcher's boy we saw in the village. How about it, Poll?"

There were three or four sleighs for the elders, but the young people piled into the big wood sledge and sat on the straw. From all over the valley came the sound of bells, church bells and sleighbells, and lights twinkled from every chalet. The half moon made lovely purple shadows on the snow. Some of the boys and girls sung snatches of tunes, but Jean was very quiet. She was wishing that her father might be here instead of way off in Russia. She wondered if he would be thinking of her, too, and decided that if she concentrated hard on wanting him to, he could not very well help it. Perhaps she could send him a thought message.

She scarcely noticed when they got to the church and everyone scrambled out; and she was still dreaming as she walked toward the church door. Just as she stepped in, Paul pushed big Fritz aside and stood directly in the way, blocking the entire door. "Meet the fate," he laughed.

Jean woke up suddenly. "Silly," she laughed, but she

didn't really mind at all.

The biggest surprise was when she came out again. There in the moonlight, as if her wish had brought him, stood her father in a shaggy fur coat. She was almost smothered in his big bear hug.

"O Mums!" she cried. "Did you know Daddy was coming?"

Her mother's eyes shone with happiness. "I wasn't *quite* sure," she said, "so I didn't tell you for fear he might not be able to get here."

It was a very radiant Jean who rode back up the mountain in the painted sleigh, squeezed tightly in between her father and mother. Snow had begun to fall gently, and from far away in the valley came snatches of song.

"Do you remember, Daddy, when I was little, I was always wanting a teddy-bear for Christmas, and a bigger one every year, to add to my collection? Well, this is the biggest one I've ever had, a real, honest-to-goodness Russian bear!"

The Russian bear only rumbled in his throat, "And the nicest?"

"And the nicest," declared Jean, settling herself more comfortably against his shaggy arm.

CHAPTER 5:
VENICE COMES TRUE

School was over. Jean and Company, Limited, had scattered in all directions, with many invitations to visit one another and eager demands that the Round Robin should fly quickly on its way. Little Jane was to stay at the convent, to see if the warm sunshine of the Southland would make her stronger. She would start the letter, and the other girls would send it along as quickly as possible, so that it might go around several times during the summer. Everyone had gone off happily for the holiday. Jane was sad at being left alone, but she clung tightly to Sister Irmengarde's hand, and they both tried hard to keep back the tears when Jean, last of all, came to say goodbye. Of course, the President of Jean and Company, Limited, must keep a stiff upper lip. Anyway she adored little Sister Irmengarde, and would try not to miss the girls too much.

First, Jean and her mother spent several weeks traveling in Italy. It seemed to Jean she could not possibly decide whether she liked Florence or Siena or Rome best. Now she was going to visit Giovanna in Venice, while her mother stayed with friends in Asolo, near by. Of course, Jean had studied about Venice in history class and had seen pictures of the Campanile and San Marco. Aunt Sally had even brought her a little silver gondola for a present. But at the convent Giovanna had never talked much about her home.

Whenever it was mentioned, she had merely looked a little wistful, going off into a blissful daydream that had made her useless for lessons or tennis for some time afterward. Even when Jean asked her mother to tell her about Venice on the train, she had only looked very mysterious and smiled. "It's like fairyland, my dear. Different from anything else in the whole world. Just wait and see!"

In spite of her impatience Jean enjoyed crossing the railroad bridge over the wide stretch of water, although she thought it very much like other railroad bridges after all. There was a distant view of domes and towers, but then every other Italian city had domes and towers. When they pulled into the station, there were the same lines of tracks and the same porters running along beside the cars that she had seen everywhere else in Italy. Venice couldn't be so very different after all, and she was perfectly sure there would not be ugly railroad tracks and perspiring porters in fairyland!

No sooner had she scrambled out of the train than she saw plump, dark-eyed Giovanna bobbing along the platform to meet her. The two girls rushed into each other's arms, and there were ecstatic hugs, kisses on both cheeks, and a most amusing mixture of English, French, and Italian words, all tumbling over each other. It was several minutes before Giovanna's governess, who had finally arrived on the scene, could get in a word of greeting, or Jean's mother, who was taking a train back to Asolo, could say goodbye. Chatter, chatter, chatter, mostly in French, as Giovanna knew only a few words of English, and Jean knew almost no Italian. It was astonishing how much faster they spoke French out of school than in school, making up in gestures and giggles what they lacked in words.

Suddenly Jean realized that they were not taking a carriage or taxi, but that she was being helped from slippery stone steps into a long, low gondola where her bags were already stowed. She sat down unexpectedly as the gondola lurched in the waves of a passing motor boat, while Giovanna and the governess laughed at her look of astonishment. Then she saw that the canal was full of other boats, long, black gondolas with high bows like the one she was in; trim motor boats; clumsy steamboats crowded with people, which were the street cars of Venice, Giovanna told her; low barges loaded with fruit and vegetables for the markets. Her eye was caught by one big boat full of beds and chairs and tables, with a marble statue and a rocking horse up in the bow. That must be a moving van, she decided. She noticed, too, that all the gondolas and barges were rowed by men who stood in the high stern of the boat and pushed a long oar, swaying backward and forward with a strong, rhythmic motion, backward and forward, backward and forward.

How thrilling it all was—the shining water, the graceful gondolas, the gentle motion, the musical calls of the boatmen! The late afternoon sky made an opalescent background for the pink houses bordering the canal, and Jean could catch occasional glimpses of vines and flowers climbing over the garden walls. She was actually speechless with excitement, and all she could do was clutch Giovanna and give little breathless squeals of delight.

Finally she found her tongue again and exclaimed, "Oh, I didn't know it would be like this. It *is* fairyland!"

Past stately palaces they went, their front steps leading down into the water, and with lacelike balconies against walls of pale pink and yellow and ivory. They slid into the blue shadows beneath the Rialto bridge; they glided noiselessly by another gondola coming around the bend, missing it by a hair's breadth as the gondoliers called musical but unintelligible things to one another. They swayed for a breath-taking moment in waves that looked as if they must surely come over the side. At last the gondola drew up to the steps of an ivory-colored palace, between tall boat posts with spiral stripes like peppermint sticks. The girls pushed at a great, nail-studded door, and Jean felt exactly as if she were opening a book cover and stepping into the midst of a most engaging fairy tale.

At the head of the wide, marble stairway stood Giovanna's mother, black-haired and gentle and gracious, as beautiful as an old painting of a Madonna. Jean loved her at once, and was delighted when she spoke to her in English, with the most charming Italian accent imaginable. Up another flight of stairs they went, and Giovanna took Jean to her room, which was next to her own. How glad she was to be alone for a little while! She sank down on the nearest chair and looked and looked, and even pinched herself to see if she were really awake.

What an unbelievable room! Walls of pale robin's egg blue; a wide, low bed with high posts and a cover of golden damask shot with blue and rose; a carved, dark wood chest that might hold the fabled treasures of the Orient; a low dressing table covered with yellow damask, and over it a mirror with a gilded, lacelike frame. Delicately painted chairs, in old ivory and rose and blue, flanked a tall, Venetian desk. There were slender candlesticks under a quaint, old painting of the Madonna and Child, and flowers everywhere. Jean gave herself a final pinch, to be sure she was not dreaming.

Suddenly she remembered the canal again and ran to the window. There was a balcony outside, and here she leaned, looking at the passing gondolas, listening to snatches of song, watching the changing colors of the sunset in sky and water, and feasting her eyes on the domes and spires all about her. It was here that Giovanna found her when she came to take her down to dinner.

The dining room was the illustration for the next chapter of the fairy tale, thought Jean, with its high paneled wainscoting of dark wood and its beamed ceiling in designs of red and blue. The long refectory table was set with creamy linen, colorful china, fragile blue glass, and tall silver candelabra. Old portraits looked down from the walls, and the windows were hung with vermilion damask.

Jean sat in her high-backed chair between Giovanna and her mother, opposite the rest of the family. There was Giovanna's distinguished father, his pointed beard and fine bearing making him look the Count that he was. Except for his present-day clothes, he might have stepped directly out of the ancestral portrait hanging on the wall above his head. A sixteen-year-old sister, slender and lovely, and a handsome lad of thirteen, as polite and courtly as his father, but with black eyes full of mischief, completed the family. The elders spoke to Jean in English, the two girls in French, and Mario knew only Italian, but Jean could understand his gestures and the twinkle in his merry eyes.

It was a gay and leisurely meal, with such good things to eat: a soup in which little round pastries floated like bubbles; macaroni cut in bowknots and sprinkled with a flaky cheese; fresh asparagus with a thick, golden sauce; chicken and green salad; a tray of cheeses, white and yellow and orange, and a great bowl of crimson strawberries. Each dish was served by itself on a fresh plate, with plenty of time for conversation between courses. In spite of an enormous appetite, Jean thought how much nicer this was than piling everything on one's plate at the same time and eating in a hurry. After dinner they walked for a while in the tiny, walled garden beside the palace, an enchanted place in the moonlight, with the flowers gleaming palely and deep blue shadows on the statues and fountain.

"If you sleep well tonight, Jean," said Giovanna's mother, "we will go out to hear the singing boats tomorrow night," but they would tell her nothing more, in spite of her eager questions.

She slept like a top in the big bed, never stirring till the maid opened the shutters and brought in her breakfast on a tray. As she sat up in bed and balanced the tray precariously on her knees, she pretended she was the Queen of Sheba. Even the Queen of Sheba would have thought it a royal breakfast, she was sure— flaky rolls, fragrant chocolate, amber honey, and a glass bowl full of cherries on the stem.

She was already dressed and back again at her post on the balcony when Giovanna appeared and said that the gondola was waiting to take them wherever they wished to go. Jean leaned still farther out, and there she saw the long gondola, graceful as a black swan, brass sea horses and dolphins shining, the high metal prow gleaming in the sunlight. She saw now the beautiful carving at the back of the seat, with the red cords and fringes along the sides. The gondolier was busy arranging cushions and a vivid piece of crimson damask which he threw over the low seats. "Why are gondolas black?" asked Jean. Giovanna told her that they had been black for centuries, ever since a great naval defeat, when the Doge had ordered all the boats to be painted black as a sign of mourning.

"In fact, everything in Venice is just as it was centuries ago," added Giovanna. "The palaces are the same, the churches, the bridges, the canals, the yellow sails, even coffee at Florian's. It is only the clothes that have changed. True, the quiet of the canals has been broken by motor boats, but nobody minds that because they are so convenient."

Just then the gondolier, in his summer suit of white, a red sash with gold fringe around his waist, and a wide-brimmed straw hat with red ribbons hanging down behind, saluted them respectfully.

"Pronto, Signorina," he called, meaning that the gondola was ready.

The girls raced down, and Jean was in such a hurry that she slipped on the wet stone steps and landed unceremoniously in the low seat of the gondola. So it was with many giggles that the girls arranged themselves to wait for the Signorina, who moved more deliberately; for Giovanna explained that she and her sister never went anywhere without the governess or her mother. Jean thought this must be a great bore, never to go out alone, and was inwardly glad again that she was an American, although, of course, she did not mention it out loud.

Off they went, Jean's eyes growing wider and wider with excitement as the Doge's palace came into view. Pale pink and ivory walls with a delicately carved lace border against the blue Venetian sky, the whole supported by fragile-looking columns, made it seem too ethereal to be real. The gondola slid silently up to the broad stone promenade. In a few minutes they were walking through an archway into a shining courtyard. Jean touched the columns slyly just to make sure they were real. They passed two great fountains, mounted a wide stone staircase, walked around the high loggia that surrounded the courtyard, and presently came to a great room whose walls were covered with murals.

These paintings peopled for Jean the Venice of olden times. Here were doges in gorgeous robes, bishops in high miters and jewel-encrusted vestments, great ladies in flowing brocades and velvets, pages in colorful tunics. Here also were ancient high-pooped and square-rigged sailing vessels, but everywhere the same palaces and churches and bridges, the same canals and gondolas and orange sails as today. How she did wish she might have lived in those grand old times! However, when the governess explained to her that slavery and poverty, cruelty and intrigue were all a necessary part of this grandeur, she shivered a little and was glad that she lived in the twentieth century after all.

"Now," said Giovanna, as they came out again into the brilliant sunshine of the square and Jean was following the substantial red brick Campanile up and up with her eyes, "you must not look until I tell you to." With that she led her down the long colonnade surrounding the great square of San Marco.

But Jean was so busy looking into the shop windows that she did not care if she never looked anywhere else again. There were windows full of cobwebby lace and delicate embroideries, pale and vivid coral, glass in all colors of the rainbow, jewelry of silver filigree, and the same kind of gondola that Aunt Sally had once brought her. It took a minute or two for Giovanna to drag her away from these captivating windows when they came to the far end of the square.

When she finally succeeded, Jean leaned against a column and did indeed look and look. There at the far end of the Piazza was San Marco, a pale golden pile of turrets and domes and delicate spires that might have been conjured up by a magician. As they walked slowly toward it, Jean saw that the opalescent color came from tiny mosaics on a golden background. Giovanna told her that the inside of the church was full of these mosaics, too. She almost stumbled over some pigeons as she walked, and suddenly she was completely surrounded by a fluttering throng of them. One alighted on her shoulder, and she stood spellbound, San Marco forgotten, afraid to move lest she should frighten it. Giovanna ran over to a man seated at a table in the square and came back with two paper cones full of yellow corn. Jean soon had pigeons on each arm, eating from her hands, and others on her shoulders and head. Then a bell struck and all the pigeons in the square, thousands of them, swept abruptly away, in a swift, slanting flight, perching on the life-sized figures carved in the high frieze at one end of the Piazza and on the galleries and bronze horses of San Marco.

"Look," cried Giovanna, as she pointed to the top of the blue and gold clock tower.

There Jean saw two bronze men slowly striking a great bronze bell with hammers. She stood transfixed till they had struck twelve times and stopped. Then she turned to ask Giovanna why the pigeons all flew away.

"When the bell rings at two o'clock every day, they are fed. So whenever any hour strikes, they fly up to see if it is feeding time."

"But there are dozens of people feeding them all the time," said Jean. "Why should they need anything more?"

Giovanna told her there were thousands of pigeons

THEY WERE SUDDENLY COMPLETELY SURROUNDED BY A
THRONG OF PIGEONS.

and it was only during the tourist season that they had enough to eat, so a great many of them had once starved during the winter. Some years before, however, a kind Venetian who loved the pigeons left money enough to have them fed. Twice each day an attendant brought a sack of feed and poured it on the pavement around four sides of a square, the pigeons covering it immediately in a solid mass. In two minutes not a trace of the grain would be left. Giovanna promised Jean she should see this sight while she was in Venice.

The shops began to close now for the long noon rest, and the gondola was waiting to take the girls home for lunch. As they slid into one of the side canals, Giovanna waved to a plump child in a doorway.

"That," she said, "is the daughter of the man who brings us milk and eggs. She has never seen a cow or a chicken. Many Venetian children have never seen an automobile. Even the new automobile bridge brings them only as far as the station, and they can never come any farther, as fortunately there is not a street in Venice wide enough for an automobile to pass through."

After lunch and the long noon rest which everybody in Venice takes during the hot hours of the day, they went to one of the lace schools to see the girls at their lace making. Jean watched while deft fingers threw the bobbins over pins stuck in the lace pillows, or wove in the cobwebby designs with a needle. In the delicate patterns she recognized many of the flowers and cupids and birds that she had noticed already in the sculpture and painting of Venice, and she realized that all these arts were closely related. She was interested in the way the designs were drawn on paper or cloth and fastened to the bolster-shaped pillows, many of them so fine that she had to bend down close to the work to make them out at all. Yet the fingers of these girls flew like lightning and they scarcely seemed to look at the pattern. Some of the smallest doilies took a month to make, and Jean saw one big piece that an old woman in a black shawl had been working at for three years. She began to realize that making a beautiful piece of lace was just as much an art as painting or sculpture.

But the glass blowing was still more fascinating, because a thing of beauty grew out of it before one's very eyes. In a few minutes a tiny lump of red-hot matter changed into a shimmering bubble of a bowl or goblet, or even into an opalescent dolphin balanced on his tail, to hold a flower or a candle. Jean felt sure that the glass blower with his pipe was merely a magician with his wand, in disguise. First he blew a transparent bubble at the end of his long pipe. This he turned deftly in the flaming furnace, and then sat again upon his bench. With a delicate instrument that was scissors or file or pincers as he chose, he made whatever he wished—an exquisite vase, a delicate goblet, a ball of glass so ethereal it looked as if it might float away on the faintest breeze.

Jean watched fascinated while a young boy dipped his rod into the red-hot mass of melted glass, drew it forth, and with fine pincers pulled at little bits of the shapeless lump until he finally held out to her a perfect glass dog, with nose, ears, feet, and a ridiculous curly tail. In spite of the almost unbearable heat of the furnaces and an increasing emptiness within that proclaimed tea time, it was only after repeated suggestions of sherbet at Florian's that she could be torn away, the green glass dog tightly clutched in one hand.

Like many other things in Venice, Florian's has been the same for centuries. Here great poets and musicians, kings and generals, rascals and villains have met to hobnob, plan the fate of nations, or hatch some new deviltry. Jean and Giovanna and the governess, however, merely ordered ices and sat at a little table on the pavement in the Piazza where they could watch the late afternoon crowd as it flowed by in colorful waves. Plump and comfortable nurses in tight-bodiced dresses of pink or blue checked material, flaunting wide bands of a plain color around the bottom of the full skirts, and aprons of fine lace and embroidery strolled past. Their costumes were finished off with snowy kerchiefs bound round the hair, and necklace and earrings of heavy gold filigree. The Signorina explained that these were almost the only traces of peasant costumes now left in Italy.

What fun it was to watch these nurses with their tiny charges, babes in arms with long, pale-blue capes, black-haired dolls of girls in ridiculously short skirts, and fat little boys in the smartest of shorts. Jean thought she had never seen such adorable children. They squealed with delight over the pigeons and ran after them with funny, fat, rolling gaits. Couples who looked like honeymooners, the girls decided romantically, tourists that must have come from every quarter of the globe, gay groups of Venetians talking with many gesticulations, bearded monks in brown robes, pretty girls, handsome youths, bent and picturesque old women still proudly wearing their black, fringed shawls made up the procession. Jean could have sat there for hours, but, of course, one must go home some time.

After dinner they put on wraps, for Venice becomes cool as soon as the burning sun disappears, and the three girls, with Giovanna's father and mother, again started off in the gondola, this time to hear the singing boats. Giovanna took her guitar and played snatches of Venetian serenades. They watched the great red moon come up, seemingly right out of the central dome of the church of Santa Maria della Salute. They drifted along to where the colored lanterns bobbed about on the singing barges, while the music of familiar Italian songs was wafted across the waters of the lagoon. It was lovely to see the dark shadows of other gondolas slipping past silently and wonder where they were going, and to watch the myriad, flickering lights reflected in the mysterious waters. For a while they moved close enough to the barges to hold on to the long string of gondolas which made a solid mass up to the singers. Occasionally one of the chorus would step from one gondola to another and pass his tambourine for contributions. If the gift were handsome enough, one might ask for one's favorite song, so when Jean dropped in her two lire she whispered something to the man, and sure enough, in a few moments she heard the familiar old serenade, *Santa Lucia*, ringing out over the water. How she wished this beautiful moment could go on forever.

However, all good things must end, and as they drifted home, Giovanna strummed dreamily on her guitar again, and Jean decided that she was rather glad after all not to have to crowd any more beauty into one day.

The next morning Giovanna, fully dressed, came into her room and told her to hurry so she could watch the boats arriving for the fiesta. Both girls hung over the balcony and watched the flower-festooned gondolas. There were barges full of fisherfolk from the outlying islands, with tables set up in the middle of the gondolas so that they might enjoy their holiday food and drink with no inconvenience, motor boats carrying smartly uniformed officers and their friends, rowboats full of excited urchins. Everything that could float was out for the great occasion.

Giovanna told her it was the Feast of the Redeemer, the most important holiday of the year in Venice. They were invited to watch the celebration from the balcony of friends who lived on the Zattere, the part of Venice which fronted the beautiful Church of the Redeemer on the Giudecca, another Venetian island. In order to avoid the crowds on the water, the girls walked to the Zattere over little bridges, down narrow streets where the roofs almost met overhead, past unexpected little shrines set in the old walls. They finally came upon the open water and the wide promenade along which were anchored larger ships than Jean had seen elsewhere in Venice—coasting vessels, fishing boats, coal barges, painted bright vermilion or turquoise blue or apple green, with yellow and orange sails lying furled on the decks. At that moment Jean longed with all her heart to be able to paint. Now she understood why artists and poets came to Venice.

"Look," cried Giovanna, pointing to a bridge built

on boats across the wide strip of water, the famous Bridge of Boats of which Jean had read. Barge after barge after barge, all arranged side by side, held a plank bridge extending from the Zattere to the doors of the great Church of the Redeemer with its beautiful dome gleaming in the sunshine. Gathered all about it were big boats and little boats, gondolas and fishing boats crowded with people. The waterside was so packed with slowly moving humanity that Giovanna's little group could scarcely push itself through to get to the friend's house and balcony.

Afterwards Jean could not tell which part of the day she had enjoyed most, the brilliant procession of church dignitaries in their gorgeous robes, marching with all the pomp and splendor of the processions which she had seen in the old paintings of Venice, across the bridge of barges and right into the doors of the great church opposite, or the colorful throngs of excited people following, or the gay pageantry of the flower-bedecked boats constantly moving on the wide expanse of water. Perhaps it was the evening itself, when the opalescent colors of the sunset faded from the sky, when every boat was lighted with bobbing paper lanterns and the air was melodious with the musical cries and songs of the happy crowd. At the last, against the thick velvet of the night sky, flamed and flared and burst into a thousand scintillating fragments the most glamorous fireworks that Jean had ever seen, she was sure. They not only filled the heavens with unbelievable splendor but were reflected in the black waters as well, a myriad of throbbing lights and colors. She dreamed that night of boats and flowers and portly priests all exploding in mid-air as fireworks and being reflected in the waters as music!

When the time came for farewells, Giovanna bemoaned the fact that Jean had as yet really seen very little of Venice, and she made her promise to come soon again. But Jean knew that what she had seen would stay with her all her life as a glimpse of fairyland. She sighed when the great palace door closed again behind her, as one sighs when closing an interesting book, still hoping to read it many times again.

CHAPTER 6:

THE STRANGE LAND OF YUGOSLAVIA

When Jean woke up that morning and stretched sleepily, her hand struck something hard. As she bounced upright in surprise, her head bumped something else. By this time her eyes were wide open and she realized she was sitting in a bunk with another bunk close above her, and she was sure she had bumped every bit of wood in both of them. Just as she began looking ruefully for black and blue spots, an absurd little toot-toot-toot brought her to the porthole, where she saw that they were passing a stately four-masted, square-rigged vessel with yellow and orange sails. Behind it the blue sea was dotted with emerald islands and queer little fishing boats with russet, lateen sails. This *was* exciting!

She jumped into her clothes, banged on her mother's stateroom door in passing, and flew up the stairway to the deck. Of course, trains and automobiles and airplanes were all right, she supposed, but certainly the most glorious way in the world to travel was by boat. Throwing back her head to let the keen wind blow through her hair, she spread her arms wide to catch the sunshine.

The sea was blue as blue, with tiny, silvery wave tips here and there. A few white-walled buildings nestled in the greenery of the islands. The little boats sped out to sea like a flock of golden birds, but most of all, the great square-rigged ship thrilled her. It might have been on just such a vessel that the Vikings set out on their adventures, or that her sea captain ancestors sailed around Cape Horn to India in those faraway days. Perhaps it was a pirate ship. How exciting it would be to stand in the bow with high boots and folded arms, a patch over one eye, a cutlass in her teeth, and, of course, a skull and crossbones on the flag flying above her.

"Oh, I'd be a pirate bold!" she sang. Whew, wasn't she feeling adventurous and ready for anything this morning!

She shook herself a little and remembered that she was really having an adventure on her own ship. It had happened this way. When the gondola drew up to the hotel where she was to meet her mother in Venice, there was her father, too, come down from Russia for a holiday. They rushed at each other with such excitement that the bell boy, coming out to get Jean's bags, tripped over the ice-cream man, who was selling ice-cream cones from a little white gondola on wheels. The gondola on wheels almost rolled into the other gondola, the ice-cream man waved his arms and hurled Italian imprecations at the bell boy, and in no time at all a crowd collected, all chattering in staccato Italian and gesticulating wildly.

Finally two gorgeous policemen in cocked hats appeared to find out what it was all about. When the uproar had subsided, Jean collected her scattered wits and introduced Giovanna and her father. Nothing would do but they must all go for tea at Florian's. Jean had to sit as close to her father as possible and could scarcely take her eyes from him for long enough to eat her *dolce*.

When quiet was restored, and everybody was full of tea and cakes, Jean's mother said, "Can you stand another surprise?"

Jean nodded eagerly.

"Instead of going to Salzburg for the entire music festival, as we had planned, your father wants to take us to Yugoslavia and Budapest."

"To where?" asked Jean, a little puzzled. Geography had never been her strong point.

"To where the language sounds like corn popping, the letters all look like pretzels, and the men wear skirts," laughed her father.

He got out his map and drew beautiful red lines down the coast of Dalmatia, up through Zagreb (Jean remembered now that was where her mother's friend lived), over to Budapest, and back to Salzburg.

Just then the clock in the tower struck five, and Jean dragged her father out to see the bronze men striking the great bell with their hammers. The girls said goodbye, with many promises of letters, and Jean and her father and mother went off to find a steamship office. They were told that the boat for Dalmatia had left that morning and there wouldn't be another for a week, which would be too late. But afterward, as they were walking along one of the quaint little streets in Venice, feeling rather crestfallen, they had passed a steamship office with posters in the window which very plainly said something about Dalmatia, although all the other words were quite impossible to read. Here they found that there was a small freight boat, with comfortable quarters for a few passengers, leaving Venice in about an hour.

They rushed back to their hotel, packed in a tremendous hurry, and found Gino, the hotel gondolier, waiting to take them out into the lagoon where the ship was anchored. In the confusion of getting off, it was some time before they noticed he was shaking his head rather dubiously and shrugging his shoulders as if talking to himself.

"What about this Dalmatian freight boat?" said Father, beginning to feel a little doubtful.

"She vera leetla sheep, Signor, and ze how-you-say Adriatico Ocean, she vera beeg."

Jean's father laughed at this, but Jean looked back wistfully at Venice, with its opal palaces and towers, wondering if she would ever see it again.

Soon Gino pointed to a white ship in the lagoon, very white and very small. As they slid up under her side and Gino shouted, several sailors with vivid scarfs tied around their heads peered out of portholes. There was something about those scarlet kerchiefs and ferocious mustachios that made Jean and her mother a little shivery—and the boat certainly did look small. However, they were soon on deck, waving goodbye to Gino, who was still shaking his head and shrugging his shoulders dubiously. In a few minutes up went the anchor and off they steamed. Gino's behavior, the queer language, along with the strange-looking men, made this a real adventure. But the polite young officer assured them, in broken English, that everything would be all right, as he showed them to their clean and shining staterooms.

As she stood on deck once more, Jean thought she had never in her life seen anything so beautiful as Venice fading in the distance under a sunset sky. And while they were eating their picnic supper— crisp rolls with Italian cheese, big strawberries from a leaf-lined basket, and white wine with plump little cakes—she was speechless with delight. Presently the full moon came up over the rim of the sea, and somewhere from the deck below rose the voices of the sailors. Jean went softly to the rail and peered over. There they were, sitting or lying about the deck, these brigands and pirates, singing songs that melted your very heart; tender, plaintive, whimsical songs, the folk songs of Dalmatia, so the captain told them. It was almost midnight before Jean could be persuaded to leave the music and the moonlight. But she had gone to sleep at last to the sound of water lapping under her porthole, and to the wailing notes of the steel-stringed guitar in the distance. No wonder it took her a few minutes to remember where she was when she awoke the next morning.

Now the steamer was coming into the crescent bay of Šibenik, the wide white sands stretching up to the amphitheater of green hills all around the little port. The buildings shone in the morning sunlight as Jean excitedly pointed everything out to her father and mother when they appeared on deck. Fisher people in bright kerchiefs and vivid costumes were moving about on the beach, the women swinging along with great, flat baskets of fish on their heads, the men hauling busily at their nets. The lateen sails of the little fishing boats made a slanting medley of color, yellow, russet, and red. While their ship unloaded and reloaded freight, the three of them wandered about the little town, lingering in the shady park and climbing to the castle on the hill. They saw with surprise that many of the buildings of the town looked as if they might have sailed over from Venice themselves.

It was interesting to know that other voyagers from that fair city had been down the Dalmatian coast before them, centuries and centuries ago. The traders must have brought architects and painters with them and even jewelers, for the jewelry that Jean saw everywhere along the way had the delicate filigree look of that which she had seen in Venice. When the whistle blew, they hurried back to the ship, their private yacht, they laughingly called it, since they were the only passengers on board.

As they drew near Spalato, Jean rubbed her eyes. First she saw an arcaded palace stretching along the water front. Then when she looked again, she seemed to see only the buildings of a town. Her father watched her puzzled expression with an amused smile.

"Think you are seeing double, eh, Jean?" he asked. "This is one of the most interesting towns in the whole world. Diocletian, a Roman emperor, built his summer palace here, back in the third or fourth century, and the columns which you see are part of that ancient structure. But about A.D. 600 refugees from Salona fled to this palace for protection and here fortified themselves against the Turks. They built an entire town inside the walls of a palace originally intended for one family and its servants, and there are now some three thousand people living within those walls. The pagan temple built to Jupiter in the third century has become a Christian baptistry. What would the slaves of Diocletian think if they could see his palace now?"

Jean could scarcely wait to get off the boat and go exploring. They poked about the quaint village, its houses, like swallows' nests, perched in every nook and cranny in the old palace. Here they picked out columns and arcades that Diocletian had built, there the tumbledown ancient dwellings of those early refugees who fled from the Turks. In the midst of all this antiquity rose an occasional modern building.

The men of Spalato wore outside vests, jingling with round silver buttons, which were a part of the treasure trove of the family handed down from father to son. The women wore queer little high caps with kerchiefs tied over them, and more silver buttons. Some of the young girls wore their dowry around their necks, chain after chain from which dangled silver coins and many strings of coral. In this way the young men could tell at a glance whether a girl was rich as well as beautiful. Jean thought this a very queer custom and rather unfair for the girls who had not much to display.

Back again to the boat! Another night of moonlight and music, and on down to Dubrovnik, once called Ragusa, the pearl of the Dalmatian coast. Shining white it rose from the blue sea, a city of gleaming opal. Around it stood tall, green cypresses and spreading palms, and in the distance the amethyst hills paled against a turquoise sky. Only jewel words could describe its sparkle and color, thought Jean.

The boat anchored in the harbor, a short distance from Dubrovnik. She and her father and mother drove in a quaint carriage through the gate above which rode Peter, the patron saint of old Ragusa, on his great carved stone horse. Such an unbelievable street as it was, with its beautiful Venetian architecture, its ancient churches and cloisters, its people in brilliant costume. On one side the houses were built so straight up the steep hillside that the streets were steps, and the roofs towered above one another to the very sky. On the other side opened the beautiful public square, almost as full of pigeons as the Piazza San Marco in Venice. Around the entire city was a shining white wall.

Jean's father told her how Richard Coeur de Lion, overtaken by a storm on his ill-fated voyage back from the Holy Land, vowed that he would build a church at the spot where he should land in safety. It was at Dubrovnik that he erected a cathedral of great beauty, which was later completely destroyed by an earthquake. He showed her the cloisters and gardens in the convents of the Franciscan and Dominican monks. He took her to the museum in a little Venetian palace where she saw a remarkable collection of native costumes, stiff with embroidery and brilliant in coloring. Why should most of the civilized world wear drab and conventional clothes, thought Jean, when every country must be rich in the tradition of vivid and beautiful costume? She was so glad that she had found one country at least where people still wore their native dress. They spent the night in an old inn, with an enchanting garden overhanging the Adriatic.

They had now left their boat for good. The next day they took a toy train which twisted and turned in hairpin curves as it carried them through fertile valleys, up barren mountain sides where boys and girls in bright costumes scrambled about the rocks with their flocks of lively goats—up, up over the very peaks where they could look away to other mountains and valleys on either side. The train was so small that Jean felt if she crossed the aisle to look down into the valley, the car might topple over. It was a breath-taking experience, this little tooting toy which carried them over the top of the world.

They came to Sarajevo next, the city where the Austrian prince was assassinated, and the firebrand kindled that started the World War. Here they saw many Muslim men in red fezzes and women in long veils. Jean's father told her that Sarajevo was now more Turkish than Turkey itself, as it had kept many of the

old Muslim customs long after Turkey had given them up. Jean was very curious about these mysteriously veiled women, and watched as they whispered their orders to the little maids who always went with them to do their purchasing for them. They themselves might speak to no man outside their own family or let their faces be seen by any other.

Jean and her mother were allowed to go into the beautiful mosque after they had put on great shuffling straw shoes over their own shoes. But Jean was told that no Muslim women might enter this church for fear of contaminating it. Women were supposed to have no souls and could worship only in the little mosques outside the city walls. She was interested in the muezzin, calling prayers from the Moorish tower, and the well near the door of the mosque where the men wash ceremonially many times a day. Sarajevo was full of the mystery of the East, with its delicate Moorish architecture, its veiled women, its strange costumes, and its stranger customs.

The Turkish market was made up of streets of open booths, with canopies over them. Here on raised platforms sat cross-legged men in voluminous trousers and tasseled fezzes, beating out shining copper bowls, making leathern slippers, or unrolling lengths of gorgeous silk, the riches of the Orient spread about them. Jean wanted to buy everything she saw and take it home with her.

At the hotel they found a room with a private bath, a great luxury for this part of the world, but as there was hot water only on Saturdays and this was Tuesday, it did not do them much good. When they asked for a

Turkish meal, they got all kinds of queer things, most of them very delicious, but Jean had to draw the line at the great bowl of thick, sour, goat's cream, which is dessert to Sarajevans.

Once more they climbed aboard a toy train and puffed and snorted off to Zagreb. They were to travel all night, but there was no sleeper, so they tried to settle themselves comfortably on the hard seats. Every time they dozed off, along came a pompous officer in uniform, who clicked his heels, bowed like a jackknife, and asked if they had any bullets. Or perhaps it was cigarettes or matches or playing cards. At any rate, for most of the night, as they crossed one border or another of the many little countries included in Yugoslavia, these uniformed customs officers interrupted their sleep to make them drag down their suitcases from the racks, spread them on the seats, and open them. Jean seldom knew what language they were speaking, and sometimes neither her father or mother could understand, either. Finally Jean's father settled himself resolutely on the long bench and only opened one eye to say, "Thank you very much, we are very comfortable," whenever a customs man appeared. The officer would sputter, command, entreat, gesticulate toward the luggage, and finally depart shaking his head. Impossible to make these stupid Americans understand!

At two o'clock in the morning they were routed out at a pitch-dark stopping place. There a strange porter went off with their bags, and they were pushed into the only lighted room in the station and locked in firmly. Several other travelers and peasants were locked in with them, but although Jean's father experimented in German, French, Italian, and Russian, none of them could understand. He then tried to find an official who could tell him what happened next, but there was no one in sight. After an hour a train came chugging in, the station doors were unlocked, and everyone made a dash to get on board. Jean's father rushed up and down the platform trying to find the porter and suitcases, but none were visible.

Finally Jean and her mother, who had raced the length of the train inside looking for their baggage, found it and a frantic porter in the front car. Jean leaned from the window and waved triumphantly. Her mother tipped the relieved porter, her father jumped aboard, and off the train went. The three of them sat down and mopped their brows, wondering if by any chance this train happened to be going where they wanted to go. There had been no one to ask. At last a conductor came through and punched their tickets reassuringly, and they settled down to more attempted sleep and continued interruptions. Jean was very grateful that her father had been with them. Traveling in a country where one could not understand the language was a great strain. But having him along made everything seem all right.

In Zagreb Jean's mother had an old friend whom she had known at school in France many years before. Although the friend had married a Serbian, she was French herself, so that they could all understand one another perfectly. Her daughter, Jovanka, was just Jean's age, and the two girls were delighted when they found that Jovanka was Serbian for Jean.

"You'll have to join our club, Jean and Company, Limited, right away," cried Jean in great excitement. "We'll send you the Round Robin and everything."

Jovanka looked puzzled at first, but was just as pleased as Jean when she finally understood. She was slim and black-haired and dark-eyed, this Jovanka. She wore beautifully embroidered dresses, adapted somewhat from the costumes of the peasants and made by girls in the embroidery schools in Zagreb. Jean's mother promptly bought one for Jean, too, so that the two girls felt as gay as they looked in their lovely gowns.

Zagreb was quite different from any of the other towns they had seen in Yugoslavia, a great modern city with wide streets, beautiful public parks, and rows and rows of apartment houses. But the streets were full of the color of more native costumes than Jean had seen anywhere else. Even the men wore beautifully embroidered blouses and jackets, and full, gathered trousers that hung about their legs like voluminous skirts.

"What did I tell you!" said her father.

It was a fête day and all the peasants from the neighboring villages had come to Zagreb to celebrate. Jean and her father and mother followed group after group about, fascinated by their lovely costumes. Gradually Jean realized that the peasants were looking at *them* just as curiously, following *them* about, nudging each other, and pointing out their strange clothing.

"Why," said Jean suddenly, "we must be just as queer to them as they are to us. I never thought of that before."

BESIDE HER WALKED A DAPPER LITTLE DANDY.

Jovanka took them to the great market place in the shadow of the cathedral where, under brilliant awnings, were spread all the wares that the peasants brought in from their villages. From one village came only dairy things, cream and butter and cheese, and at these booths the peasants all wore exactly the same kind of costume. In the next booth were strawberries and cherries from another village, the peasants also being dressed just alike. In another part of the market were chickens and ducks and eggs only, and these women wore a still different style of clothing, typical of their own village. As she watched, Jean saw a great, strapping woman come striding in with a basket of live ducks in either hand and another balanced on her head. She turned her head from side to side easily as she walked and talked, while the ducks quacked and stretched their necks. But the basket on her head never even wobbled. Beside her walked a dapper little dandy, much embroidered and beribboned, swinging his cane, but carrying nothing else.

"Why doesn't he help her?" asked Jean.

Jovanka looked at her in astonishment. "Here women carry everything to market. It would be beneath a man's dignity to do it," said Jovanka. Jean thought how John would chuckle if he could hear this. She must be sure to mention it in her next letter.

Her mother was not half so interested in the cheeses and ducks and strawberries as she was in the costumes that the women wore, and before the morning was over, with the help of Jovanka's mother, she had bargained for a blouse and cap, a gay skirt, and a brilliantly embroidered apron. It was not easy to persuade the women to part with these treasures. They were not just dresses as we know them, but were traditional costumes identical from one generation to another, embroidered by each bride on homespun, hand-woven linen, to last a lifetime of feast days and market days. But there were some younger women who now preferred the newer dresses they could buy in the shops, with the money given them by these foolish foreigners who wanted somebody else's clothes. Jean wondered how she would feel if some casual traveler in America tried to buy her clothes.

Jean and Jovanka could not get to sleep that last night at Zagreb. And in spite of various mild protests from their elders, they talked and talked and talked. There was so much left to say! Jean told Jovanka again about some of the girls who belonged to Jean and Company, Limited. Jovanka wondered how soon she would get the Round Robin and how many of the letters she would be able to read, for, of course, they might be written in several languages. Jean asked question after question after question about Yugoslavia, and Jovanka wanted to know all about America.

Finally, long after midnight, there was a loud knock on the door. In came the two mothers, arm in arm in their dressing gowns, both looking very stern.

"We have decided," they said severely, "that if this midnight talking isn't stopped—"

The girls looked crestfallen, wondering what would come next. "But we have so much to say," they pleaded, "and we may *never* see each other again, at least not for years and years."

"That if this talking isn't stopped," continued Jean's mother even more severely, "Jovanka will have to come with us to Budapest, so that you may carry on your conversations at more reasonable hours."

It was a moment before the girls understood.

"O Mums," cried Jean, leaping out of bed and almost smothering her mother with a hug. "Do you really mean it?"

Then she plumped herself down on Jovanka's bed. "We hereby swear that we will never again even so much as whisper after midnight," she recited, holding up Jovanka's right hand.

"'What, never?'" teased her mother, with one of their favorite quotations from *Pinafore*.

Jean grinned. "'Well, hardly ever!'"

CHAPTER 7:

THE DANCING CITY OF BUDAPEST

Jovanka came up spluttering and gasping after her ducking in the first big wave, and looked around for Jean, who was diving neatly through the following one. Quick as a dolphin, Jovanka leaped after her, caught her by the foot, and pulled her under. There was a momentary struggle. Then Jovanka scrambled up the ladder and fled around the marble portico, with Jean in hot pursuit. They avoided several leisurely strollers in brief bathing suits, almost fell over a portly female sunning herself in a steamer chair, and simultaneously dove from the diving board and slid down the slide. Arriving in the water at precisely the same moment, amid the cheers of the spectators, they disappeared from view beneath the waves and bobbed up again on opposite sides of a very fat gentleman who was floating placidly about, his luxuriant white beard billowing in the wake of his elevated chin. This was too much for the girls, and they swam for the tiled steps.

"Voilà Papa Neptune," chuckled Jean, as they sat down on a cold marble bench to drip contentedly and watch the other bathers. Jean was sure she had never seen so many different kinds of people at one time. There were tall ones and short ones, thin ones and fat ones, dark ones and fair ones, beautiful ones and ugly ones. Without the usual amount of conventional clothing, all their individual characteristics stood out much more sharply. The only similarity was in the briefness of the bathing suits and the broad expanses of richly tanned skin.

Those who were not bathing were basking in the sunlight, with obviously nothing in the wide world to do except bathe and bask. Mattresses were even provided for those who wished to sleep comfortably between swims. Back of the marble portico in which Jean and Jovanka sat, they could see green hillsides and terraced gardens rising to the sky. Between them and the great Budapest hotel was at least half an acre of restaurant tables, some in the sun, some shaded by gayly striped awnings. As the girls watched, the waves died down, and the pool was quiet again. The little children and timid bathers who had rushed for safety when the waves broke, now slid back into the smooth water. In fifteen minutes, when the mechanical surf would begin again, there would be many who would not hear the warning gong, and once more there would be a great scurrying and squealing as they were caught in the first unexpected waves.

"I suppose Mums and Daddy are still soaking in that hot pool," remarked Jean in French. Fortunately Jovanka spoke French, even though she knew no English, so that the girls understood one another readily. "I think I shall have to try it just for fun, although I don't much like the idea of a hot swim. Come on."

They walked through the open-air restaurant and down the stairs to another marble pool, a smaller one this time, with two tiers of galleries around it. Jean put one foot in rather cautiously.

"Not bad," she announced, as she felt her way down to the bottom step. The water was cool and clear, and somewhat warmer than in the big pool. Still warily, she walked out into the deeper water. Suddenly she squealed and jumped, for she had stepped into a bubbling spring of warm water that tickled the soles of her feet as it gushed from the bottom of the pool. She backed away to the wall, only to be showered with more warm streams that came from the edge of the tank. When she had recovered from her astonishment, she swam across to her mother who was watching her with amusement from the far end of the pool.

"Where's Daddy?" she called.

Her mother laughed. "He decided to get his money's worth from this hotel, so he's gone to be thoroughly boiled in a still hotter bath, and have a good rubdown afterwards."

"Do they have all those things here?" asked Jean in amazement.

Her mother nodded. "And doctors and nurses and mineral waters. People come from all over the world to be cured of rheumatism and heaven knows what." Jean looked about nervously. "Don't worry. There are at least eighty other places in Budapest to 'take the waters' as they call it, and most of these people here are no more sick than you or I. They just come here to rest and swim and sit in the sunshine. Some of them who like the horrid stuff even drink the warm mineral waters, too."

Jean groaned. "Not for me, thank you. I don't even like to swim in it. Goodbye," she called, as she swam back to Jovanka. "You'll find us in the ocean waves."

When they returned to the big pool, it was quiet again. The surf had changed to still water, and the children were once more paddling in the shallow end.

"How about a siesta?" suggested Jean. "We ought to try everything once."

So an attendant brought them each a mattress, and they went peacefully to sleep, stretched face down in the hot sunshine. Jean was awakened by a rhythmic pounding in the region of her left elbow. She opened one eye, and could scarcely believe what she saw. There was a fat puppy, wriggling ecstatically as she showed signs of life, and thumping her elbow with his stubby tail. He was a comical little fellow, with big flopping ears, and black spots all over him.

"Jovanka," she called. "Look what's here."

"He's a Dalmatian," said Jovanka, as she rolled over. "Oh, you cute thing!" He wriggled and leaped about, and the girls romped with him delightedly.

"Do you suppose he's lost?" asked Jean. "Perhaps we ought to tell the attendant."

The attendant only shook his head doubtfully and started to carry him away.

"Oh, no," cried Jean. "Let us keep him until you find his master."

The girls watched with interest as the attendant told the bellboy to write something on a blackboard mounted on a stick. He then walked silently round and round the pool with it, and everybody read it with interest.

"That's the way we tell people if they have telephone calls in the hotel," explained the attendant.

But when, after fifteen minutes of advertising, no master appeared, the attendant, to the girls' horror, picked the puppy up and dropped him calmly over the marble balustrade to the lawn beneath. "No dogs allowed here," he remarked coolly and went about his business.

The girls were crestfallen. "Poor little fellow," they said. "If only we could keep him."

Just then the gong sounded, the quiet pool rose into great waves, amid much squealing of escaping children, and the girls dived in. "We'll drown our sorrows, anyway," they said, and swam and dived, and swam and dived, until they were quite breathless.

They had been sitting only for a moment on the marble steps in the sunshine, when Jean felt a little nudge in her ribs from behind, and a warm nose poked itself through her elbow.

"Sh!" she whispered warningly to Jovanka. "Bring me my bath cape."

Together they wrapped the wriggling puppy in the big, blue cape and strolled out to the restaurant. "It's almost lunch time," said Jean. "Let's find a table in the corner and wait for Mums and Daddy. Perhaps they'll know what to do with this little rascal. We can't let him go again."

In a few minutes they were all ordering melon and Hungarian goulash and corn on the cob, while Jean tried to keep the bouncing puppy out of sight under her voluminous cape.

"You seem so restless, Jean," said her mother. "Is anything the matter?"

When the waiter had safely disappeared, Jean let the puppy's head just show above the table. "Sh!" she whispered. "No dogs allowed. What shall we do with him, Daddy?" Then she told him the tale of the morning.

Her father thought for a moment. "If you could get him to your room and tie him on the balcony, I am sure I could think of some way to find his master."

"All right," agreed Jean. "We'll join the fashion parade," and she and Jovanka walked off through the tables, arm in arm, the puppy wrapped securely in the cape between them.

"It's lucky they can't see his tail," laughed Jean's father, for it was wagging madly with excitement, entirely free from the enveloping folds that concealed the rest of his body.

Fortunately everybody else, except the head waiter who saw everything, was too engrossed in luncheon to notice. But when they reached the main lobby of the hotel, the little fellow managed to escape and went gamboling about under chairs and sofas, with several bellboys in pursuit. Jean and Jovanka pretended they had never seen him and marched up the wide stairs with as much dignity as possible. In a moment they heard scurrying feet, and there was the puppy racing up the stairway beside them, while the bellboys still hunted him below.

"Quick!" whispered Jean, gathering him once more in the folds of the blue cape. No one had seen her catch him, and so they got safely to their room. Together they rigged up a leash with a suitcase strap, tied him securely to the balustrade of the iron balcony that ran across the front of their room, and with a promise to bring him goulash, went back to lunch.

Everyone was sitting around in bathing suits, slacks, or lounging pyjamas, thoroughly enjoying the meal in the sunshine.

"They even have tables in the porticoes of Parliament House in the evening," said Jean's father. "The whole world eats out-of-doors in Budapest. A Hungarian who has been to Washington asked me why there were no open-air cafés there. He thought the Capitol Plaza would be such an excellent place for one."

When they had finished luncheon, Jean gathered the scraps of goulash together on one plate, and Jovanka took the cream pitcher. The head waiter looked at them suspiciously as they went out. "For a sick friend," said Jean guiltily, and the head waiter winked with great solemnity.

After luncheon the girls romped with the puppy on the balcony and looked across the river to the towers and spires on the other side.

"That is Pest, the modern town, over there," explained Jovanka. "My father has told me about it often. Buda, the ancient city, with the royal palace and fortress, is on this side." She pointed to the citadel above them.

"That must be the grotto, with the statue of the Virgin, where all the pilgrims come," added Jean.

Even as she spoke, a crowd of girls in peasant costume were climbing up the hill to the grotto. They were dressed in bright kerchiefs, brilliantly embroidered bodices, and gayly swinging skirts that stood out around them like bells. Behind them walked an old man with a long mustache and a great white cape covered with gorgeous embroidery.

"And look," cried Jovanka, clutching Jean with delight, "the men wear skirts, too, just as in Yugoslavia."

Sure enough, young men in jaunty, high-crowned derbies trimmed with flowers went striding up the hill in flowing, white trousers as big as skirts.

"Next week is Saint Stephen's festival, and I have heard that all the peasants come to town to celebrate, so perhaps we shall see more costumes than at other times," said Jovanka hopefully.

That afternoon Jean's father took an open car, and they explored Buda. As they left the hotel, they heard suspicious, whining sounds from the balcony above, but they resolutely turned their backs.

"After all, we can't play nursemaid *all* the time," said Jovanka. "We mustn't spoil him."

They stopped first in a public square beside a bubbling fountain, where Papa Neptune, now in sober black, with his long, white beard neatly combed, was wandering up and down under the trees, a cane in one hand, a large paper cup in the other.

"What is he drinking?" asked Jean. "It looks good."

"Wait and see," said her father. He climbed out of the car, spoke to a woman who was filling cups on a long stick held in the fountain, and brought back a cup to each of the girls.

"A dime for the one who finishes first," he laughed.

Jean took one sip and flung the cup as far as it would go. "Ugh!" she exclaimed, shuddering. "I've never tasted anything so awful in all my life."

But Jovanka drained hers to the bottom and held out her hand for the dime. "It's not bad. We get it in bottles at home. It's really very healthful."

"Well, I, for one, would rather die than drink it," groaned Jean as they drove on.

They saw the Fisher's Bastion, a high, balustraded terrace climbing up from the river, with towers and pinnacles at the top. They visited the Coronation Church, admiring its tall, Gothic spire from without. Inside, the columns and ceiling were richly oriental in their brilliant coloring, and the girls could picture in their minds the great doors opening to receive the coronation procession with its music and banners, uniforms and regal robes.

At the palace, they were fascinated by the antics of the royal guard. He marched back and forth at the top of the steps, turning abruptly at each end. Before starting again, he paused, raised one knee high, and fell forward upon that foot, like a jointed, wooden toy. Then he righted himself and marched off stiff-legged again. Jean could scarcely wait to get back to her hotel room to try it herself.

"I wish John could see him," she thought, remembering that John had been a royal guard in a play at home the year before. Strange how often she wished that John could be seeing things with her! Anyway, she could draw a picture in the next letter, with dotted lines showing how the guard's legs worked.

To the right and left of the palace gate as they entered, sat two lions, erect and cheerful. Inside the gate were two more lions, apparently plunged in the deepest gloom.

"The Hungarians say that the lions outside the gates always smiled a joyous welcome to the Emperor, who came so seldom. But the ones inside wept as he departed, fearing that it would be a long time before he came again," explained Jean's father. "Budapest has another lion story, too. On the bridge which we will cross going to Pest, there are other lions. The young sculptor who made them forgot their tongues. So much fun was made of him that he leaped from that very bridge into the river, drowning himself in despair."

Inside the royal palace they wandered through one great room after another, each one seemingly more gorgeous than the last. Jean had not known there was so much gilded furniture, so many marble pillars, so many crystal chandeliers in the world. To find them all in one palace was quite overwhelming. She felt that her eyes would shortly pop out of her head.

The only rooms which looked at all friendly and livable were those in the private apartments of the Empress Elisabeth. Even though they were dowdily Victorian, in the fashion of the Empress' day, the girls thought them charming. Jean's mother had told them much of this beautiful and tragic woman, who hated the pomp and ceremony of being an Empress and, whenever possible, escaped her queenly duties to spend her days writing poetry, taking long walks through the forest with her dogs, or riding the spirited horses that she loved so much.

Whenever she had to appear in public, she suffered agonies of shyness, carrying a fan and a parasol to hide her face from the staring and curious crowds. The girls could see from her portraits and statues how exquisite she must have been, with her thick braids worn as a coronet, her delicate features, and her graceful, slender figure. And they were sure that if they had been as lovely as she was, they would have wanted everyone to see them. They stood on Elisabeth's balcony and looked down over the garden she had planned, where she had been happier than anywhere else in her great kingdom.

Toward dusk they drove up to the high citadel, which had for so long been the barrier between east and west, Christian and Muslim. As they sat overlooking the two cities, the old city of Buda and the new one of Pest, Jean's father told them a little of the history of Hungary. First the Romans came. There were the remains of an early Roman settlement on the banks of the Danube a little way above Buda. Then came Attila, the Hun, with his hordes of barbarians, overrunning all Hungary. Four hundred years later came the Magyars, under Arpad, the picturesque forerunners of the present Hungarians. At various times the Turks swept up from the south and the Mongols down from the north, but all feudal Europe combined with the descendants of Arpad to keep the them from crossing the Danube and overthrowing western civilization.

He told of the wandering nomads who brought their herds on to the great steppes of eastern Hungary, and whose children's children now ride magnificent horses over their boundless cattle ranges; of fertile fields and forests and mountains; and of all the wide lands that eventually belonged to Hungary, including Czechoslovakia and parts of Yugoslavia.

He told of the bitterness of the Hungarians over the loss of these countries with their rich resources, at the time of the Versailles Treaty after the Great War, and their longing to get them back again.

He told of the national motto, which appears everywhere, from the small signs in the street cars, to the public parks where it is written large in flowers, and which, freely translated, means, "We believe in God, we believe in our country, we believe in divine justice, and in the ultimate restitution of greater Hungary."

When they got back again to the hotel, there was no puppy to be found. He had gone, leaving half a baggage strap and a well-chewed overshoe as the only evidences of his occupation. The girls were crestfallen, hunting high and low, without, of course, daring to question any of the hotel staff.

"Well, I suppose he's gone forever," decided Jean, sinking down on the bed at last. "We've looked everywhere, but I don't see how he could possibly have gotten out, unless he squeezed through the railing of the balcony. It's probably better after all, because I don't know what we should have done with him." But she was a little sad, nevertheless.

In the evening they all walked along the water front, watching the lights of the farther shore reflected in the river and the little pleasure boats that went up and down. The girls giggled over the unpronounceable signs that they saw everywhere, words seemingly a yard long and letters all decorated with umlauts and accents and circles. It looked like no other language that they had ever seen.

"Is it like Russian, Daddy?" asked Jean.

"No, it is not related to any other language in the world except Finnish. Probably the two countries have some remote Asiatic ancestors in common. Even the greatest students of language rarely study Hungarian, so that a very beautiful literature is practically lost to the outside world. Franz Josef himself, Emperor of Austria-Hungary for more than sixty years, never learned to speak easily to his subjects in their own language. But his wife, the Empress Elisabeth, loved

Budapest more than any other place in her kingdom, and so studied Hungarian until she could speak it perfectly. As a consequence, the Hungarians adored her, and she served as mediator for them with the Emperor."

The girls were amused at the glass telephone booths in the middle of the streets, and especially at the gesticulations of the conversationalists within.

"Can you imagine doing that in New York," said Jean, "at the corner of Fifth Avenue and Forty-second Street, for instance?"

They exclaimed over the meticulous cleanliness of the city—a garbage can on every corner—and Jean's father told them that a friend of his had once been arrested in Budapest for dropping a cigarette wrapper in the street.

They heard music coming from a big café, dropped in to see what was going on, and stayed to eat ices.

The orchestra was made up of gypsy boys, many of them quite small, who were dressed in blue trousers, brightly embroidered vests, and long, flowing, white sleeves. The music that they played was now wild and joyous, now plaintive and sad. Jean noticed that none of the boys used any notes, although some of the things that they played were very difficult, like Liszt's *Hungarian Rhapsodies.* From time to time one of the smaller boys stood up on a chair, where he could be seen by everyone, to direct the orchestra, and one tiny lad played an entire piece with his violin upside down. Jean and Jovanka could almost imagine themselves out on the great plains, beside the gypsy tents, dancing and singing in the moonlight. For that was where these dark-skinned boys had come from, bringing with them the mystical, plaintive quality of the gypsy music.

As they played, Jean's father told the girls fascinating tales of the wandering gypsies, who built their fires and pitched their tents on the high steppes of eastern Hungary. He told them, too, of the herdsmen who followed the sheep and cattle over the great plains, dressed in long sheepskin cloaks which they wore with the fur inside to keep out the cold in winter, and with the fur outside to keep out the heat in summer. He spoke again of the beautiful Hungarian horses and their dashing riders, some of them descended from ancient kings, who owned these vast cattle-grazing ranges. But, most exciting of all, he told of the famous bandits who once roamed these plains.

When the girls went to sleep that night, their heads were still full of gypsies and wild horsemen and fearless bandits. Suddenly Jean awoke. She had a queer feeling that she had heard something unusual. Cautiously she raised herself on one elbow, not making a sound. Her heart leaped into her throat. There, silhouetted against the window, was the unmistakable outline of a head, peering into the room. Very, very slowly it moved from side to side, then disappeared.

"Oh, heavens," thought Jean, "it's one of those bandits, who has climbed in over the balcony. What *shall* I do! At least, I must let Jovanka know."

She leaned over to Jovanka's bed, putting one hand firmly over her mouth, and fairly hissed in her ear, "Sh!" Jovanka groaned sleepily, but Jean cautioned her again, shaking her a little this time.

Both girls now sat bolt upright in bed, and Jean pointed to the head that was once more being cautiously raised just outside the window. This time there were faint sounds of scraping, too. The girls dared not whisper for fear of being overheard, but Jean reached for the brass candlestick on her table and prepared to use it as a weapon, while Jovanka did the same. With gestures they indicated to each other that they would throw them straight at the French door, if the intruder ventured to come in. Each could almost hear the beating of the other's heart, but somehow neither of them thought of screaming. They were much too frightened for that. Now the shadow was rising higher and higher. The girls waited, candlesticks poised. At that moment the fearsome bandit turned his head slightly and made a queer sound. As he did so, he was seen in the brilliant moonlight to have long, flopping ears and a wiggly nose.

"It's the puppy," exclaimed both girls at once. Dropping the candlesticks with a clatter, they hopped out of bed to rush for the balcony. Sure enough, dragging his strap behind him, the puppy had evidently squeezed in again through the same opening he had gone out. Relief made the girls welcome him even more rapturously than they would have otherwise. It was only after a royal romp that he could be persuaded to curl up and go to sleep at the foot of Jean's bed.

"Whew, what an adventure *that* almost was!" murmured Jean, as she pulled the covers about her head. "I'm not even going to *look* at the window again."

The next day they were up bright and early, to drive out to Mezőkövesd, for the Sunday display of costumes. At breakfast they discussed what to do with the puppy, describing the blood-curdling experience of the night before.

"Master or no master," said Jovanka, "I think he ought to have a name. We can't even give him away without calling him something."

"Let's forget the master," said Jean's father. "As long as you found him, and have 'loved, honored, and cherished him,' why not name him for yourselves?"

Jean beckoned to the head waiter. "How do you say John in Hungarian? We want to name—" she hesitated guiltily, then, as she saw the twinkle in his eye, "our sick friend."

He was quite solemn as he told them that "John" was Janos, but "Little John" was Jani.

"Jani it is," cried the girls.

"He can be mascot for Jean and Company, Limited," suggested Jovanka.

Jean shook her head thoughtfully. "No, Ioannochka is our real mascot, but we might have Jani on a coat of arms or something, like those the heralds used to wear on their shields."

"I have it," announced her father, "a Dalmatian rampant, on a field of azure, with crossed bones, and a bowl of milk!" Producing a pencil, he drew a coat of arms on the back of the menu.

"A little cream for the sick friend," suggested the waiter tactfully, bowing quite low, and presenting a tray to Jean.

In their room again they decided that Jani should be given to some child who wanted a dog. But how could they find one, and would it not be better for him to be brought up in the country rather than in the city?

"Let's take him with us today," suggested Jean's mother. "He would like the ride, and we might find him a home in Mezőkövesd."

This time he was not smuggled out in the bathing cape. No, indeed, he marched proudly through the lobby in his new green leather collar, studded with brass nails, which the girls had bought for him the day before.

"If they say anything, he's just leaving," declared Jean pertly.

It was a beautiful, sunshiny morning. Jani sat with his paws hanging over the edge of the car, his pink tongue lolling out, barking excitedly whenever they passed a flock of waddling geese or an amiable, wide-horned cow. They flashed by broad fields of yellowing wheat, quaint villages with their roofs set endwise to the single street, long rows of Lombardy poplars, and tall wellsweeps with arms lifted against the sky. Now and then a blue cart loaded with colorful peasants drew aside as they approached, or a shepherd in a vividly embroidered cloak carefully guided his flock into a huddle at the roadside, and stood watching, pipe in mouth, as they passed.

It was a long ride, and they ate lunch in the car, arriving at Mezőkövesd in the early afternoon. The girls hopped out, with Jani in tow on his green leash. Here was a fashion parade indeed, and Jean and Jovanka were all eyes as they followed the throngs of strolling villagers about. The girls and women moved arm in arm, in a constant stream, chatting gayly as they walked. They were dressed in finely pleated, bell-shaped skirts, layer upon layer of them, that tilted coquettishly above their high, red-leather boots. Their aprons and velvet bodices were covered with brilliant embroidery; their white underblouses had short, puffed sleeves. The young girls wore high crowns of gold and silver lace, studded with semiprecious stones and tied with a cluster of vivid ribbons that hung down behind. The older women had darker dresses with more somber embroidery, and dark kerchiefs tied over peaked head-dresses.

Behind them followed the young men, in full pleated, white embroidered trousers, with long, voluminous sleeves to match. Their vests were of felt, appliquéd in brilliant colors, and their bright blue aprons were gayly embroidered, too. Their crowning glory was a jaunty, high-crowned derby decked with ribbons or flowers, and held in place over one eye with an elastic around the back of the head. The older men wore cloaks of felt or sheepskin with the fur outside, flung over their shoulders, the sleeves hanging loosely and the cuffs tucked into vividly decorated pockets. Even the youngsters were dressed in replicas of the costumes of the grown-ups.

Jean and Jovanka were so fascinated that they followed first one group and then another. But Jani was somewhat more interested in the dogs and cats of Mezőkövesd than in the costumes. However, being firmly attached to the girls by the green leash, he went with them for the most part unprotestingly; and behind him followed, hand in hand, two plump cherubs in full Hungarian regalia. Whenever he stopped, they overtook him and patted him joyfully. Whenever he continued his promenade at the end of the leash, they pursued him patiently.

Jean's mother finally mentioned it to the girls. "Do you see who are following you? They haven't taken their eyes off Jani for the last half hour. They look exactly like animated dolls, but I suppose they are real. Perhaps they were sent by heaven."

"Oh, the darlings!" cried Jean. "I've been so busy watching the procession of costumes that I haven't seen anything else. Do you suppose they'd like to have Jani?"

"Why not find out?" suggested her mother.

So Jean and Jovanka sat on the end of a fountain and beckoned to the children to come and pet Jani. They tried to ask the youngsters by signs if they wanted to keep him for their own, but the children did not understand. Finally Jean picked Jani up and put him in the little boy's arms, and Jovanka gave the end of the

JEAN PUT JANI IN THE LITTLE BOY'S ARMS.

leash to the little girl to hold. At last they understood, and their faces fairly shone with delight. They called to their mother, who stood in a group near by, and told her what had happened. She, too, was overjoyed. She curtsied shyly to the girls and tried to thank them. Then she beckoned to them to follow her, leading the way to a thatched, whitewashed, picture-book cottage, with flowers in the window boxes.

"O Mums," begged Jean, "may we go in?"

Her mother nodded. "We'll wait for you here."

The girls clutched each other with delight as they stooped to go through the low doorway. There was the bed, hung with gay curtains and piled to the ceiling with brightly embroidered puffs and pillows. There were the great chests and cupboards decorated with fat hearts and birds and flowers. Even the beams were painted in vivid colors, and around the walls were rows of bright bowls and plates.

The housewife motioned to the girls to sit on the painted bench beside the table, and she spread before them a beautifully embroidered cloth. On it she placed two pottery bowls filled with milk, and a plate of poppyseed cakes. She put another bowl of milk before Jani, who lapped it up with noisy appreciation. As they ate, the girls pointed out various things about the room, admiringly. The woman could see that they particularly liked her embroideries. Proudly she opened the great chest and brought out one lovely bodice and apron after another. Last of all she showed them a pleated, crimson skirt trimmed with row after row of gold and silver ribbon. With gestures they asked her how she made such exquisitely fine pleating. She laughed, laid the skirt on the table, and from her great oven took several round loaves of bread, still hot. These she packed about the pleats of the skirt, and then stood off to watch its effect on the girls.

"Of course they wouldn't have electric irons," said Jean, "but who ever heard of pressing in pleats with loaves of hot bread?"

Meantime the cherubs romped with Jani, who seemed to feel that this was to be his future home. At last, tired with his play and fairly bulging from his huge bowl of milk, he flopped suddenly onto the blue cushion that the children had arranged for him in the corner and went contentedly to sleep. They whispered together, tiptoed to the great cupboard, took out two bones, and crossed them carefully on the floor beside Jani, where he would see them the moment he awoke.

"Wait a minute," said Jean softly. Going to the door, she beckoned to her father and mother. "Daddy," she whispered, pulling him in, "you must see Jani now. 'Dalmatian rampant, on a field of azure, with crossed bones, and the bowl of milk *inside*.' Could anything be more perfect?"

While Jani slept, they went out again into the dazzling sunlight of the little street, the brilliant costumes and the window boxes glowing against the whitewashed houses. The girls slept, too, during most of the drive home through the cool darkness.

During the following week in Budapest, they explored Parliament House and the museums, had tea on green St. Margaret's Island, visited enchanting shops, swam in several of the famous pools, and ate sturgeon and apple pastry to the tune of the orchestra in the City Park.

Most thrilling of all, they went to see the pageant of costume and dance given by the peasants of the many Hungarian villages in honor of Saint Stephen's festival. This series of folk dances was called the Pearly Bouquet, and it included, indeed, all the colorful flowers of the rich Hungarian folklore. The girls did not miss a single evening of it, in the great hall where the costumes in the audience were almost as brilliant as those on the stage. This was indeed the dancing city of Budapest.

The next Sunday morning they rose at five o'clock so that they might find a good place from which to watch while the sacred hand of Saint Stephen, which had blessed so many people a thousand years before, was carried through the streets in glittering procession, a fitting climax to a perfect week.

Now it was all over, this colorful interlude in their trip. And Jean and her mother and father were getting ready to leave. There had been no folk costumes or folk dances left in Italy, where they had started, nor would there be much in Austria, where they were going next. Jean wondered why so much of the world had lost its traditional color and uniqueness. If only every country could preserve its ancient and lovely customs and costumes as Hungary had done, the world would be a much more colorful place in which to live, they all decided.

Perhaps Jean was depressed only because she was leaving this enchanting city; perhaps she was lonely because Jovanka had left the day before to return to Zagreb with a friend of her mother's. Perhaps she could not bear to have her father go back to Russia, after their beautiful holiday together. At any rate, tears came to her eyes as she tied together the broken suitcase strap, and wished she had not given Jani away. She knew that the one picture she would take away with her, of all she had loved in Hungary, would be that of a spotted puppy asleep on an azure cushion, in a room besprinkled with painted hearts and birds and flowers, and presided over by two plump cherubs in picture-book costume.

CHAPTER: 8

THE SINGING CITY OF SALZBURG

Jean and her mother settled themselves comfortably in the bus. It was a very elegant bus, Jean reflected, upholstered in red leather, with little shelves that popped out from the back of the seat in front, to hold a book or a purse. They had decided that it would be more fun to take this bus trip over the new highway from Budapest to Vienna than to go by train. Both of them were still feeling a little sad after seeing Jean's father off for Russia; it had been so hard to let him go.

There were outwardly cheerful farewells as he climbed into the plane. In the din from the propellers and motors, Jean put her thumbs in her ears and waved goodbye with her fingers. Her father, looking down from his window, thought she looked like a jolly young donkey, and hoped she would not burst into tears. She did her best, but as the plane rose, pulled in its landing gear, circled around the field, and made off for the northeast, she had had trouble with an enormous lump in her throat. It was just as well that it had been necessary to dash off to the bus in a taxi.

Jean still missed Jovanka, too. And so did her mother. The landscape was so interesting, however, that soon they were absorbed in the view from the windows and were chattering busily together. The road ran along the Danube, and Jean's mother pointed out Czechoslovakia on the other side.

"That is the land which the Hungarians consider their own and want to win back again," she explained. "And there is the boat that goes to Vienna. Sometime I should like to travel that way."

Now and then they passed a monastery or a ruined castle on a hill, but for the most part the way lay through level country and small villages. The houses were all more or less alike, one-story cottages, with peaked roofs set endwise to the road. On one side was a long porch overlooking the yard, and in the back were the sheds for animals. There were picturesque hay carts, flocks of waddling geese, pots of flowers on the window sills, but no people.

"I know why," said Jean, "it's Sunday. There are the church bells now, and look what's coming."

She and her mother almost fell out of the window trying to see the vivid costumes on the peasants who were walking along the road to church. The full skirts of the women stood out like barrels, layer after layer of swaying petticoats. And such bonnets and ribbons and embroidered blouses and colored stockings! The men were just as gay as the women, with their high felt derbies, brilliant vests, and shiny boots.

"If the bus would only stop," groaned Jean, "so that we could get pictures of them."

But the real adventure came later on. They stopped an hour for lunch in one of the larger towns. After the meal, which happened to be entirely fruitless, Jean's mother announced that she was going back to a shop she had seen along the way to get some peaches.

As it was raining, and they had only one umbrella between them, she suggested that Jean should wait for her in the bus. Jean watched her depart with some misgivings, especially as the driver presently climbed into his seat again and started tinkering with some of the gadgets. Sure enough, off he started, so gradually at first that Jean thought he was just experimenting with the car. Soon, however, she realized that everybody but her mother was back on board, and that they were gathering speed. She jumped up and rapped on the glass, signaling for him to stop, but the driver shook his head and kept serenely on his way. Then she turned frantically to the conductor, explaining to him in English and French that her mother had been left behind. He made a wide gesture and responded cheerfully in words which meant nothing to her, but still the bus went on.

"My mother," she cried, "mia madre, ma pauvre mère, meine alte Mutter," pointing back at the village and trying in every language she knew to say that they must wait.

Gradually the other women in the bus had become interested, and now they were all jabbering together, gesticulating backward and forward, and arguing with the conductor. He murmured something, which an indignant German woman translated as saying her mother could take a taxi, and went on punching tickets.

Jean tried to collect her wits. She was so angry that she did not feel in the least like crying, but it was a last resort. She burst into a perfect deluge of tears, working herself up to a frenzy of hysterical woe. The conductor was really concerned now. He rapped sharply on the window, signaling the driver to stop. Jean continued to sob loudly until, peeping out between her fingers, she saw her mother, rain streaming from her umbrella, at last over-taking the bus. She arrived, breathless and apologetic, much distressed by Jean's evident collapse. Jean, however, between sobs, managed to wink at her mother. In fact, she was quite cheerful again in a few minutes, when she thought it was discreet to stop crying and pass the peaches to her benefactors. She said, "Thank you," in as many languages as she could, but when she got to the conductor, she handed him a wormy peach. She simply had to get even some way!

At the frontier they were cross-examined, and their papers, money, and baggage inspected. The suitcases came sliding down a chute from the top of the bus, but when they had been examined and closed again, Jean was horrified to see a sturdy official swing every bag back and forth two or three times and heave it upward to another official on top of the bus. She expected each suitcase to miss the mark or burst open in transit, and she breathed a sigh of relief when they all landed safely.

The bus trip was a great success, adventure and all. Jean and her mother stopped in Vienna for the night, but hurried on to Salzburg by train the next day, to be there in time for as much of the festival as possible. They came now into mountainous country, green valleys, rolling hills, and blue and purple peaks in the distance. Here and there were prosperous villages in the lowlands and old palaces or monasteries on the mountain tops, now turned into hotels for summer tourists or winter sports. At last the train came rolling down into a flat, green valley, with mountains all around it, and a river, like a silver ribbon, winding through it. Exactly in the center, on a low hill, was an ancient fortress.

"O Mums, what is it?" cried Jean.

"Salzburg at last," sighed her mother. "I thought we would never get here."

Jean beamed. "Now may we eat? I'm simply starved!"

At the Austrian stations along the way boys had run out to the trains with big trays full of foaming mugs of beer and thick buns with enormous sausages in them. Jean and her mother had not been tempted themselves, but they had been interested in seeing fat Germans squeeze themselves halfway out of the tiny train windows to clutch the beer and sausages. Some of them seemed to do it at every station, and Jean began to understand why they were all so round and jolly. She thought it would be fun to know these people. Her mother explained to her that in spite of beer and sausages, Austrian cooking was almost the best in the world, delicate and finely seasoned like French cooking.

An hour later Jean agreed with her. They sat at a little table under a tree outside an old tavern in Salzburg where they had an omelet so fluffy and light that one hardly knew it was an omelet and not a puff of down. They ate dainty fried cakes, too, that her mother told her were flat elderberry blossoms dipped in batter and browned. They ended up with crisp cornucopias of pastry as thin as paper, filled with whipped cream and tiny, wild, red strawberries. If it had not been that there was so much to see, Jean would have gone on eating indefinitely, she was certain.

After the final scrap of whipped cream had been eaten, they went out to the shady walk along the river, enchanted at the beauty of the scene. They stopped in the center of one of the wide bridges and looked up and down and all around them. Tree-bordered walks lined both sides, and the river was kept between its banks in the spring freshets by high, stone embankments. Just below her Jean saw a man in rubber boots who stood on a low stool fishing away out in the shallow part of the river. She had never seen a man stand on a stool to fish, but evidently it was the fashion in Salzburg.

"Wouldn't Daddy love to fish here?" she said sadly. "Do you suppose there are fish in Russia?"

It was interesting to see how the people dressed. The men wore sturdy, short, leather trousers with embroidered suspenders, and pointed, felt hats with ornaments that looked like shaving brushes. Even their heavy knitted socks were queer, like golf stockings in two pieces. There was a very short sock for the shoe, several inches of bare ankle, and then some more stocking around the calf of the leg. Their coats (when they wore any) were short, waist-length ones of heavy hand-woven linen, with big silver buttons. Many of them smoked long, curved pipes with china bowls, which rested comfortably on their stomachs. The girls wore checked or calico *dirndls*, the German name for dresses with tight bodices and full skirts. Sometimes the bodices were of black velvet laced down the front, with embroidered blouses underneath and bright flowered skirts and gay aprons. Others were dressed

in suits of heavy homespun linen with jackets cut like a man's, and pointed hats with more shaving brushes. Jean begged her mother to get her one of these outfits to take home.

All around them the church spires and domes of the city gleamed in the sunlight. High on one side of the river was the old Capuchin Monastery, its long wall peeping out here and there among the trees. On the other side was the highest hill of all, its picturesque fortress, which they had seen from the train, perched on the very top.

Away in the distance surrounding the flat and fertile valley were snowy mountain peaks.

"How beautiful," breathed Jean. Then, "Let's go and find Hannah now, and ask her to show us everything."

It was the same Hannah who had been with Jean at the French convent, and whom Jean had promised to look up if she ever got to Salzburg. It would never do to pass by one of the famous members of Jean and Company, Limited! They found Hannah in an apartment overlooking the river: it must have been an old palace at one time. The girls rushed at each other joyously, and Jean chattered in a mixture of French, German, and English, while plump Hannah beamed. Hannah's mother insisted that Jean and her mother should come and stay with them for as long as they could. So they sent a taxi for their bags and moved into a home such as Jean had never seen before.

Hannah's father was an artist and designer of modern furniture, and their apartment opened a new world to Jean. The walls were covered with gayly colored murals of strange animals and stranger-looking folk. If one looked at them from a distance, one scarcely saw any figures at all–just color and design. But Jean liked to look closely at the queer, distorted animals and strange trees and flowers, and Hannah's father explained to her that when he painted them, he was thinking of a beautiful whole, something fine in line and form and color and not of the figures and flowers themselves. Jean thought that rather odd, but, strangely enough, she seemed to like odd things.

The furniture in most of the apartment was of pale-colored wood cut in geometric lines, with low couches and deep chairs. There were square cushions, and the curtains were of heavy hand-woven fabrics, falling very straight and stiff. The room she liked best, next to her own bedroom, was the hallway in black and white and silver, but she thought it looked more like a movie setting than a real home. Hannah told her that people in Austria and Germany like what they call modern architecture and furnishings. Jean wondered if all Europe was not perhaps a little tired of old things. So many countries seemed to be trying out new kinds of government, as well as furniture.

After a rest they all went off for late tea, or rather coffee, at a little place called the Glockenspiel, which Hannah told her meant "chimes." Here Jean saw men and women and even children drinking coffee at little tables out-of-doors. Everybody was arguing seriously or talking gayly to somebody else, or reading newspapers and magazines which the waiters distributed. Jean and Hannah had ices, while the three older people drank coffee. From where she sat she could look up at a stately tower in the open square. Suddenly quaint, melodious chimes began to play up at the very top. They sounded like familiar folk songs just a little out of tune, but she thought it most fascinating—like an old music box suddenly tinkling in the sky. When she looked closely, she could see the bells of different sizes, swaying and playing.

No sooner was this over, than another marvel began in this city of music. From still higher up, this time from the gray fortress on the lofty hilltop, came the sound of an organ. Hannah clutched Jean by the hand and together they raced across the square to the

HANNAH AND JEAN SLIPPED INTO A HIGH-BACKED PEW.

far corner where a crowd of people stood looking up. At the top of the fortress tower a little window swung open like the window in a cuckoo clock, and it was from this high place that the heavenly music came. Mozart himself, whose boyish statue was in the square below, had helped to install the mechanical organ which played each night at sunset—ghostly, faraway melodies with no player at the keyboard. After a few minutes the window flew shut again and it was over.

While Jean was still asking Hannah about this strange music, another organ began so suddenly behind her that she jumped. Hannah led her inside the Dom or great cathedral. They slipped into a high-backed pew, listening quietly while the organist played exquisite pieces by Haydn and Mozart, written especially for the organ. The dim light filtering through the stained-glass windows, the people slipping softly in and out, the occasional priests moving around the altar, the flickering candles in the dusky chapels—all made a deep impression on Jean. She now began to understand why at school Hannah had loved only the fine, old music, and why she had played so well. One could not live in Salzburg all one's life and not be full of it.

Hannah showed her the square in front of the cathedral which once a year is turned into a great theater. She explained that the architecture of the Dom is not Gothic like most of the cathedrals in France, but Baroque, a later and more elaborate type of architecture, with domes instead of spires and lofty columns and porticoes like the old Greek and Roman buildings. Here once a year the medieval morality play, *Everyman*, is given by some of the greatest actors in the world, the columns and steps of the cathedral serving as a background. The benches were already set up in the open square in preparation for the performance. In fact, during the entire month of August there is a music festival held in Salzburg where many operas are sung, with famous singers and conductors, and people come from many countries to hear them. But the quaint chimes, the music from the fortress tower, and the organ concert in the Dom play every day of the year.

That night they all went to an open-air production of Faust, where they sat out-of-doors facing a steep and rugged cliff in which galleries and caves had been cut many years ago. Below it was built a tiny stage village with real flowers and hedges growing in Marguerita's little garden, and overhead were twinkling stars in the blue vault of the sky. Jean thought this much jollier than hearing people sing and seeing them act inside a theater. When she was told that the idea was that of one of the best known theatrical directors of the world, the great Max Reinhardt himself, and somebody pointed him out to her, she almost burst with excitement.

The next morning when she awoke and looked at her deep, sky-blue walls and ceiling with little silver stars and moons scattered over them, she thought she was still seeing the real sky of the night before above her. But a cunning maid in a snug *dirndl* dress of red and white checked gingham brought her a fragrant cup of thick chocolate with whipped cream on top and a crisp roll, and Hannah came bouncing in with her own cup of chocolate at a perilous angle to perch on a plump floor cushion beside her. Before they had finished, the maid hurried in again with an enormously fat letter for Hannah.

"The Round Robin!" they both shrieked at once. What fun they had for the next hour, reading the letters from all the Jeans now scattered about in various countries, some of the letters written in English, some in French, and some in German.

Later on the two girls started off alone, for in Austria one need not always be followed about by a mother or governess. They took a comical-looking little funicular train, and climbed straight up the mountain side to the old fortress. At the entrance they were greeted by dogs and cats and children, for several families lived in the old barracks. They scrambled up dark, circular staircases to towers and high rooms where many generations of ruling bishops had lived in almost regal splendor. From every window was a beautiful view, out over the flat, fertile, green valley to the encircling mountains. They had something cool to drink on a terrace overlooking the city and they talked about all they had done since they had left school. Jean told Hannah of her thrilling visit in Venice with Giovanna, her discovery of Jovanka in Yugoslavia, and the adventures with Jani in Budapest. She told Hannah that she was going to stay a few days in Rothenburg with a friend of her mother's. Hannah wished she could go too, but Jean said that if she lived in such a beautiful city as Salzburg she would never want to go anywhere else. They looked down on the domes and towers of the churches and the lovely old streets and squares lined with houses of gray and silver and soft rose, mellow in the noonday sunshine.

Instead of returning in the queer mountain train, they walked back along the mountain top, past picturesque country houses, through parks and forests, and down this time in an elevator as high as the mountain, which brought them down to the flat part of the city. Then they walked home beneath the wide-spreading horse-chestnut trees by the river.

In the afternoon they drove out through a shady country road to Hellbrunn, an old palace outside the city. Hannah tantalized Jean all the way with mysterious hints about what they were to see, until Jean was tingling with excitement. They drove up a wide avenue past cream-colored walls, and houses smothered in climbing roses on both sides, to the stately palace at the end. The palace was now a museum and everything in it was interesting to Jean, but it was the garden that she was to remember best. "Hellbrunn" means clear water, and Jean loved the lagoons full of swiftly darting fish, the grottoes and caves, dusky and cool, with springs of water bubbling or spouting or standing in still pools. This clear water did such astonishing things. It seemed to provide power for everything in the palace grounds. At the end of the garden was a great marble banquet table. When the guests sat down, a fountain sprang up all around them. In one grotto a forest full of birds suddenly burst forth in song. In another a single spout of water raised a golden crown in the air and held it suspended. Along a shady walk droll little mechanical figures, the smith with his anvil, the potter with his wheel, all suddenly started turning and moving their arms and legs and looking very human. Each time these amazing things happened it was because the guide had merely turned on a water spigot just as one would press an electric button.

At the end of the garden was the biggest surprise of all—a stage set with miniature houses and hundreds of little figures. When the guide turned the magic tap, an organ played and the figures in the village all started walking, bowing, courting, dancing, grinding flour, drinking beer, or building houses. Jean and Hannah would have needed a dozen pairs of eyes to see everything. Then suddenly the music stopped and the figures stood quietly, as if Sleeping Beauty's wicked fairy had put them all to sleep again. The girls begged the guide to do it once more, for they were so afraid they had missed something the first time.

Most exciting of all was when spouts of water sprayed up from the sidewalks or steps at unexpected moments as they walked along. The guide was careful not to let the girls really get wet, but he gave them all the surprises he could. Jean had always thought that old-time people who lived in palaces were very dignified and solemn, but now she began to understand that they must have loved fun just as much as any of us today.

For the rest of the afternoon the girls rambled in the great park which was beautifully laid out with flower beds and shaded walks and cool lagoons. Up on the mountain side lived deer with their spotted fawns, and at the top of the mountain, reached by a forest path, was a huge stone amphitheater, partly natural and partly cut out of solid rock, where the first opera ever given in Austria was performed. Back at the palace once more Jean and Hannah had ices at a table under the trees, and listened while someone somewhere played Mozart. They fed the birds that hopped up to their feet for cake crumbs, and they wished that all the girls of Jean and Company, Limited, could see the magical gardens of Hellbrunn.

That night they went to hear an opera in the lovely historic Festspielhaus. It was there that Jean made up her mind she was never going to waste any time on cheap music again. Real music was so much more lovely.

More dreams beneath blue ceilings with silver moons and stars, more sight-seeing to fascinating places, more ices at little tables under trees with orchestras playing Viennese waltzes full of haunting melodies. Then an hour's shopping for a linen suit with silver buttons, a red challis blouse, a red Tyrolean hat with a shaving-brush ornament, all for Jean, as Hannah had them already.

In the late afternoon Hannah and Jean drove with their mothers out to Klessheim, formerly the Archduke's palace, park and hunting lodge, now the Elizabeth Duncan School, for tea with Elizabeth herself and all the children. Jean had danced with the Duncan School in America and this was one of the places that she most wished to visit. They drove in through a high iron grilled gate, pushed open by a sturdy, small boy at the lodge, up the tree-shaded avenue with a glimpse of three tall girls in long, straight, Greek costumes, walking arm in arm over the lawn like the Three Graces themselves. They were greeted at the summer palace by Elizabeth, sister of the great Isadora, looking very tiny as she stood in the high doorway. This was the school where for many years she had taught children and young people to dance and think and live beautifully.

No wonder, thought Jean. In such a setting one could live only in beauty.

They had tea on the lawn in the dusky shade of the cedars and afterward saw dozens of children dancing on the green, in and out of the long shadows and golden sunlight of the late afternoon. In their brief, blue costumes with flower wreaths in their hair, they looked like so many wood sprites. The visitors had supper at a country tavern near by with "Tante," as the children all affectionately called Elizabeth, and afterward in the moonlit park Jean saw what made her heart almost stop beating for sheer loveliness. Max Reinhardt put on a performance of *Midsummer Night's Dream*, bringing with him his own actors and actresses, and Tante's children danced as Titania's fairies. Instead of having a stage and changing the setting for each act, pages with banners and torches led the audience from place to place for the different scenes. One act was given on the lawn, another in the forest, another on the steps of the great palace, another in the lofty ball-room. It was such fun wondering what would happen next.

Then came the goodbye to Tante and the children. The sight-seers drove home in the moonlight past vineyards and fragrant hayfields, through villages with little lights in the high windows, past outdoor taverns where peasants were singing folk songs or waltzing in their bright costumes. Then back again to the quiet-flowing river and the deep velvet shade of the horse-chestnuts, to go to bed once more in the silver-starred blue room.

But not to sleep! Jean had had a wonderful idea as

they drove home and was much too excited about it to sleep. In a few days it would be time for her to go back to the convent in southern France for another year, while her mother went on to Germany, Czechoslovakia, and Poland, and perhaps even Russia, to gather material for her book. Jean could not bear to think of leaving her again. This summer had been such fun, and she had met so many interesting people, and her mother had always known the most thrilling things to see everywhere. It was an education just to travel with her, Jean thought. Besides, she was sure that she could learn as much by studying history and geography on the way around Europe as she could in school. She would read everything she could about every country she was in, and she would work at her French and German, speaking them as much as possible. Of course, it would be harder to keep up her Latin and geometry, but she could make them up some way when she got home again. She would not even mind it if she had to drop back a year in school. At least, she would not mind *much*!

Softly, very softly, she reached over to her mother's bed.

"Mums, are you asleep?" she whispered.

The bed creaked. "No, not yet. I was just thinking."

"So was I," sighed Jean. "Mums, you may think I'm a little crazy, but couldn't I travel with you this winter, instead of going back to the convent?" She told her her whole plan for studying history and geography in each country as they went along, and keeping up her languages. "And, Mums, don't laugh, but I've always wanted to write a book, too. Perhaps I could do it this year, and that would be practice in English and grammar."

Her mother did not laugh. She patted Jean's head in the dark. "I've been thinking about the same thing myself," she replied. "I even talked over some such plan with Daddy at Budapest, to see if he approved of the idea of having you travel with me this year. Although you still turn backward somersaults occasionally, I'm sure you are old enough now really to work hard and get the most out of the kind of things we should be doing together. I came abroad for the first time when I was fifteen, and I still keep in touch with many of the friends whom I made then, and remember the places that I visited. It has colored all my reading and study and travel ever since. But your father said—" she paused.

Jean was very quiet, waiting. "What did Daddy say?" she breathed, finally, almost afraid to ask.

Her mother smiled in the dark. "He said, 'Don't make plans for the young lady. See if she thinks of the same thing herself, and then let her do as she pleases!'"

"Hooray!" cried Jean. "She pleases to go with you!"

The other bed creaked this time, and dimly, where a shaft of moonlight shone against the wall, Jean's mother could see her grown-up daughter standing on her head.

CHAPTER 9:
THE TOWER OF ROTHENBURG

"**O**nce upon a time there was a princess who lived in a tower. Once upon a time there was a princess," the words repeated themselves over and over in Jean's head. Presently she pinched herself on one arm, then very carefully on the other. Then she reached out her finger experimentally and touched the heavy stone sill upon which she was leaning. Yes, she was awake, this was a real stone tower where she was standing, and she was just plain, ordinary, everyday Jean and not a princess in a magic tower. She looked around and smiled apologetically to her mother and Tante Hildegarde, as if they might have suspected what she was thinking. But they were absorbed in looking out of another window, and were not the least bit interested in Jean's private fairy tale. So she went on in her own mind, remembering all the romantic stories of Rothenburg that she had read. She had planned to write a book. Why not begin now?

"Once upon a time there was a princess"—no she was not a princess, that would be silly. "Once upon a time there was a beautiful maiden, and her name was Johanna (that would be German for Jean), and she lived in a tower. Her father was a soldier, and all around the gray walls of the city of Rothenburg were

THE TOWER OF ROTHENBURG.

other soldiers, hundreds of them. From her tower window she looked off across the wide, green valley. There she saw, far away, columns of more soldiers marching along the winding river toward Rothenburg, armor gleaming in the sunlight, and banners flying. She knew that there was going to be a great battle."

Suddenly she turned to the others. "Tante," she cried, "tell me the story of General Tilly and how Rothenburg was saved. Please tell it to me right here, where I can look out of this tower window and imagine every single thing just as it actually happened."

Tante Hildegarde was one of her mother's friends whom Jean had always looked forward to meeting. Her mother had known her years before when they were both studying art in Munich, and they had kept up the friendship ever since, writing often to each other. Jean's mother had not painted for years, but Tante Hildegarde had continued with her sculpture. Jean hoped she was going to see some of her work.

But already Tante Hildegarde, in perfect English with only the barest German accent, had begun to tell the story.

"Long ago, three hundred years and more, Rothenburg looked exactly as it does now, its gray walls, stately gables, and red roofs rising high above the Tauber River and its green valley. It was a proud and prosperous city, and everybody who lived there was comfortable and happy. Each morning the shepherds took their flocks out to feed on the green hillsides, bringing them back again at night to the shelter of the walls. Each morning the children danced and played in the public square, while their elders, in wide lace collars and plumed hats, filed solemnly into the church for early Mass.

"All day long the men and women of the town were busy with their various peaceful occupations. Many of the inhabitants had built for themselves great houses with high gabled fronts and overhanging upper stories, finished with crisscrossed timbers and plaster walls. Some of these houses had glass bay windows where the plump master of the house might sit and enjoy his morning pipe and his mistress keep a watchful eye on what the neighbors were doing. They all had plenty to eat, and they were famous drinkers. There are still to be seen in the museum some of the huge flagons and tankards from which the burghers drank their ale.

"Rothenburg was so far away from the other little towns of that day, where there were no automobiles and no railroads, of course, that it seemed very peaceful and secure, guarded by its walls and towers. But soon there began to be rumors of troublous times. Soldiers gathered in the little town; under the walls and in all the streets they were encamped. One city after another in the Tauber Valley had fallen before the victorious Imperial Army of the great General Tilly. At last came the long-expected day when his army, with tall pikes and streaming banners, marched up the hill, and in spite of brave resistance, Rothenburg, too, fell into his hands.

"Now General Tilly was a ruthless victor and had burned villages and killed and driven out their inhabitants without mercy. When he marched into the city of Rothenburg with his triumphant army, he

went straight to the city hall, or Rathaus, where he commanded all the city councilors to appear before him. He announced that he would not sack the city if four generous persons would volunteer to have their heads cut off, whereupon the sturdy councilors as a body stoutly said he must take all of them or none.

"Meanwhile the women of this hospitable village had set before General Tilly and his officers huge flagons of ale and had gently urged them to drink. As the argument went on and the genial ale went down, General Tilly became more jovial and amenable. Suddenly he reached for the biggest tankard of all, said to have held several quarts, and challenged his enemies. 'If anyone of you can drink this entire flagon of ale without once stopping, you may keep your heads, your walls, and your towers.' Burgomeister Nusch, so the story goes, stepped forward and with a single gulp drained the tankard to the bottom. It was the Master Drink, and in spite of General Tilly and his victorious army, Rothenburg had won."

Jean listened spellbound. "O Tante, it's such fun to hear the story away up here where I can look over the very same walls and towers and imagine the battle. Now let's hurry down and see the Master Drink. It's almost twelve o'clock."

Jean hurried ahead down the steep tower stairs, and was out in the sunlight looking up expectantly, long before her mother and Tante appeared, somewhat breathless from the descent of almost two hundred steps. They were just in time, for there on the high gable at noonday was enacted again the *Meistertrunk*, a mechanical burgomaster raising a great flagon jerkily to his lips and draining it at a single gulp. And Tante told them that if they would come back at Whitsuntide sometime they could see the whole story acted out as a pageant in the great upper room of the town hall.

If she were going to write a book (and fifteen was not a bit too young to begin, she was sure), Jean felt she must really explore Rothenburg. The view from the tower had shown them how the town lay. Now they wandered about the streets where the half-timbered gables almost met overhead, read the swinging iron signs about the little shops, walked along the top of the walls, and climbed one or two of the smaller towers, while Jean kept on imagining she was Johanna in the story. Suddenly she began to feel a dreadful hollowness.

Tante laughed when she vaguely murmured something about lunch.

"I was wondering when you would wake up enough to be hungry," she remarked, leading the way to the ancient Architect's House, one of the most interesting buildings in the main square. Such a house, (Johanna could do something exciting there!) dark paneling, leaded casement windows, a mysterious staircase, and a tiny courtyard surrounded by balconies all the way to the top. They found a place in a corner where they could see everything that went on. Jean loved the dark wood tables that looked as if they had been there for hundreds of years. She was amused by the quaint Bavarian chairs with high, slender backs and narrow seats, almost too narrow to sit on. They ordered lunch and there for the first time Jean could leisurely watch the people. Outside she had found too many other things to see. There were a few tourists, of course, and several prosperous-looking Germans in conventional dress. There were occasional sturdy, bearded Bavarians in leather "shorts," bright linen jackets, pointed, felt hats with tall pheasant feathers, and long-stemmed pipes resting comfortably on their round stomachs.

Suddenly Jean was transfixed. Two black-suited men, their backs to the room, were holding open the door and bowing. Squeezing through it was the strangest figure Jean had ever seen. In it rolled a perfectly enormous woman shaped like a pyramid, starting with a tiny pointed hat and tall feather perched on the top of her head and sloping down past a tightly tailored jacket and flaring skirt. No feet were visible. The woman advanced down the room, puffing heavily, supported on both sides by the two gentlemen, who, it now appeared, had long, white beards. Jean watched over the top of her napkin with round blue eyes, while the woman looked from the narrowbacked chairs to the narrow-seated benches against the wall. Finally she spied a corner where two benches met and toward this she sailed. Her escorts let her down gingerly, half on one bench and half on the other, and seated themselves on each side of her. Waiters hurried up to push in a table for her convenience. The table had a square corner, but the lady was so plump that it was impossible to get it close enough for her to eat from, without stabbing her at a vital point. Finally a round table was triumphantly produced which could be pushed near enough for practical purposes. When Jean and her mother finally got out to the street again they burst into unrestrained laughter. Even Tante joined. "You know," she said, "plump women are much admired in Germany, but I do think that this one rather overdid it."

They wandered over to the market place, where all kinds of fascinating wares were spread out and watched over by old women in voluminous skirts and gay, flowered shawls. Sounds of tinkling music and children's laughter came from a side street and here they found an itinerant merry-go-round in full swing. Jean dropped a penny in the slot and climbed on a spotted pony, just as excited as the children. Around and around the youngsters went, holding on for dear life, eyes shining, red cheeks glowing, pigtails streaming out behind. Even after she had tired of the spotted pony, Jean wanted to stay and watch the fun for a while.

The children were adorable, she thought, round-faced, freckled-nosed boys with close-cropped fair hair and a little tuft in front. Their tight trousers stopped halfway between the knee and ankle so that Jean had a queer feeling they must be either too short or too long, but they were all that way. The little girls' skirts were the same odd length. They wore tight bodices, and above their polished red cheeks were wide, blue eyes and surprised-looking eyebrows which seemed to be supported in the middle by the tightness of the yellow hair brushed back into two neat pigtails. Sometimes the older girls had their pigtails wound in quaint rolls over their ears.

Suddenly Jean cried, "Please, Mums, give me all the pennies you have," and off she dashed to a group of shabbily dressed youngsters who had been only looking on. She showed them her shining pennies, then led them all, solemnly wide-eyed, to the merry-go-round, where she helped them on to the ponies. Such radiant faces they had as they started off, and how they squealed with delight as the merry-go-round went faster and faster.

Finally the three of them wandered off again, visited a medieval kitchen in an old nunnery, looked into an antique shop or two, and stopped in the welcome shade of an ancient tree. Here they sat at a little stone table in a courtyard beneath the level of the street, and were served coffee by a picturesque old woman who brought it out of her quaint cottage in the corner. Jean did not like coffee much, but she liked beer even less, and there seemed to be no other alternative. However, it was lovely just to sit there on an old wooden bench with sunlight sifting down through the branches of the great tree, and continue her dream story, while her mother and Tante talked of their days in Munich together.

Later they sauntered off down the hill to the picturesque bridge over the Tauber, looking back, as they strolled, at the gray walls and towers and steep red roofs of the city on the hilltop. The valley was sprinkled here and there with odd houses that looked as if they must have fallen from some child's toy village. Jean began choosing the illustrations for her book—this glimpse of the tower and that cottage for the house where Johanna lived.

"And now," suggested Tante, "will you come home with me?"

Jean and her mother had arrived in the middle of the morning and Jean had begged first of all to see everything there was to see. So Tante had sent their suitcases on to the house and had gone sight-seeing with them. The little city was beautiful in the later afternoon light. As they came back again through one of the tower gates, they turned to look at the sunset, slanting in shimmering rays across the valley. Tante pointed out her gabled house with its ancient lanterns and oriel windows up the narrow street. At the gate stood the sweetest little grandmother, in a cap and kerchief, waiting to greet them. She welcomed them gently in German and led them into her tiny garden where her knitting and a comfortable cat lay on a small bench. Jean wished, oh, how she wished, that she had a German grandmother in a cap, too. Of course, she would not give up her own two beloved grandmothers for anything, but she would have liked to include a third. Of course she could put her in the story, anyway.

Inside the house were picture-book rooms with paneled walls and furniture painted in quaint designs, the colors mellow with age. There were carved chests, glossy old pewter, shining copper. Upstairs they entered a high-ceilinged room with busts and statues of children along the walls.

"A studio," exclaimed Jean. "O Mums, isn't this exciting!"

She dropped on her knees beside a low table full of exquisite figurines and cried with delight, "O Tante, Tante, did you make these?" There were plump little angels holding tall candles and shepherds with tiny lambs and Mary kneeling beside a fragile Christ child.

"Mums, these are like the little figures in the French crèche at Christmas time, only much lovelier. What do you call it in German?"

"The Krippe," said Tante, watching her. "I make other things too, but these little figures I love best of all."

She brought more of the tiny models out of a cupboard, kneeling angels, sheep and lambs, the ox and the ass, Wise Men bearing gifts, all modeled in simple lines and painted in soft colors.

"At first I made them for my own little boy. See, here he is," said Tante, pointing to the head of a child. "He is almost grown up now and away at school. Then other people saw them and wanted them, too. Now girls come and work with me every day in my studio. We make hundreds of figures to send all over the world, to help children in every country celebrate Christmas. Tomorrow you may work with us if you like."

Then came dinner with the small grandmother at the head of the table, and a tight-bodiced little maid, with cheeks like polished apples and golden "buns" over her ears, serving. Jean and her mother enjoyed to the utmost the special dainties that had been prepared for them, most of all the little cakes for which Rothenburg is famous, and which were made there long before Burgomeister Nusch took his famous drink.

The last thing before she hopped into bed, Jean leaned for a long time out of her high, gabled window, looking down at the little town beneath her, where rosy lights glowed behind latticed windows and twinkled in iron lanterns hung outside. Then she looked far off over the valley to where the faintly gleaming Tauber wound its way under the clear starlit sky. How fortunate she was! She jumped into bed with a sigh of utter contentment, curled up like a kitten, and started dreaming. "Once upon a time there was a beautiful maiden who lived in a tower...."

CHAPTER 10:

PRAGUE AND GOOD KING WENCESLAUS

Jean was wakened by a great jerking, jouncing, and shouting. Vaguely she realized that the train was stopping in a station. She was so sleepy she could only dimly remember stumbling out of the little compartment and being steered to a waiting cab by her mother and a porter through what seemed like miles of station, where everybody jabbered in a strange language. It really was dreadful the way European trains always seemed to arrive at important places in the middle of the night. She had dozed off again in the cab and had wakened only long enough to fall into a comfortable bed in somebody's house. When she really awoke the next morning, the sun was streaming in her window, making bright patches on the floor, and all sorts of street noises came floating up from below.

"Oh, dear," she thought, "here I am wasting a perfectly thrilling morning in a new place by being a sleepy-head."

She sat bolt upright and looked about her. Her bed was enormous, and very soft, with a fat, feather mattress making plump billows all around her. The bright embroidered coverlet billowed, too, and the woodwork was painted blue and decorated with gay flowers and birds. A big clothes cupboard painted in the same way and a chest with quaint little figures on it stood in opposite corners. Even the linens were embroidered with bright flowers, and gay calico curtains fluttered in the morning breeze. It was such a jolly room—sunlight and breezes, birds and flowers all brought in for her particular delight.

But what was that over on the chair in the corner of the room? It looked for all the world like a fancy dress costume. Jean sprang out of bed and held it up. Why, it fitted! There was a striped skirt with several bright petticoats, a tight, blue bodice, and an embroidered white blouse with enormous sleeves. A bonnet with a huge bow of wide, flowered ribbon hung down the back, and an embroidered apron and neckerchief completed the costume. Jean didn't waste a moment; quick as a flash she slipped into the dress and spun around and around before the long glass, her full petticoats whirling about her.

"What fun it would be to dance in a dress like this," she thought, as she whirled and bobbed and stamped in one of the folk dances she had learned in Yugoslavia. Then she heard her mother's laugh at the door.

"I thought you would like a Czech costume of your own," she said, "so I asked a friend of mine to get one for you. Perhaps you would like to thank the lady yourself," and who should peep shyly around the corner but little Janesika!

Jean was breathless with excitement. "O Mums," she cried, "I've been asking you all the time if you thought we could see Janesika in Prague, and here she is already. Can't she come every day to see me?"

Her mother smiled mysteriously, Janesika giggled, and Jean looked more and more puzzled.

"This happens to be Janesika's own house, and we are going to stay here all the time we are in Prague," answered her mother.

This was too much for Jean. First she hugged her mother and then Janesika, and then she started all over again. "What a surprise! What a marvelous surprise!" she cried. "And you didn't tell me, but I'm glad now you didn't. It's much more fun this way."

Her mother went on to explain to her that this was the beginning of her travel school. Through the Mother Superior of the convent, she had gotten Janesika's address and had written to her mother to find if she knew a place where she and Jean might live in a private family in Prague. Janesika's mother had replied that Janesika was not going back to the convent because her father had died in the early summer, and she could no longer afford to send her away to school. For the same reason, she was planning to take paying guests herself. Would Jean and her mother care to come to her?

There had been more letters back and forth, and it had finally been settled that Jean and a French-speaking governess should stay in Janesika's home for a month, while Jean's mother traveled about Czechoslovakia collecting her material on folk costume and music. The girls were to study in the mornings and go sight-seeing in the afternoons. Even though Janesika was three years younger than Jean, there would be many things that they could study together, with the help of the governess. The plan had been kept a secret from Jean, for fear it might not finally work out. Even at the last her mother had decided that it would be more fun to surprise her, for Jean loved surprises, she knew.

Jean sighed happily. Indeed she did love surprises. "School is all very well," she thought, "but Janesika and a governess are much more exciting. After a few weeks here I will not have to worry about the geography and history of that unpronounceable place called Czechoslovakia. I'm so glad Mums is letting me travel with her this year instead of really going to school. I'm going to keep my promise to study the history and geography of all the countries I visit, and I'm going to work hard on my French, so Mums won't be sorry."

The two girls were very shy when they were first left alone together, but Jean pointed to the various things about the room, and told Janesika in French how much she liked them. Then Janesika took her to the

window and showed her the boats on the wide river, the great palace and cathedral on the opposite hill, and the beautifully arched stone bridge with statues all along it. For some time they watched the boats moving up and down the river between the emerald islands, the swimmers on the farther shore, the people walking along the banks below, or sitting on the benches in the tree-shaded park along the water's edge. Janesika told Jean the Czech words for "boat" and "water" and "bridge" and "horse," and they almost fell out of the window with excitement over a little dog.

Then Jean told Janesika about the puppy that she and Jovanka had found in Budapest. She told her, too, about visiting Giovanna in Italy, Hannah in Salzburg, and about receiving the Round Robin while she was there. There was so much to tell that it wasn't long before they were chattering away as if they had never been separated. Janesika helped Jean get her costume straight, with all the ribbons in the right places. Then she taught her a Czech dance, in which she turned and turned until her bright petticoats stood out like the petals of a flower all about her, and shy little Janesika was whirling and stamping with her.

A plump maid suddenly appeared with a tray full of beautiful china and bright glass. Even the tray was sprinkled with painted flowers. It was like eating color, Jean felt, and she couldn't afterward remember whether there had been any real breakfast at all.

Then the governess appeared, and with her Janesika's twin brother. He was named Jan, which was spelled so much like her own name that Jean had to know all about it. The governess explained that the greatest character in Czech history was not a king or warrior, but a poor preacher named Jan Huss, who dared to teach freedom of thought and religion to his people, and who was burned at the stake for his courage. That was more than five hundred years ago, but many Czech children are still named for him. So, of course, Jean tried to pretend that she was partly named for him, too.

Jean enjoyed immensely that first day of exploring. They drove in an open horse cab to the square in front of the Town Hall and waited with great suspense for the clock in the tower to strike. Jean was afraid to take her eyes away lest she might miss the thrilling moment. As the hour struck, a window in the tower suddenly flew open, and there began to move across it in stately procession the almost lifesize figures of Christ and the twelve apostles, each one turning a little as if to look out. At the end a bobbing cock crowed lustily. The two girls laughed merrily at that.

Jean was amazed to see how many other people were also watching the clock. Delivery boys had put down their packages; shop girls were standing with eyes upturned. Dozens of business people of the town, besides carriages full of visitors, had gathered to see this wonder in the old tower. When it was over, they collected their various bundles and wits and went again about their respective businesses.

Jean looked around her as they drove slowly along. They stopped for a moment before the statue of Jan Huss in the public square, and it gave Jean a real thrill to know that her name had the same origin as his. She decided to read all she could about this interesting man.

She loved the high, sloping roofs of the city, the mellow walls of gray stone, the flattened Gothic towers like spires spread sideways. These beautiful towers were everywhere and she understood now why Prague was called the city of towers. They crossed the Charles Bridge with its lofty entrance arch and the statues all along both sides of it. Jean knew she would come back to it many, many times and wander its length to look again at the statues and gaze down on the peaceful river and lovely green islands. They drove through the quaint and narrow streets of the Mala Strana, full of ancient, gray houses and little bridges over canals, and then up the hill to the lofty castle and cathedral.

There was not time to see everything on the first day, but they had a glimpse of the great cathedral in its Gothic splendor, empty now except for a few tourists. They saw the Byzantine tomb of King Wenceslaus, inlaid with gold and precious stones. Jean was surprised to learn that good King Wenceslaus of Christmas carol fame had been a national saint of the Czechs for over a thousand years.

They walked through the great gold and white ballroom of the palace which was set with a hundred crystal chandeliers, and they tried to imagine how it might have looked filled with mighty lords and exquisite ladies in the olden days. They wandered down the narrow Golden Lane, unchanged since the days when King Rudolph the Mad had housed in these toy buildings alchemists from all over the world, who came there claiming to be able to make gold for him out of the baser metals. Once they complained that their experiments suffered from lack of air in these tiny houses, so King Rudolph had iron cages made and slung from the trees in the garden, with an unhappy alchemist in each one.

The governess knew the old stories connected with each special spot. While they stood at the palace wall overlooking the river and the many-towered city beyond, she told them the legend of how this great city came to be called Prague. Libussa, the earliest queen of the Czechs, stood on a great rock across the river and pointed up to this hill, uttering these prophetic words, "I see a city of glory which will reach the stars." She sent messengers across the river to find a woodsman in the forest who was working at the threshold of a house. This was to mark the site of the future city, and the name of it was to be Praha or as we know it, Prague, which in Czech means threshold. The girls looked up at the lofty spires of St. Vitus' Cathedral behind them and thought it was indeed part of a glorious city which almost reached the stars. It was hard to go down again.

Their carriage left them at the foot of a high hill near the river. They took a funicular train that pulled them straight up the side of the mountain, and there in a tea garden almost hanging over the edge of a wooded hillside, they had ices and little cakes, while the governess told them more of the ancient history of Prague. Jean wanted to know all about St. Vitus for whom the cathedral was named. She had heard of St. Vitus' Dance and wondered if there was any connection between the two. The governess said that he was a martyred saint of the fifth century who was supposed to be miraculously able to cure epilepsy and the nervous disease now known as St. Vitus' Dance, and that good Roman Catholics still pray to him for this. She told the girls they would see a statue of him on the bridge going home. She told them, too, of the Roman ruins beneath the modern city of Prague and of the traditions centering about King Wenceslaus in medieval times.

Jean began very softly to sing "Good King Wenceslaus." Sitting there in the late afternoon as the shadows lengthened about them, she taught Janesika the words of the old English carol.

Still singing, they walked down the mountain through the beautiful public park, stopping at an ancient palace, now a public museum, to see its famous collections of native costumes and furniture. There, too, Jean decided she would come again many times to study. It was twilight when they came back to the Charles Bridge, and the lights were beginning to twinkle along the banks. They watched the people coming and going—neatly dressed shopgirls, important-looking business men, Jews with beards and ringleted hair from the Jewish quarter, clerks with bundles and briefcases, smart women whose frocks might have come from Paris shops, sweethearts strolling arm in arm, and a group of lace sellers in bright peasant costumes. They all, like themselves, paused to look out over the river and up the hill to St. Vitus' Cathedral, and Jean was sure they all felt the quiet beauty of the twilight hour.

In Janesika's comfortable and charming home they gathered about the dinner table, Janesika and her mother, her twin brother Jan, Jean and her mother, and the governess, who translated for them. The roast goose was most delicious and Janesika told her it was a famous dish at Prague. There were mushrooms, too, but best of all were the sweet rolls stuffed with prunes. After dinner they sat around the fire and the governess told them the Czech folk tale of the mushrooms.

"Once upon a time when Christ and St. Peter were walking over the hills, a beautiful young woman was going from village to village carrying a basket of cakes and inviting everyone to her wedding. Christ said to Peter, 'We will not take her cakes, for she is very poor. We will thank her and say we have just eaten well at the Inn.' But Peter was tempted by the cakes, they were so plump and brown and sugary. When Christ was not looking, he took three. He walked behind Christ and bit into the first cake. Christ said, 'Peter, what are you eating?' Peter replied, 'Nothing, Lord,' and threw the cake away.

"A little later he took a bite from the second cake. Christ asked again, 'Peter, what are you eating?' and Peter answered again, 'Nothing, Lord,' and threw the cake away. But a third time he was tempted, and this time he took a big bite from the last cake. Christ said, 'Peter, if you have eaten nothing, you must be hungry. Go then and gather up what you see along the path behind us and bring them to me.' So Peter went and gathered great handfuls of mushrooms, plump and brown and delicate as the little wedding cakes. Christ took them and said, 'This is the food you have thrown away. As you took the cakes from the mouths of the poor, so these shall feed the poor forever more,' and that is how mushrooms came to be."

Jean went to sleep that night and dreamed that good King Wenceslaus was picking mushrooms in the forest when he came upon Jan Huss working at a threshold, and that together they had built a golden tower that reached to the stars with a little window opening in heaven. One head could scarcely hold all that she had learned!

Each day was busier than the last, the girls working away at their lessons in the morning and exploring the city in the afternoon with the governess. They enjoyed visiting the fascinating shops or wandering through the tiny streets with quaint houses lining both sides. Sometimes they stopped to admire the strings of sausages festooning the butcher's windows, and sometimes they wandered through the mushroom market and read the poster that told which kinds of mushrooms were safe to pick and eat and which ones were poisonous. Sometimes they bought ice cream from the girl who pushed her little cart about the street. Or they walked around and around the lace sellers, looking at their lovely peasant costumes.

Two or three times, on feast days or market days, they drove out to the neighboring villages which were brimming with life and color and interest. Finally the day came when they went to visit Charles' Castle, the Citadel of Jewels. They spied it in the distance, a lofty palace perched on the topmost peak of a mountain of rock above a beautiful river valley.

"Here," thought Jean, "is the castle I shall put into my book. I can imagine it filled with all the heroes and heroines I have ever read about, Aucassin and Nicollette, Melissande, Roland, Robin Hood, and the Knights of King Arthur. Or I can make up a new hero to go with Johanna. What a castle!"

THE CITADEL OF JEWELS.

There were the great gates that used to have a moat before them, the high walls, the soaring pinnacles with their heads almost in the clouds. There was the watch-tower where once the guard stood who called out each hour, "Let everyone keep away from the walls. Death to those who come near the walls."

Charles built this castle nearly six hundred years ago, as a treasure house for his jewels and archives. Jean and Janesika clutched each other in the dark passages, gasped over the four great doors and twenty locks that guarded the treasure in the olden days, and stood in silent awe in the exquisite chapel. Blocks of semiprecious stones formed the walls, and faded paintings of saints and kings rested against a gilded background. They saw the tiny wicket where Charles received his penitential ration when he had retired here for meditation and prayer. They saw, too, the cupboards, each emblazoned with the coat of arms of the knights whose sword and armor it once held.

Around every corner they half expected to come upon a princess with golden hair or a sighing lover with his lute. Both wished that those days of knights in clanking armor and languishing ladies in towers might come again with all their romance and splendor. On the way home Jean pretended she was a gallant troubadour and Janesika her lady love, and they both giggled over their own nonsense.

The month flew by in no time at all and the last night came. Jean's mother had finished her work, and now they must go on to the next chapter in this progressive geography book, which would be Poland for Jean's mother, but Norway and Sweden for Jean.

Jenny had asked her to visit her in Bergen, and an alluring invitation had come from Greta, who had finished at the convent the year before, and who was a year older than Jean, to spend six weeks with her.

Jean and Janesika sat in the deep window overlooking the river and watched the little boats as they drifted by. In a comical mixture of English, French, and Czech, signs and giggles, sighs and smiles, they talked over all the good times they had had together in Prague. Janesika promised to come some time to visit Jean in America. They wondered about all the other Jeans, and especially frail little Jane, and baby Ioannochka. They hoped that Jean and Company, Limited, would continue to flourish at the convent and that the Round Robin would come regularly. Finally, after the last good nights were said, they went up the wide staircase arm in arm, singing "Good King Wenceslaus" together, softly and a little sadly, for it might be the last time for many a long day.

CHAPTER 11:

NORWAY AND THE LONG WINTER NIGHT

Jean was annoyed! She had wasted three whole weeks in a hospital in Berlin, just having measles. For the first week she hadn't really cared, for she had been too sick to think about anything. But the second week, when she was allowed to sit up and admire her departing rash in a hand mirror, she began to be very impatient. It would be two weeks more before they would let her out of the hospital. Meanwhile she was delaying her mother, who had planned to take her up to Oslo, and then come back to Poland and Russia by boat. And she herself was missing much of her visit with Jenny in Norway.

Well, anyway, she could get books on Norway and Sweden and study very hard, so that her mother would not regret letting her travel instead of going to school. When she suggested this, however, there was another bitter disappointment. It would be some time before she could read, the doctor said, because of the effect of measles on the eyes. On top of everything else, she hated being laid up with such a childish disease as measles. Perhaps when she added her letter to the Round Robin this time, she would merely say that she had been very ill, in a foreign hospital, with an obscure complaint which had affected her eyes, and then everybody would be sympathetic, and not laugh.

However, she practiced her German on the doctors and nurses, and her mother read aloud to her when she had time, and she mentally added several chapters to her book.

They had had no intention of stopping in Berlin, but because Jean began to feel sick and feverish on the train, her mother had decided that they should have a night of rest in a Berlin hotel. When the doctor arrived the next morning and pulled up the shade, he found Jean's face just one blotch of red, and so he hurried her off to the contagious ward in a big hospital. During their enforced stay in Berlin, Jean's mother had looked up some old friends and discovered that one of them was planning to go to Oslo at about the time that Jean would be ready to start. She said she would be delighted to chaperone Jean, which meant that her mother could go on to Russia, without taking the extra trip to Oslo.

A few days later a letter came from Jenny saying that Jean would get there just in time to go to a cousin's wedding with them, a real country wedding, where all the old customs would be carried out. Perhaps something else exciting would happen, too, something that her grandfather had suggested, Jenny concluded. It was all very mysterious, which made it rather difficult for Jean to concentrate on the annual rainfall in Bergen or the mean temperature of Hammerfest, about which her mother was reading that afternoon.

Nevertheless, the time passed some way. Almost before Jean knew it was gone, she was landing in Oslo in a heavy snowstorm, with Jenny a bright spot of color on the pier, in her crimson jacket and vivid scarf and cap. Jean said proper "thank yous" and "goodbyes" to her mother's friend and rushed down the gangplank into Jenny's arms. They were such comfortable arms, Jenny was so big and quiet, and Jean had wanted so much to get there. She sighed a long sigh of satisfaction, while Jenny patted her shoulder, greeting her in singsong English. Jean had always loved Jenny's English. The words were correct, but the tune somehow was different.

These two were the best friends imaginable, perhaps because they were so entirely opposite. Jenny was older than Jean, and had finished at the convent the year before. She had really been the senior member of Jean and Company, Limited, and had always been the one to smooth things over and straighten them out, when the other girls got excited or bothered about anything. She was so strong that she had often lifted small Jane in her arms, carrying her upstairs like a baby when she was tired, and tucking her comfortably into bed. When little Ioannochka was ill, it was always Jenny who rubbed her back and sang to her softly, cradling her in her arms until she went off to sleep.

On the other hand, Jean was as restless as a grasshopper, hopping from one interest to another, exclaiming over this, adoring that, organizing something else, and always with contagious enthusiasm. She found it very difficult, try as she would, to be properly dignified and serious—witness the somersaults! Yet she and Jenny had always been together at school, and the girls had laughed and said that Jean was like an excited fox terrier yapping and jumping about the genial and deliberate Saint Bernard, that was Jenny.

The lights of the city came on as they drove home through the early twilight. Jenny pointed out the Royal Palace, its yellow walls gleaming palely at the end of a wide avenue. She showed Jean the Royal Theatre, the Park, and the University.

"I'm so glad you got here today," she said, "because tonight the students will have a torchlight procession in honor of the first snow, with skating and coasting. Thorwald will take us," and her pink cheeks grew rosier still.

"Hurrah for the measles!" cried Jean. "If I had come any earlier, I would have missed all this fun!"

"Tomorrow my friends will go to the country for the first skiing, too, but we shall miss that, as we must start the long railroad journey to the wedding at Hardangerfjord. After that—shall I tell you the surprise?"

Jean was too excited to speak. She could only nod, her eyes shining like stars.

"My grandfather is a doctor, and every year he goes to visit the hospitals all up the west coast as far as Hammerfest. This year he had planned to take me, too, and a telegram from your mother this morning says that you may go with us."

"And see the North Cape?" cried Jean. "And the Lapps and the reindeer?" She hugged Jenny's arm. "But won't we freeze to death? How can boats sail in the dark? And what about icebergs and polar bears?"

Jenny smiled. "How funny you are! Here in Oslo it is very cold in winter and in the mountains, too. But on the west coast, among the fjords and islands, the Gulf Stream makes it warm. In winter Hammerfest is no colder than New York or Paris. As to the boat, the Royal Mail Lines run all through the winter, taking letters and freight to the little villages all the way up to the North Cape and around the top of the world, into the Arctic Ocean. When it is moonlight, it is very beautiful, and sometimes there are Northern Lights, too."

Jean was just about to ask some more questions, when she saw they were stopping in front of a tremendous apartment house, unlike any that she had ever seen. It was built solidly of cement with rounded ends, a flat top, and open balconies on every corner. In the center was a great courtyard, with a garden and trees, and below it was spread the bay with all its shipping, big and little.

"Soon the bay will freeze over, and then no more boats can come in for several months," said Jenny. "You arrived just in time."

Inside the apartment they were greeted by Jenny's grandfather, a distinguished-looking old gentleman with snow-white hair and square, white whiskers parted crisply in the middle.

"Welcome, young American," he said, in singsong English. "I am happy that I can return the hospitality that America has so often shown me."

Over the dinner table he told Jean that when he was younger, he had several times been to visit relatives in Minneapolis and Saint Paul. "There are now more Norwegians in America than in Norway," he said. "Sometime I want to take Jenny over."

Neither of them mentioned Jenny's father and mother, but Jean knew they had died at sea, lost in a great storm when Jenny was a baby. She had been saved with a few other passengers and brought back, a tiny bundle, to her grandfather, with whom she had lived ever since. Norway itself began and ended with the sea, thought Jean, and so did the lives of her people.

Jenny had been to the best schools in Norway, finishing with the year in southern France, to perfect her French. This winter she was to spend traveling with her grandfather and tutoring in special subjects.

"When I come to America," she said, "I want to go to college for two years—to the University of Minnesota, I think, where some of my cousins have studied."

Her grandfather made a comical face. "And what will become of me?" he asked.

"You can study, too," she laughed, "model housing conditions and modem architecture. You know," she turned to Jean, "my grandfather built this modern apartment house and several others. His dream is to build them for all the poor in the city of Oslo, with every modern improvement, at a rent that everyone can afford."

Jean nodded over her prawns, which she was cracking carefully, as the others did, and pulling off the hard pink shells. Prawns look like shrimp but have black eyes, and they were hung enchantingly by their natural curves over the edge of a little glass, heads inside, tails out. In the glass was a sauce in which to dip them. As Jean swallowed the last one whole, she almost choked. She had an idea!

"Then you can both visit me in America," she cried. "Oh, do come soon."

She was interrupted by the arrival of delicious fish, smothered in a golden sauce. Later, as she was about to attack a chicken so small she thought it must be a squab, in burst a tall youth, a regular Viking, blond of hair and broad of shoulder.

"I came to tell you to hurry," he cried. "The torchlight parade has begun."

"This is Thorwald," said Jenny to Jean. "Have some chicken with us first, Thorwald, and then we will get ready quickly."

In no time at all the girls were dressed in ski suits and bright sweaters. "I can't wait to get a whole Norwegian outfit," cried Jean. "Will you take me shopping tomorrow?"

Jenny's grandfather beamed on them all as they rushed out of the door.

"I thought this would be quicker," laughed Thorwald. "Jump on." Jean looked dubiously at a very little sled. "Jean, you sit on Jenny's lap and both of you make yourselves as small as possible. Pull in your feet."

Before Jean knew what was happening, they were off down a steep hill, Thorwald skilfully dodging the few automobiles on the street and shouting at pedestrians to get out of the way. Jean had coasted before, but never in this blood-curdling way, rounding breath-taking curves, missing cars by a hair's breadth, weaving in and out between boys and girls with skates slung over their shoulders. Several times she shut her eyes as they came sickeningly close to something in their way, and opened them with surprise when she found she was still alive. If Jenny hadn't clutched her firmly, she would have fallen off, she was sure. As it was, when they got to the bottom, her mouth and eyes were full of snow, her cap had blown off, and her curls stood out in every direction.

"Whew," she cried, "What a ride! I've never been so scared in my life. *How* did we make those curves? I thought you two big Vikings were going to run me right into the Skagerak."

Thorwald grinned. "That was just a modest sample of a much advertised winter sport in Norway. I can do better," and he showed her how he had steered the sled by means of a long pole under his arm, which he dragged behind like a tail.

They trudged along beside the sled, coasting down every convenient hill, but none was quite so terrifying to Jean as the first. They finally sailed triumphantly into the midst of the torchlight procession, scattering shouting students and waving torches here and there. Jean and Jenny and Thorwald were pulled into the parade and marched along with it, singing as lustily as the others. They stopped at last at an outdoor skating rink, where the ice had been swept, and joined the skaters. Thorwald introduced the girls to a number of boys, and what a good time they had! While Jean could not skate so well as the young Norwegians, she found that waltzing on skates was new to many of them, and despite the fact that she was not yet expert herself, she had great fun showing them how it was done.

Later they wandered off to a hill and watched some skiing, and it was a very weary Jean that was finally dragged home on the sled by Jenny and Thorwald—to make up for treating her so badly at the beginning of the evening, they said.

The next day Jenny helped Jean shop for all kinds of winter clothing, and they rushed home to pack just in time to make the late afternoon train.

Although it was dark for most of the dozen hours that they traveled from Oslo to Bergen, Jean had exciting glimpses of this high, wild country. Fortunately it was moonlight, and she could see the snow-covered mountains dimly, the rambling cottages smothered in whiteness like Christmas cards, the great, flat expanses that were lakes, the fir trees black against the snow. Sometimes they could scarcely see over the drifts piled along the snow fences of the railroad or newly pushed from the tracks by the snowplow. Jenny's grandfather said that he had known the drifts to be as much as thirty feet deep in this mountainous part of the country. The lights of many villages twinkled brightly in the darkness, and occasional clusters of farmhouse lights shone out on the hillsides. Jean longed to see it all by daylight, but she found it difficult to sleep, even in her comfortable berth. It was absolutely necessary to look out the window of their compartment!

Meanwhile Jenny was a bit apologetic about the wedding. She had hoped until recently that the bride would wear white satin and a veil, but evidently, so Jenny explained a little condescendingly, she wanted to carry out the old customs and have a real country wedding. Her whole family was like that. The bride's father owned enormous fishing industries, and they could have lived wherever they liked, in Oslo or Bergen or Trondheim, but they all preferred the quiet farm near the Hardangerfjord.

Jean, however, was delighted, and said so in no uncertain terms. It was exciting enough to see a wedding anywhere, but a real Norwegian one would be most thrilling.

When they got out at the little station, they joined the crowd of people flocking up the hill. There was less snow here, barely enough to fold everything softly in a white blanket. It was only beginning to be light, although it was well along in the morning. Lamps still shone in some of the log houses that they passed, and an occasional torch flared in a barnyard. Many of the women wore wide white headdresses and white aprons. Under their heavy jackets, Jean could see, they had on bright red, beaded bodices. The men were more conventionally dressed, many of them in black Sunday suits, and hard, round derbies. The few in picturesque knee breeches and bright vests made Jean wish that all of them still wore Norwegian costume.

Everyone seemed to know Jenny and her grandfather, and all were very polite to the American girl. One of them asked her if she knew his cousin, Hans Hansen, who had gone to America. He could not remember where he lived, but he was very tall and had a fine mustache. Perhaps she might have met him!

Presently they came to the church, a queer, pointed building with the roof extending into the steeple as if someone had stretched the peak upward. It was built of logs, with a narrow balcony running all the way round, and the whole painted with tar.

"It is because of the tar that this church has lasted so many hundreds of years," explained Jenny's grandfather. "And there are no windows because the people used to come to church armed for defense, and the building was a fortress as well. It is said that the women even brought shrouds to the service, in case someone should be killed before he got home again."

"But why—?" began Jean. At this moment the bridal procession appeared winding up the hill. At the head of the procession marched the fiddler, fiddling merrily and dressed in knee breeches, white stockings, and a green vest under his dark coat. Behind him came the bride, mounted on a fat, cream-colored pony. On her head was a wide, flaring crown. As she came nearer, Jean could see that dozens of bright bangles twinkled about the crown, and she wore a great brooch, with more shining bangles. Her short fur coat was open, and underneath Jean could glimpse a crimson beaded bodice. Fluttering ribbons hung from her waist over her richly embroidered white apron. Beside her walked the groom, in city clothes.

"She couldn't get *him* into a Hardanger costume," giggled Jenny.

A crowd of young people brought up the rear, the girls in bright costumes, the boys in soberer clothing. Against the shining snow, the procession was a never-to-be-forgotten sight for Jean.

Only a few of the near relatives, Jenny and her grandfather and Jean among them, followed the bride into the church, for it held but a handful of people. Jean was surprised that a Lutheran church had such a high altar and that the ceremony was performed by what looked like a Roman Catholic priest in richly brocaded robes. She must learn more about the history of the Lutheran Church.

Later they all followed the bridal procession back to the great old farmhouse. It was built around a hollow square, the buildings of brown logs, with carving over the doors and windows. Some of the

AGAINST THE SHINING SNOW, THE PROCESSION WAS A
NEVER-TO-BE-FORGOTTEN SIGHT.

smaller buildings had turf roofs, with bits of grass still sticking up through the snow. The great hall had dark beams, heavily carved, and a loft at one end, under the pointed roof.

"That is where some of the guests will sleep tonight," said Jenny, "as they did in the old days."

The walls were hung with bright, woven tapestries in quaint designs, and benches were placed all around the room against the walls. Down the center stretched long refectory tables, loaded with every kind of food: brown goat's cheese, sliced meat, sausages, goose and chickens, smoked eel, prawns, lobster, fish, stuffed eggs, salads, and piles of pumpernickel bread.

Jean following the example of the others, took a plate and fork and walked around the table, heaping her plate with food. Then they all ate standing up, refilling their plates as often as they were empty. At a table in the corner were puddings of sweetened cream cheese and bottles of schnapps.

After luncheon the tables were taken away and all the young people danced, the fiddler standing on a bench as he played. Most of the dances were square dances or figures that looked like the Virginia Reel. Jenny's grandfather led Jean on to the floor, pulling her and pushing her into the right steps and winking at her when she made mistakes. It was great fun even though she was not expert, and she was sure that she had the handsomest partner there.

Later Jenny took her to explore the rest of the farm buildings while it was still light. There was the storehouse, built on piers, the second story wider than the first. Next it were the sleeping quarters. Downstairs was a white-washed fireplace built out at the corner of the room, with one slender column to hold up its sloping hood. In the corners built-in beds, very short and wide, were heaped with huge pillows and puffs. Bright pottery filled a hanging cupboard, and pictures were painted on the wall. Upstairs, by way of an outside staircase, were two smaller rooms, under the eaves. Each one had a small four-poster bed and a row of painted chests.

"These are the bridal chests," explained Jenny. "See, they are full of embroidered linens and woven rugs and dresses. After the wedding party is over (it may last three or four days), the bride will take them to her new home. I wonder what she will do with all these headdresses and beaded blouses in the city, where she is going to live? Perhaps she will keep them to wear when she visits the farm."

The small building next to the storehouse was the smokehouse, then the bath house where there were steam baths in the old days. From there they went to the great barns full of cattle and cream-colored ponies and two-wheeled carts.

"No wonder they like to live here," said Jean. "I'm sure I should never go to the city, if I could stay here always."

The dancing and feasting went on alternately until far into the night. Some of the people who lived near by went home for the night, to come back again the next day. The young men who were left slept along the benches and in the loft of the great hall, and the girls went over to the sleeping house. Jean and Jenny and another cousin all squeezed into one of the big beds, curling up under the feather puff. They had to curl, partly because the bed was too short to stretch out in and partly because it was the only way for the three of them to stay under the single puff.

A fire burned on the low hearth all night, and what with the firelight dancing on the ceiling, and the laughing and whispering of the girls sleeping in the other built-in beds and on mattresses on the floor, there was not much sleeping that night. Jean wished she could understand Norwegian and know what all the fun was about. Besides, there were occasional snatches of song and laughter from the great hall, where evidently the boys were not sleeping too soundly either.

Jean and Jenny wanted to stay as long as the wedding festivities lasted, but they had to leave the next morning for Bergen, to catch the mail boat. All Jean could remember about Bergen afterward was the hair-raising trip up a perpendicular mountain side in a funicular, to a charming restaurant overlooking the city. From there Jenny's grandfather pointed out the steamship pier and the fish market and the Hanseatic House which dated back to the fourteenth century. Most of the city, he said, was comparatively new, as it was built entirely of wood, and had been frequently swept by fires. It was a splendid way to see the city, which was spread like a map beneath them, with the ocean almost surrounding it and a lake in the middle.

It seemed to Jean that the meal consisted chiefly of national anthems by the orchestra, although she remembered a few hasty mouthfuls between times. As they came into the restaurant, Jenny's grandfather spoke to the head waiter, and very shortly thereafter she heard the strains of the "Star-Spangled Banner."

She rose, as did the others. After the first course, the orchestra played an American medley in her honor, including "Old Kentucky Home," "Dixie," and "Home Sweet Home," ending, naturally, with the national anthem. A little later, the strains of an accordion wafted in from outside, and what should it be but the American anthem again! This time Jean stood up with less enthusiasm, for it took her so far from the chicken. In despair she asked Jenny if there was no such thing as a Norwegian national anthem, whereupon there were whisperings among the musicians, and they burst into the strains of a stately hymn. This time everybody stood and sang. Jean tried to be very polite, for it really was magnificent music, but she seemed to feel distinctly less patriotic than at the beginning of the meal.

As they came out of the funicular again, it was raining, a cold and dreary drizzle, which glistened under the early lamplight. Jenny laughed as she put up her umbrella.

"They say that it rains in Bergen for three hundred and sixty out of every three hundred and sixty-five days in the year," she said. "The horses are so accustomed to umbrellas that they only shy at people without them."

Her grandfather added, "There is a story that a Bergen seaman came into the harbor one day when the sun was shining brightly and immediately put to sea again, thinking he must have made the wrong port."

The boat which they took that afternoon belonged to the Royal Mail Line. Norway is so broken by deep fjords and high mountains and wide lakes, so covered by snow and ice in winter, that there are many places which the railroads never reach. But the mail boats, winter and summer, penetrate the harbors and fjords, and touch at the islands along the coast several times a week, carrying mail and freight. The coast of Norway stretches a thousand miles as the crow flies, but counting the length of the shore line in and out of the deep fjords, it is more than twelve thousand miles long. All of this Jenny and her grandfather gradually explained to Jean as their ship wandered along the coast.

In Bergen there were several hours of daylight, but as they moved northward, there was less and less. The ship was lighted most of the time. The channels and fjords were marked by lighted buoys, and each village was brightly illuminated, for there is electricity all over Norway. Jean and Jenny loved to hang over the railing and watch the eager faces of the people on the pier as the boat drew in at every town. It was the one excitement these northern villagers had and, day or night, they all seemed to gather there. The girls saw plump, blond children in bright sweaters or hooded jackets, sturdy young men and women who looked like direct descendants of the Vikings, picturesque old men and women, bronzed and wrinkled by their lifelong struggle with the sea. Often the three of them got off the boat and wandered about the brightly lighted piers and streets, watching the shipping, looking into the unadorned shop windows, buying here a gay scarf and there a pair of wonderfully patterned mittens. Jenny even bought a fur coat in a fascinating shop where a stuffed polar bear stood guard outside.

The villages themselves were bleak and dreary, made up of plain timber buildings and streets bare of trees. The shores were lined with ugly docks, miles of fish-drying frames, and piles of cod-liver oil barrels. But the chief characteristic of them all was the smell, that of thousands of dead fish through countless centuries past, so Jean and Jenny decided. In some places they noticed small, black heaps set at regular intervals, and Jenny's grandfather said that these were piles of peat cut from the peat bogs and set up to dry. Norwegian flags were everywhere, waving in the chilly breeze. Jenny explained that Norway was so proud of her recently gained independence that she lost no opportunity of waving a flag and saying, "We are now a nation." The chief disappointment to Jean was that there were no native costumes left in this part of the country, but she was glad that she had seen them at the Hardanger wedding, at any rate.

The brief daylight was almost gone now, but fortunately the moon was full, and cliffs and crags and snow-capped peaks looked wilder and more weird in its clear, cold light. The cliffs stood out blue-black against a silver sky. The mountain tops gleamed palely as if touched with phosphorescence. Here and there clusters of lights twinkled against the deep purple of a shadowed hillside.

They sailed into narrow fjords, where the towering crags on either side seemed ready to topple over on their tiny ship. They threaded their way between rocky islands so steep that they were almost like the cliffs of the mainland, and so narrow that there seemed no opening to pass through. Jean could imagine the mighty gods of Norse mythology hurling their thunderbolts from crag to crag, and she could almost hear the cry of the Valkyrie as they rode the lightning.

She determined to read these myths again. Meanwhile Jenny's grandfather told her as many of the legends as he could remember, of Thor and Odin and the great gods of the Northland.

Only once or twice did they feel the force of the wintry sea outside the islands, and then they stayed in the ship's cabin, drinking strong coffee and listening while the captain, who had once been head of a whaling fleet, spun yarns of his deep-sea days. He told of cod fishing in the early spring, when hundreds of boats go out to the wild waters of the Lofoten Islands, to meet the great shoals of cod. Sometimes these shoals are a solid mass of fish a hundred or a hundred fifty feet deep. He told how they pulled them up in nets, brought them to shore, and spread them to dry. The bodies were cleaned and salted, cod-liver oil was made from the livers, and the heads were dried for fertilizer and cattle food.

He told, too, of the capricious herring, which might arrive at any time of the year, or not at all, but the fisherman must be ready in any case. The girls enjoyed best his tales of whaling adventures in the Arctic Ocean—tales that described the courage of these men in facing the rigors of snow and ice and wintry seas as well as the monsters of the deep.

Sometimes the three travelers took a stock-jaerre in a village, the two girls sitting on the main seat, while Jenny's grandfather occupied the driver's seat behind, flapping the reins of the cream-colored pony between their shoulders. Occasionally they tried a sleigh, and twice they went overland by automobile, meeting the boat again at the next stop. In one village the girls joined

a torchlight skating party at a little inland lake, and at
another time they skied off over the hills for an hour.

By the time they came to Tromsø, there was only an
hour of daylight left, the sun cutting a brief, golden arc
along the horizon. It was here that the first Lapps came
on board, men and women dressed alike in flaring, blue
felt tunics and long, blue trousers tucked into pointed,
reindeer skin boots. There were touches of vivid color
in the great tassels on their square caps, in the girdles
low about their hips, and in the braided bands with
which their boots were bound about their ankles. Some
of them wore reindeer-skin jackets, trimmed with
bright colors. The men were not more than five feet
tall and the women even less. But the babies were the
most interesting and colorful of all. The Lapp mothers
carried them in brightly painted cradles slung about
their necks in front, the rosy, round-eyed babies half
smothered in fur robes.

Jenny's grandfather said he was sorry that they had
not arrived the week before, so that they might have

skied over to see the great Lapp caravan coming in to the winter market at Skibotten—reindeer herds, tents, sledges, and all. But he had another thrill for them. They skied out to a Lapp encampment near by, where they hired sledges and reindeer. Each of them had a short sledge, like a half boat, in which they sat flat on the floor, their feet stretched out in front of them, a reindeer hitched in front. Jean, remembering her other experience on a Norwegian sled, was a little skeptical, but she did not falter. They all started at once, three in a row, the Lapps holding both sledges and reindeer until the last moment. Then off they went, the sledges rolling and bouncing like little boats in a high sea, Jean and Jenny squealing with alarm, the reindeer swinging their great horns as they ran, the Lapps shouting and racing along behind.

Of all the concentrated excitement and action that Jean had ever had in her life, she was sure this was the greatest. She tried to steer with her reins and put on brakes by sticking her pole into the ground, as the Lapps had shown her, but nothing made the slightest impression on her galloping steed. Jenny's sledge, which was a little ahead of her, tipped over at the bottom of a small incline, and Jenny rolled out shrieking, while the bewildered reindeer was skilfully lassoed by a Lapp. Jean had a fleeting moment of triumph, thinking she had lasted longer than Jenny, before her jouncing, bouncing craft came to a stop against a fence. By some miracle, she was still upright, and she could not help feeling a bit superior as she ran back to see if Jenny were safe and sound. She found her ruefully rubbing an elbow and a knee, but otherwise unhurt, except for her feelings.

"I'll show that reindeer," she cried, as she climbed firmly into her sledge again to drive back to the encampment. But Jean decided that she preferred walking. Jenny's grandfather had disappeared completely into the twilight regions. Meanwhile the girls ventured into the Lapp tent, a tepee made of reindeer skins sewed together, to warm themselves by the fire. At first they were almost smothered and blinded by the smoke, but gradually they began to see things around them. The fire was built in the middle of the tent. A Lapp mother sat cross-legged on the ground, nursing her baby. A couple of children rolled around on a white bearskin bed. A great kettle boiled over the fire. Chunks of smoked reindeer meat and strings of dried fish hung in the peak of the tent.

At first the girls were a little nervous about being alone with these strange-looking people, with everything about them so smoky and dirty, but it was exciting, too, to see how the Lapps really lived. Before Jenny's grandfather returned, they had watched the women spinning by wetting the thread in their mouths and rolling it against their skirts. They had seen how they sewed their leather boots and wove their bright-colored braids. They had watched them as they scraped and pounded the reindeer skin, preparing the leather. At last, much to the relief of the girls, Jenny's grandfather appeared, leading his reindeer by a rope. As he warmed his frozen fingers, he told them how the Lapps followed the reindeer in their great treks across Norway in search of pasture, while the women and children stayed in tent encampments or sod huts, their cows and dogs under the same shelter. Finally he gave the children some candy, paid the men for the doubtful pleasure of the sledge trip, and they all skied back again to the boat in the moonlight.

The day they reached Hammerfest, the sun appeared for only a few moments, an angry, red ball rising halfway above the horizon and then apparently going down in a rage. The town was bright with electric lights, which would shine continuously, day and night, for the next four months. The following day the sun could not be seen at all from Hammerfest, but Jean and Jenny joined a group of young people who climbed to a high hill near by for a final glimpse of the great, golden disk. Meanwhile Jenny's grandfather visited the Hammerfest hospital, in which he was much interested, a hospital for sailors and fishermen. The nurses were nuns, willing to face a lonely life for the sake of helping even more lonely men. All along the coast Jenny's grandfather had been visiting hospitals, many of them the only stone building in the town. Several of them were very large, as each one must serve a wide area of land and ocean.

Jean asked him why so many hospitals were needed in a land where the people seemed so sturdy and healthy. Grandfather explained that, strangely enough, even in this land of outdoor living, there were many victims of tuberculosis. The other great scourge was insanity, the result of extreme hardship and continuous isolation, especially among the women. Jean tried to picture to herself what it must be like to be a woman on one of these isolated farms, snowed in for the winter, often alone in the warm summer months as well (because the

209

menfolk were off in the fishing fleets and the children were away at the centralized schools), with no outside interests and amusements, nothing but drudgery and loneliness.

That night Jean saw her first aurora borealis, a breath-taking display of darting, scintillating rays and streams of light. It started as a golden glow along the horizon, like the reflection of a great fire on the earth, flared into a vibrating band of color, and burst finally into fiery flames that swept toward the zenith. It disappeared at last in red fragments, which darted across the blue sky and even colored the snow with its rosy reflection.

After that they sailed almost entirely by the stars, as the moon was now only a golden sickle. Jean at last really had the feeling of the long, winter night.

At the North Cape they anchored in the open ocean, sailing in to the shore by a tender. It was very exciting, trying to climb from the ship's ladder onto a tiny craft that came rushing up the side of the boat in a terrifying way and then sank again in the trough of a great wave before one could leap into it. Guides armed with torches led the way up the steep, zigzag path against the black cliff. It was a long, cold climb in the chilly twilight of noon. But Jean stood at last on the snow-capped tip of the North Cape, looking out over the wildly tossing Arctic Ocean, the waves faintly illuminated in the clear, crisp starlight. She pulled her coat more closely about her and shuddered as she thought of all the intrepid explorers who had braved that treacherous sea to find the top of the world and had never come back. But she thrilled, too, with the thought of the great adventure of meeting the unknown and conquering it. Perhaps she had some Viking blood in her veins, after all!

Surely this was the high point of her trip, she thought, this one moment of facing the elements, longing to make of her life something strong and courageous and new. Out of darkness to search for light and find it. To reach into the unknown for knowledge, and then give it as a gift to the world. She tried to tell Jenny what she was feeling, but her lips were stiff with the cold, and a great wind blew the words back into her throat. She wished her father were standing beside her, because he would understand without the need of words.

She was very quiet as they climbed down the dim, zigzag trail to the little ship whose lights were bobbing in the harbor. She wanted to keep in her heart that moment of exaltation. The rest of Norway did not really matter.

CHAPTER 12:

SWEDEN AND LILLA MORMOR

J EAN pulled her head out of a snowdrift and shook it vigorously. She brushed the white flakes from her eyes with a vividly embroidered mitten and wriggled about until she could look back over her left shoulder. There she was, lying headfirst down the mountain side, her left shoulder still buried in soft, smothering snow. Her new scarlet ski suit was covered with it, as were her striped scarf and sash. A long, red stocking cap lay like a crimson pennant on the snow near by. Some distance up the hill, or so it seemed from her confused point of view, were her tasseled socks and her shiny skis.

She began to feel herself cautiously from top to toe. No arms broken, no legs broken, even her curly head intact, though it now looked like a powdered wig. She rolled over carefully, trying not to sink too deeply in the soft snow, and managed to raise herself to a sitting position. She found she was movable from the waist up, but her legs and feet and skis and ski sticks were hopelessly entangled. What on earth had happened to her! Oh, yes, she remembered now. She had been flying like the wind down the steep hillside a little behind the other boys and girls and she had not been able to make that last curve. For some strange reason she had slipped off to one side, shot out over a high drift, and landed headfirst in the soft snow. Anyway, she was glad she had not screamed and showed she was a tenderfoot. Now she could brush herself off, put on her cap, straighten out her skis, and sail off around the trail after the others. She could follow their tracks, and they would never know what had happened.

But no such luck. She found that one of her ski straps had broken and refused to be adjusted. First she tried walking on one ski and one foot, but the ski kept going faster than the foot, and the foot always sank in deeper than the ski. Then she tried sitting down on both skis together like a sled, but that did not work either.

The group had disappeared as if by magic, Greta in her bright jacket, Jenny in her vivid Norwegian sweater, Nils and Per with their gay caps and scarfs. Suddenly she wished for John, good, old, American, freckle-faced John. He would not have gone off and left her. At least he would have known it the moment she had fallen and would have rushed back to help her. Nils and Per were very nice, but they were so accustomed to girls doing everything the boys did on skis that it never occurred to them that she could not do it, too. Greta and Jenny were ahead and had not missed her, either. Jean sighed and then brightened again.

It had been such fun having Jenny come with her to Greta's. Jean and Jenny had left the Norwegian mail boat and Jenny's grandfather at Trondheim and had come by train straight to Stockholm, where Greta had met them. This had seemed the proper time for Jenny to visit her cousin Greta, and as the three of them had been together at the convent, it was a great reunion. Everything had been fine until just now! Jean sighed again with discouragement and began to wish that she had screamed, after all. Then suddenly four little figures whizzed into sight on the plain far below, one after the other, like brilliant spiders scudding along the smooth snow and gradually coming to a stop. She watched them when they discovered she was no longer with them, look all around, up and down the pine-clad slopes. Tying her bright scarf to a ski, she waved it, and they saw her at once, gesticulated encouragingly, and started back again to rescue her. They were good sports, after all, thought Jean.

She knew it would be some time before they reached her, as they must climb the hill at easy angles, zigzagging back and forth and pushing themselves along with their ski sticks. So she made a comfortable seat for herself on her skis and settled down to enjoy the view. These wooded hills around Lake Siljan were really not mountains. Black pines stood on thick clumps or like single sentinels against the shining slopes. Away in the valley at the edge of the lake clusters of red cottages lay half hidden in the snow. Here and there a church spire raised its queer, onion-shaped top. Through the crisp, clear air she could hear the distant tinkle of sleighbells, and she watched eagerly till she could see the tiny red sleigh swinging along a road deeply banked on either side with snow. On some of the lower hills she saw children tobogganing in their gay snow suits, and heard their shouts of laughter. If only she had a toboggan, it would not take her long to get down.

Flying figures on skates, no bigger than insects, and an occasional ice boat, like a graceful butterfly, skimmed along the lake. Suddenly she heard laughter and shouts above her, and she looked up to see a half dozen swiftly gliding figures. But they were gone without seeing her, so intent were they on the great slope before them. The other hillsides were filled with them, too, bright bevies of snowbirds, sweeping into sight, disappearing again around the curve of the mountain or behind a clump of pines, sliding out into the valley far below. She watched some beautiful ski-jumping, a group of boys who rose into the air, leaped out from the mountain side, and alighted skillfully without once losing the sense of perfect flight.

Soon the rescue party came in sight below her, shouting to know if she was hurt. She stood up on her ski bench and did a highland fling to show them she was safe, ending disgracefully when she fell off and was almost smothered again in the snow. Now was her chance to watch them climb and so be able to do better herself the next time. As they helped themselves along by pushing with their ski sticks, she noticed their smooth skating motion. When there was a sharp corner to turn, she watched how each skier lifted one ski hip high at right angles to his body, turned his foot entirely around in the air and put the ski down so that it faced in the opposite direction. He then turned the second ski in the same way. She had tried to ski ever since she could remember, and she had had some practice in Switzerland at Christmas time and a little in Norway. These young people, however, had the advantage of her, for their winters lasted much longer, and there was less sunshine than anywhere she had ever been before. The days were so short even now that twilight was beginning to fall almost in the middle of the afternoon.

At last they arrived, Greta and Jenny, Nils and Per, breathless from the climb, their cheeks like polished apples. Nils produced an extra strap from his pocket, which he carried for just such an emergency, and in no time at all they were merrily sweeping off again down the mountain. Lights were beginning to twinkle in the village when they sped out on the plain below. They hailed a passing sleigh which happened to belong to Per's father, and all piled in, the sleigh suddenly changing to a multicolored porcupine bristling with skis and making sweet music of laughter and bells.

Jean and Greta and Jenny jumped out in front of a little gate half hidden in drifts, and waved goodbye to their companions. Jean loved the little red wooden cottage almost buried in snow, its welcoming lights gleaming out through the small-paned windows. It was not like a real house at all, she decided, but much more like a picture in her favorite book at home. Even when she was a tiny child, her mother had let her turn the pages in the book of drawings by Carl Larsson. She could still remember how heavy it was. When she was so small that her feet stuck straight out from the huge, winged chair, her mother carefully had laid the big book open on her knees. Her eyes never tired of the enchanting pictures of Swedish children and Swedish houses, but sometimes her feet got very tired from holding the big volume. Tonight she felt as if she had moved into the pages of the Larsson book.

It might have been Larsson himself who opened the door—Greta's tall father with the pointed, blond beard, ruddy cheeks, and genial smile. Over in the corner by the big tile stove sat the tiniest and merriest little old lady in a striped apron and white cap with a flowered shawl over her shoulders. She was the great-grandmother of Greta and Jenny. She was almost ninety and had grown up in Dalarna, the home of the Dale folk of Sweden. Since she was a tiny child she had lived in this same quaint red cottage and she still loved it better than the luxurious city houses and country places of her children and grandchildren where she went sometimes to visit. She loved, too, her native costume and always wore it at home. Greta and Jenny called her *Lilla Mormor*, which means "little grandmother." Jean felt honored because she let her call her that, too.

The girls disappeared to take off their heavy ski suits, and when they hurried back again to the warm tile stove, they, too, were dressed in bright peasant costume. Greta always kept one to wear when she visited Lilla Mormor. She had lent one to Jenny, and Jean had bought one to take back to America with her. They got as close as they could to the big stove, and while Jean warmed her nose and fingers, she examined again the colored tiles, each one a picture. There were fat, red hearts and full-blown roses, spirited reindeer and birds with ridiculous topknots.

The walls of this big, central room were painted a soft blue-green, and against them stood red furniture decorated with birds and flowers. There were pictures on the cupboard doors, pictures on the brilliant bits of china and pottery ranged along a high shelf, and out of each window was a cheery picture of candlelight gleaming on snow-covered fir trees, the whole framed with gay, checked curtains. Coziest of all were the friendly pots of red geraniums that graced every window sill.

Jean compared it in her mind with the great rooms of the old castle in south Sweden where Greta lived most of the year, and where she and Jenny had already visited her for several weeks. That fortress-castle, four hundred or more years old, contained much of the grandeur of the past: rare furniture, priceless tapestries, painting, and sculpture of olden times. Mingled with them were the finest treasures of the present day: etched glass, delicate china, gleaming copper, fine carvings, and a gallery full of modern paintings and sculpture.

Neat maids, at least a dozen of them, so it had seemed to Jean, in traditional blue dresses with white caps and aprons, kept the castle spotless. There was the cheery one with long, blond braids who came early in the morning, curtsied, and built a fire in Greta's bedroom while all three girls snuggled down in the big four-poster bed for their morning gossip. There were the very dignified ones who served so perfectly at the long dining table, and the rosy, windblown ones who took care of the garden. There were still others in the great washhouse by the lake where they were doing all the autumn laundry when Jean and Jenny arrived. Greta explained to her that even in the wealthiest homes the laundry was done only four times a year. Then, not merely the sheets and table linen which had been used in the last three months must be washed, but all the unused linen as well, to keep it white and exquisite. She had seen the loom house too, not so much used as formerly, but still ready, with weaving

on the great looms and piles of flax to be spun when any of the maids had extra time.

Jean remembered the mellow beauty of the old brick walls and towers reflected in the wide moats. Some of these had been filled up and planted with rose gardens, but in others stately swans still floated. She and Greta and Jenny had loved to imagine the days when beauteous maidens had watched from the towers for the return of their knights in armor, and had thrilled to the clanking of the drawbridges let down to welcome them.

All about the castle now were miles upon miles of rolling farm land, quaint farmers' cottages nestling here and there along the lake or in the groves of trees. Some were of mellow, red brick half-timbered in brown, others were of white plaster or painted boards, but all of them were picturesque. Nevertheless, they were not so enchanting as these red log houses of Dalarna, that lay half hidden in the snow.

When dinner was announced, Jean was still thinking that even though the castle in the southland was very grand, she loved better this cozy cottage presided over by rosy Lilla Mormor, whose face was seamed with tiny wrinkles, all of them looking as if they radiated from her merry smile. With her bent figure and her gay costume and her cane, she went tapping before them to the dining room.

Although the little grandmother lived in a cottage, her three country maids in caps and striped aprons were quite as efficient and much more friendly than the dignified ones at the castle. Lilla Mormor prided herself on her table, which was well known throughout the countryside for its special Swedish delicacies.

"Why wouldn't it be?" she laughed. "When one has eaten for ninety years, one knows what is best to eat."

Jean never could get over the fact that everyone in this family, from Greta to Lilla Mormor, not only spoke English, but French and German as well. Even the little children study several languages in Scandinavian schools. It was in the French convent, where Greta had been sent to perfect her French, that Jean had known her. She had not been one of the charter members of Jean and Company, Limited, because her name happened to be Greta. But Jean and Jenny had shared the Round Robin with her, because she knew all the girls who had written it, and they had decided that she ought to be an honorary member, at least, especially as she was Jenny's cousin. Neither was it really her fault that she had not been christened Hannah. Her parents *had* thought of it.

No wonder Lilla Mormor prided herself on her table, after so many years of practice in feeding sturdy sons and daughters, grandsons and granddaughters, and now great-grandchildren. In a country where everyone continually skis and skates in winter, hikes and climbs and swims in summer, and where even the tiny children indulge in the strenuous gymnastics for which Sweden is famous, eating has become almost a ritual. There are four to six meals a day, beginning usually with several varieties of cheese and cold meat at breakfast, and ending with a midnight lunch in the long, summer evenings. But the chief meal in the country is served in the late afternoon, and Jean was as ravenously hungry for her dinner as the others.

It was such fun, this Swedish dinner. First of all came the smörgåsbord, a sort of Swedish hors d'oeuvres. It reminded Jean of the wedding feast at Hardangerfjord. Spread out on a long table at one side of the room was a surprising array of different dishes: caviar and anchovies, stuffed eggs, goosebreast, cheese, fish, smoked eel, and dozens of others. From these each one filled his own plate, choosing his favorite delicacies, once, twice, several times, and ate them standing up. At Jean's first meal in Sweden she had eaten so much of the tempting smörgåsbord that she had had no room for the rest of the meal, but she was wiser now.

Then came the meal itself. Lilla Mormor and Greta's father sat at the ends of the table, and Greta and Jenny and Jean at the sides where they could kick each other under the table when something especially good appeared. Jean was so busy with the soup, the liver pâté, the roast goose, and the delicious pudding, that she scarcely had time to notice the hand-woven table linen, the gleaming red glass, and the quaint peasant china.

But she loved them all, especially the charming formalities that have grown up about the Swedish meal. She watched with interest when Greta's father lifted his wine-glass, caught Lilla Mormor's eye, and said, "Skål," while he drank a toast to her. She had discovered that no one in Sweden ever drank without toasting someone at the table. After the meal Jean kissed Lilla Mormor's hand, bowed politely, and said, "Tack för maten," which means "thanks for the meal." She learned that all young people and children thanked their mothers after each meal, and guests politely shook hands with the hostess and said the same thing. It would be very rude, even in the simplest home, to omit this little ceremony.

After the meal, Jean and Greta and Jenny begged Lilla Mormor to tell them about the ancient customs still followed in Dalarna. So they sat at her feet by the tile stove while she told them about the Dale folk who, more than anyone else in Sweden, cherish to this day their old customs and costumes.

First she described Midsummer, the festival that celebrates the day when the sun climbs highest into the sky and shines all night long. It is then that the young people in each village raise Maypoles, made from the tallest trees that can be found, sometimes sixty or seventy feet high, and deck them with flowers and green birch branches. They dance around them all day and all night, the girls in their colorful folk costumes, varying with each village, but all of them gay with striped aprons and flowered shawls, red skirts, or caps. Even the young men condescend on that day of the year to put on yellow breeches, tasseled stockings, and bright vests, while they dance the old folk dances to the tune of gay fiddling. Each dance tells a story, one of weaving, another of sowing and reaping, another of making love. The young people dance with gusto, eating and drinking a great deal in between times in the outdoor cafés among the flowers and trees.

Then she told about weddings as they still take place in Dalarna, and Jean thought of the interesting one she had just seen in Norway. The customs here were somewhat the same. All the countryside is invited, and each guest brings cheese and cake or wine so that there may be enough for all. The bride puts on a silver crown hung with shining pendants, the same crown which has for generations been worn by all the brides in the village, and her bodice is covered with flowers and brooches. The guests gather at her house before the wedding, following her as she rides on horseback to the village church. She carries a prayer book, which the groom has given her, wrapped in the wedding handkerchief she has herself embroidered. The groom wears the shirt which she has made for him under his long green coat. Behind them come the musicians, also on horseback, and perhaps a few young men with guns and pistols to shoot off at intervals, a relic of the days when the bridal party was protected from enemies on its way to church. The other guests follow on foot, the girls dressed in their gayest costumes, the young men with bright ribbons flying from their hats.

At church they pass through a triumphal arch of green boughs. When they go home again, there is another arch of boughs waiting for them, and the young people dance, sometimes three hours, sometimes three days, until the provisions are all gone. This depends somewhat on the wealth of the family and the generosity of the neighbors. When that time comes, the hostess passes a highly spiced rice pudding, which is the equivalent of saying to the guests that the party is over. Sometimes they "dance the crown off the head of the bride." The bride is blindfolded and all the maidens present dance around her until she takes her crown off and places it on the head of one of them. This girl will, of course, be the next one to wear it as a bride, and she in turn will play the game again and pass it on to someone else. Jean told Lilla Mormor that in America the bride throws her bouquet after the ceremony, and the girl who catches it is supposed to become the next bride.

Lilla Mormor said, too, that in summer the Dale folk go to church in the church-boat, sometimes as many as thirty or forty of them rowing across the lake in a long, pink boat with a high bow and stern. The men row, the children stand at the bow, and the women sit in the stern. Jean could almost see the now frozen lake coming suddenly to life in the warm sunshine of a midsummer morning, with the descendants of the Vikings rowing their way to church. Only now the men had on yellow breeches, tasseled stockings, long dark coats, and square-crowned hats, and the women, who always sailed with the Vikings in the olden days, so we are told, now dressed in scarlet and white caps, flowered kerchiefs, and striped aprons. Lilla Mormor said that one could tell the village from which the women came by the types of caps and aprons they wore, and whether they were married or single. The young girls had red caps and the matrons white ones. When the boys met their sweethearts in church, they always said politely, "Good-day, thanks for the last meeting." But their eyes said they were grateful for this one as well.

She described Christmas, a season as much loved in Sweden as in other countries. For days beforehand the children buy all sorts of things in the market, toys and candy, and especially the little ginger cakes shaped like pigs, to commemorate the boar which was always sacrificed at this season in heathen times. Among older girls it is the tradition that at least once before Christmas they must sit up the whole night through making gifts. On Christmas Eve there is a Christmas tree, of course, with gold and silver balls, flickering candles, and the Swedish flag on top. But instead of Santa Claus, it is the Christmas gnomes who bring the gifts, a little old man with a big, white beard and red cowl, ringing a bell, and a little old woman carrying a basket full of gifts. In the late evening there is a Christmas feast, first a specially prepared fish, then a roasted pig or ham, and then a fat goose. The dinner ends with a Christmas rice pudding (not so good as a plum pudding, Jean thought), in which an almond is hidden. Whoever finds it will be lucky during the next year. But nicest of all, it seemed to Jean, is the sheaf of grain set up for the birds beside the snowy gateway, so that they, too, may have their Christmas tree.

Lilla Mormor described also some of the Dale folk who had lived in this beautiful valley. There was Anders Zorn, the famous artist, who painted beautiful women, blond, blue-eyed, and ruddy, clad in their bright peasant costumes or splashing in the lake in the golden sunshine. He surrounded himself with all the beauty and color and luxury of which he was capable, a brilliant setting for such a colorful genius.

She told, too (and here Jean held her breath with interest), of Carl Larsson, who also lived in this lovely dale, in a cozy, homelike cottage surrounded by his household and loving most of all the simple things of every day. They enjoyed hearing about how he painted his own candlelit windows at evening, his own garden covered with a riot of blossoms, his own small boy scrubbing the back of his neck, his own wife rocking her baby. All the enchanting and intimate scenes of his own home, from the kitchen full of bright copper to the nursery filled with toys and cradles, plaid curtains and patchwork quilts, were familiar to Jean from his books.

Lilla Mormor related the story of Gustavus Vasa, the ancient hero of the Dale folk, who led his people against a cruel tyrant. His career was almost as exciting as English King Alfred's, for he, too, burned the good dame's pancakes and hid in her cellar beneath a trap door concealed by a huge wine keg.

"And Selma Lagerlöf, does she live here?" asked Jean. "She's wonderful, too."

"No, she lives in the Varmland, farther south," said Lilla Mormor. "She is a dear friend of mine. Sometime I will take you all to visit her."

Jean sat quietly for a long time, seeing before her a great panorama of all Sweden past and present, its heroic deeds, its great artists, and its traditional country ways. She saw the color and strength and vigor of a people who had never been slaves, had never been conquered by another country, and which for one hundred years had never had a war. Here boys and girls grew up with strong bodies and healthy minds; here men and women lived in peace and plenty and were proud of their glorious past as well as their prosperous present. Jean had noticed in Stockholm that there seemed to be no poverty and no slums such as she had seen in other cities. As has been done in Norway, new and modern apartments had been built, which rent for a few dollars a month. The streets and the people were shiningly clean, and everyone was busy and happy, as if there were enough work and food and clothing for all.

"And now," concluded Lilla Mormor, "you three must go to bed early, for tomorrow is the festival of Santa Lucia." Jenny beamed with delight at the thought, and Greta and her father smiled mysteriously, but not any one of them would tell Jean what it was all about, only that she must get a good sleep, so she would not mind being wakened early. Giggling excitedly, the girls mounted the ladder into the big attic bedroom with its bright walls, painted furniture, and checkerboard curtains, and went to bed in the great sleeping cupboards. It was almost like going to bed on a pantry shelf, thought Jean, as she pulled the fat quilt around her cozily, while Greta and Jenny scrambled up to the bunk above. Outside the snow

IT WAS LILLA MORMOR HERSELF!

swished softly against the roof.

It was still very early and very dark when Jean heard the sound of footsteps and whispers and saw a bobbing light. Could it be a birthday cake, she wondered, this little circle of flickering candles nodding its way toward her? She sat up in bed, her knees under her chin and the quilt drawn up around her. Now she remembered! She had seen it in Carl Larsson's book, the vision of Santa Lucia in a white robe, with long, fair hair, a green garland on her head and candles set about it like a starry crown. But this was a tiny Santa Lucia, with apple-red cheeks and pale hair, more white than gold. It was Lilla Mormor herself! Behind her came the three maids, beaming with pleasure, each carrying a tray with coffee and little saffron cakes. Her crown still flickering, Lilla Mormor seated herself beside Jean's low bunk, to which Greta and Jenny had now descended, too, wrapped warmly in their quilts. They all drank coffee and ate little cakes together as she told them the quaint legend of Santa Lucia.

Santa Lucia was a beautiful virgin about to be married, who admired the Christians so much because of their courage that she gave all her dowry to them. She became a martyr when her furious lover informed against her, and she was condemned to be burned at the stake. But the flames came up all around and did not burn her. That is why her festival is celebrated with a circle of candles.

Soon there were shouts below and the girls recognized the voices of Nils and Per. They jumped into their clothes, scrambled down the ladder, and found Santa Lucia's breakfast feast spread for them.

Everybody was very gay and tried not to remember that they were separating today. But as Jean looked around her and thought of all her good times with these jolly boys and girls and Lilla Mormor, tears sprang to her eyes. She brushed them quickly away, and in sweet wine toasted every one of them in turn, saying "Skål," as she caught their eyes, and trying to look as if she had done it all her life.

Just as breakfast was over, they heard jingling bells outside, and there was Per's father in the red sleigh waiting to drive Jean and Greta and her father to the train. Jenny would stay on for a few weeks with Lilla Mormor, who was lonely in the long winter. The others would go back to the south of Sweden, and Greta's father had promised to get Jean to Paris by Christmas, where she was to meet her own father and mother.

There were goodbyes all around but Jean saved the last for Lilla Mormor, who slipped something into her hand as she stood on tiptoe to kiss this tall American girl. It was not until Jean was on the train that she found she was still clutching the little package. When she opened it, there lay the loveliest pair of silver skis. She started to pin them into her scarf, then impulsively pinned them over her heart instead, turning to wave a last goodbye to the little red cottage half buried in the shining snow.

CHAPTER 13:

HOLLAND FROM A CANAL BOAT

What a clattering and clumping and what shrieks of laughter! Jean's mother pulled back the crisp, white curtains of the tiny cabin window, moved a pot of crimson tulips, and looked out. It had been a long time since she had seen her daughter so young and carefree. During the last few months in Paris, Jean had been living up to the dignity of her sixteen years, wearing city clothes, toning down her voice and actions to the older people she had been with, tutoring in French and history, studying art, going to the opera, being altogether a sophisticated young Parisian. Her mother had begun to feel that she herself, in spite of her thirty-odd years, was quite the younger of the two.

Even when Jean's father had been with them at Christmas time, he had stood a little in awe of his grown-up daughter and had been almost afraid to attempt anything so undignified as their usual exchange of puns and practical jokes. Nor did she bounce on to his lap any more or tweak his ears or treat him with her former affectionate disrespect. Altogether, she was an extremely serious and correct young lady. So now it was with relief and amusement that Jean's mother saw her daughter behaving normally again.

There on the little deck Jean and Jan were clumping merrily about in a Dutch dance, now swinging this way and that with their hands on their hips, now slapping their knees and clapping their hands together, now jumping high into the air and coming down in their wooden shoes with a tremendous thump. Jean's full skirts were billowing so madly in the wind that her mother was afraid she might go up like a balloon at any moment. The little wings on her crisp, white cap blew this way and that across her rosy cheeks, and her apron kept flying up and hiding her face completely. Jan's full black trousers blew tightly against his sturdy legs and his blue jacket flapped in the wind, showing the bright, cerise blouse and silver buttons underneath. Once his black fur cap blew off and he and Jean chased it down the deck with shrieks of laughter, rescuing it just before it rolled into the water. Jan clapped it on his head again at a rakish angle, catching Jean's hands again in a dizzy whirl.

But Jean was not so lucky. Off flew one of her wooden shoes, splash into the water! Jan seized the boat hook and deftly fished it out and then dodged about the boat, Jean stumbling along after him with one wooden shoe and one red-stockinged foot. Finally she sat down breathless, and Jan produced from his capacious pocket a pencil, three or four elastic bands, and a bit of yellow sail cloth, with which he turned the wooden shoe into a quaint little sailboat. He attached a string to it and, bending suddenly, dropped it into the water again, defending himself with his other hand while Jean pommeled him soundly. But she could not help being fascinated by the jolly toy boat, and presently both of them were lying flat on their stomachs, quite regardless of their adult dignity, watching the shoe bob along on the water beside the big boat.

Jean's mother turned to Jan's mother in the snug cabin where they had retreated from the cold spring wind. They laughed together over their knitting, and began to talk of the time, many years ago, when Jean's mother had visited Jan's mother and Jan was still a rosy-cheeked baby. They were happy that their grown-up children were having fun together now. Jean was sixteen; Jan was three or four years older and had been to school at Oxford, so that he spoke perfect English. For days Jean had been longing to wear the Dutch costume that Jan's mother had given her, and she had teased Jan to put on his, so this was a hilarious masquerade for the duration of their canal-boat trip. In Amsterdam, of course, everybody dressed in conventional clothes, as in any other great city. But in the villages to which they were going there would be so many Dutch people in native costume that they would not feel conspicuous at all. It was really a triumph that Jean had been able to persuade Jan to join in this lark. Along with his city clothes he had discarded his usual Oxford dignity and was having just as much fun as Jean.

While her shoe dried in the sun, she and Jan sat on top of the now horizontal mast. It was bent down against the cabin of the boat like a shut-up jackknife in order to pass under the bridges, until they should get out into the open waters where the sail could be hoisted. Meantime they chugged lazily along with a little motor. All that long, bright morning they had loitered past low fields checker-boarded with yellow, scarlet, and purple tulips nodding primly in orderly rows. The water was so much higher than the land that they looked down on all the surrounding country.

Jan explained that The Netherlands, Holland's real name, meant lowlands, and he told her that all these fields had once been at the bottom of the sea. For centuries Holland had been patiently building dikes of earth and sand and straw around section after section of ocean and then pumping out the water with windmills. Jean watched with new respect the wind turn the great yellow and orange sails of the mills as she realized that they were constantly pumping to keep the water from overflowing the tulip beds and green pastures.

Jan told her that sometimes in great storms the dikes were broken and all the men and women and children rushed out to build them up again, filling bags with sand, piling up logs and stones, and even bringing their own straw mattresses to stuff the holes and so hold back the threatening sea. He told her again the story she remembered having read in school, about little Peter who saved Holland by thrusting first his finger into a hole in the dike, then his arm, and then trying to stop the flow of water with his little body, being rescued only when he was exhausted and almost frozen.

But sometimes there was no help for it and whole villages would be inundated and the people drowned or rescued in boats from their red roofs or chimney tops. At one time during the siege of Leyden the Dutch king broke the dikes and floated his warships up to the walls of Leyden to rescue the beleaguered city. Jan told Jean that, in many places, great electric pumps had taken the place of windmills and that more land was constantly being reclaimed from the sea for new gardens and pastures.

Jean was glad to see that they still passed numbers of these gayly painted red, blue, and green windmills beating their great arms against the sky. They also passed rows of trees, their tops cut off, and only the tall trunks with a tuft of green at the top remaining. Sometimes the road ran along the dike, along which automobiles raced, entirely out of keeping with the slow movement of the clumsy canal boats. Now and then there was a picture that Jean especially loved, a milk cart with shiny copper cans drawn by a patient dog, while beside him walked the milkmaid, her skirts blowing in the wind. Sometimes they stopped at a door to pour foaming milk into the housewife's shining, copper pans. Most amusing of all were the Dutch boys and girls who raced merrily along on bicycles, skirts and trousers ballooning in the wind and clumsy wooden shoes speeding around and around on the whirling pedals. Jean thought they must be more skillful than she was at keeping their wooden shoes on, and she told Jan she would not be happy until she had tried that feat herself.

She loved, too, the quaint villages with their step-roofed houses rising into peaks along the water front. Sometimes these houses were tall enough to make deep reflections in the canal, but sometimes only the upper story with its bright front door opened on to the top of the dike, and the lower floors wandered down to the meadows back of the house. The houses were painted in the gayest colors, here a green door opened into a red and white house; often a blue and yellow house had a red roof, and always there were crisp curtains and pots of tulips or hyacinths in the windows.

Jan told her that he thought Holland must be the wettest country in the world, for not only was it full of lakes and rivers and canals, but it rained or was foggy much of the time.

As if they did not already have enough water around them, Dutch women threw pails of it over their tiled floors, front steps, and even the cobblestones in the street, scrubbing and mopping from morning until night. Jean thought she had never before seen such shining cleanliness as here in Holland. Even the rosy cheeks of the buxom housewives shone as if they had been polished. She almost fell off the boat with excitement when she saw a plump little maid standing on her tiptoes to scrub a tree trunk with a big brush, while her brother dipped the family chairs into the water one by one and very solemnly rubbed them dry. In another place a girl of her own age, with cap wings bobbing energetically, was polishing a pile of copper pans in the sunshine.

She never tired of watching the fat Dutchmen with their hands in their voluminous pockets, and buxom housewives with their hands folded under their aprons, clattering over the cobblestones. Most of all she loved the roly-poly children, dressed in miniature Dutch clothes, toddling plumply along in their big shoes. Jan told her that boys and girls dressed alike in skirts and aprons until they were four years old. It was only by the kind of cap they wore that one could tell which was which. An occasional sturdy milkmaid with a wooden yoke across her shoulders from the ends of which hung two pails, and now and then a man with a bright cart load of tulips or cheeses attracted Jean's attention.

But most of the vehicles were in the water. Clumsy blue and green barges towed by horses along the banks, squat sailboats with yellow or red sails furled about their prostrate masts made their way along. Smartly polished little motor boats threaded their way through the slower traffic and occasionally a rowboat or a ferry crossed from side to side. Some of the barges were loaded with pots and baskets full of bright tulips, some with yellow and orange cheeses like enormous oranges and grapefruit, some with piles of square peat blocks, some with logs for the sawmills, and one proved to be a moving van filled with household furniture and with a goat tied in the bow.

On many of them were gay little cabins painted blue and yellow or green and white, with crisp white curtains at their miniature windows, and pots of tulips and hyacinths on the window sills. Here and there a colorful family wash billowing in the wind fluttered from a clothes line. In front of the boat cabins, as in front of the house doors, the housewives sat knitting, their children playing around them. Numerous pets, terriers that bounced from one edge of the barge to the other, barking at everything in sight or a great cat asleep in the sun completed the family.

Jan told Jean that many families lived on canal boats all the time, except for a few months of the year when the children are required by law to go to school—cruising from one end of Holland to the other, from Friesland in the north to Zeeland in the south, wandering through canals and rivers and inland seas. This sounded like a tremendous distance to Jean, from one end of the country to the other. But Jan told her that on a clear day one could see the entire land of Holland from the high tower of Utrecht in the center of the country, and he had heard that Holland was no larger than her Massachusetts and Connecticut put together.

Jean watched with the greatest interest whenever they came to a drawbridge, to see the keeper take toll in a wooden shoe let down on a string. Some of the sailboats dipped their masts as they went under, while the helmsman pushed with a long pole. Where the bridge was narrow, the traffic was sometimes very thick, and it needed skillful handling to steer the clumsy boats.

When they finally came into the Zuider Zee, Jean was delighted that the motor stopped and their mast sprang upright like an opening jackknife, sliding them unceremoniously to the deck in a heap. But when the great henna-colored sail was raised, she leaped to her feet and spread her arms to the wind and sunshine, so delighted was she to be in the open sea. The bright blue water was alive with bobbing whitecaps, and the sails of the little fishing boats leaned precariously in the wind like so many diagonal yellow, red, and orange patches against the horizon. Over Jean's head white, puffy clouds scudded before the wind. Jan stood beside her, pointing out the villages as they sailed past. They saw Broek in the distance, and Jean remembered that Broek was where Hans lived, in *Hans Brinker, or the Silver Skates*, and she wished she might see it more closely. Farther on was the little island of Marken, visited by tourists from all over the world, where the people still wear their quaint Dutch costumes and carry out many of their early Dutch traditions.

At Volendam they furled their sails and landed. By this time they were ravenously hungry and Jan's mother, a twinkle in her eye, said she would see what could be done about it. Jean and Jan raced up the dike, ran along the road at the top of it, stopped in front of a cunning cottage painted bright blue and yellow with a red door, and waited for the others to arrive. Much to Jean's astonishment Jan's mother pulled the polished brass knocker, and who should appear but one of the jolliest, plumpest housewives one could imagine.

"Did we surprise you, Katrina?" asked Jan's mother. "I have brought my good friends to see if you would give us some of your delicious fish and waffles for luncheon."

Katrina beamed from one bonnet wing to the other as she welcomed them eagerly to her little house. Until she married a Volendam fisherman, she had been a maid in Jan's household, and, while Jean and Jan were still arranging their wooden shoes in a neat row on the front doorstep, she ran to a high cupboard and brought out Jan's favorite sweet cake. They all stood on the top steps munching the cake and looking down to where the little fishing fleet lay anchored, its nets spread out to dry. They saw Katrina run down with her basket to pick out several shining silver fish from the latest catch, and they knew that soon there would be a delicious aroma of cooking fish.

Two young people on bicycles rode past them along the dike, and Jan hailed them, asking politely if he and Jean might have a ride. They stepped into their

wooden shoes again and with many shouts and much laughter tried riding the bicycles. Jan was expert, but Jean's big skirts blew into the wheel, her apron fluttered over her face, and her clumsy shoes just would not stay on the pedals. Finally she collapsed in a heap on the cobblestones, all tangled up with the handlebars and surrounded by a solemn group of children who had been looking on politely and silently. But when Jean started to laugh, they all laughed too, and helped her up again.

By this time the most tempting odors were coming from Katrina's front door, and Jean and Jan hurried back again, once more leaving their shoes on the front step and padding into the kitchen in their heavy, red wool socks. A great tile fireplace covered with Biblical pictures, brightly scoured tile floors, gleaming copper pans hung against the walls, potted flowers on the window sills, a heavily carved high cupboard against one wall made up the furnishings of this little room. Jan pointed out that here was the whole house in one room, a dining table and chairs before the fireplace, a high shelf where the good man kept his long Delft pipes and cans of tobacco, a basket with Katrina's knitting, and a cupboard full of blue and white china.

Showing behind a sliding panel were the fat down quilts and embroidered linens of a great bed. Above the bed was a smaller bed built into the wall, and it was not until this moment that Jean caught a glimpse of a fat, round cheek and a chubby hand above the coverlet. At the same time she heard a contented gurgle, and Katrina let her climb up and lift down a perfectly adorable baby. To Jean's delighted surprise she was dressed like her mother in a little white cap, full skirt, and an apron. Off she walked like an animated Dutch doll, clutching at the furniture and occasionally sitting down suddenly among her plump petticoats.

While Jean was still following little Betje about, Katrina called them all to the table and set before them fish, fried a golden brown, a bowl of kaas, or fresh cheese, and a great pile of crisp rolls. As she ate, Jean watched Katrina bending over the fire with her long-handled waffle iron. By the time they were ready for them, there was a pile of pale golden waffles, crisp and crunchy. With a final hug for little Betje, whom Jean would have loved to kidnap, they thanked Katrina for their luncheon and went back to the boat.

All afternoon they sailed along the shore, watching the fishermen come in, the motor boats flying by on important business, an occasional pleasure yacht with great white sails skimming over the blue water. Their own henna-colored sail caught all the wind and sunshine, and Jean could hardly bear to think that sometime she must be a landlubber again. Gradually the wind died down, the sun sank lower and lower, and it was almost twilight when they saw Hoorn rising from the sea like an enchanted city of the East with its spires and harbor towers. Jean wondered if they could ever enter the elusive harbor, which seemed to be entirely cut off by a long green strip of land. But they found the opening at last and glided into the romantic port while the sunset gilded the housetops. They were all very quiet as the sail was furled, looking out on the dreamlike harbor where boats of every kind were moored for the night.

In the early dusk they walked through the quaint town along the main canal, where the grave and dignified façades of the step-roofed houses seemed to be leaning forward as if to see their own reflections in the water. On the side streets stood rows of gay little houses, bright in color and much more frivolous than the dark and stately mansions which they had just passed. They wandered about this picturesque village until dark, watching the lights twinkle out in the windows and the little boats come home to rest. At last they stopped at a brightly lighted café where they had enormous oysters and stewed duck with apricots, topped off with cheese and the hard cake which is typical of Hoorn. Jan said he had been in Hoorn once for the kermis (the fair), when each customer had been allowed to take only as much cake as he could chop off with a hatchet, and sometimes the would-be buyer had to go away empty handed. When they reached the boat again, Jean and the two mothers slept in bunks in the cabin while Jan rolled up in a big blanket on deck and slept soundly until morning.

The next day, bright and early, they had "little breakfast," coffee, rolls and jam, in the cabin. With a last lingering look at Hoorn, they wandered off in their boat through the canals to Alkmaar, to see the cheese market. On the way they passed clumsy barges laden with golden cheeses, and along the dikes they saw brightly painted horse-drawn and dog-drawn carts going in the same direction. Jean told Jan that she would never be able to look a cheese in the eye again as long as she lived, she had seen so many at once.

But Jan only laughed and said, "Wait until you get to Alkmaar."

Halfway through the morning they stopped to visit a friend of Jan's in a great old farmhouse, where Jan said they kept the hay in the attic and where the cows lived on the first floor. As they came along the canal, near it, Jan whistled shrilly on his fingers a very special signal that only Peter knew. Suddenly plump Peter himself appeared, rushing up to the dike all puffing and breathless and almost falling into the canal in his joy at seeing Jan again. Nothing would do but that they should all come in for "second breakfast." Jean's mouth fairly watered at the thought, and she was eager, too, to see if it were true, as Jan told her, that cows did live in the same house as the family.

Peter it was who showed her the great, tiled cow room where rosy-cheeked milkmaids were scrubbing the floors, where crisp curtains hung in the windows, and where there were flower boxes all about. Even the mangers were made of bright-colored tiles, and the great room was fragrant with the smell of sweet hay and fresh milk. Jean looked out of the door to where dozens of black and white cattle grazed in the green meadows, and Peter told her that the cows, too, were frequently scrubbed from head to foot. Jean thought she would not mind living in the cow house herself.

A tinkling bell now called them to breakfast, this time in a great beamed room with heavily carved furniture and more beautiful tiles. The table was set with fine linen and exquisite blue and white Delft china. There were piles of pancakes with dents in them, glasses full of foaming milk, sausages and jam and steaming hot coffee, about three times as much as anyone could possibly eat anywhere except in Holland. Jean wondered if she could eat six big meals a day as the Dutch did. Little breakfast, second breakfast, lunch, tea, early dinner, and late supper. She knew she was getting plumper by the minute and she wished she could keep right on living in Holland all her life, where plumpness was considered beautiful, and dresses were designed to accommodate curves. As they were finishing breakfast, Jan whispered to Peter, who disappeared and then reappeared playing an accordion—such a gay tune that Jan brought Jean her wooden shoes, pulled her to her feet, and whirled her around and around and around in a gay, Dutch dance. But no matter how hard she tried to hold her shoes on in the high jumps, even curling her toes and lifting her eyebrows in the effort, they *would* fall off.

"What you need is practice," laughed Jan. "We'll have to see about that."

When they finally took their leave, Peter stood on the bank and played for them until their little boat had disappeared around a bend. For the rest of the day they meandered peacefully along.

As they came closer to Alkmaar, they noticed that the canals were crowded more and more with cheese-laden boats. Jan told Jean that on Thursdays all the cheeses were brought in from the country for the Friday market. They watched as the boatmen threw their golden balls to be deftly caught by the porters on shore in their white uniforms and gaily beribboned caps—a baseball game made up exclusively of pitching and catching. Suddenly Jan clutched Jean by the hand, leaped with her to the dock, and dragged her breathless and protesting to where a crowd of people stood on a little bridge looking up. Jean looked, too. As the bell in the Weigh House tower struck four, a mechanical trumpeter blew upon his horn and out popped two little mechanical knights in medieval armor, who flew at each other with their spears in the most realistic manner. This was more fun than even a cuckoo clock, thought Jean and begged Jan to bring her to see it every hour. They found quaint and charming places for tea and dinner, and Jan and Jean explored the town from end to end. That night they slept again on the boat so that they might wait over and see the cheese market in the morning.

At ten o'clock it began. There were piles of golden cheeses neatly arranged on barrows or carrying trays, with aisles between and porters standing quietly at attention. For half an hour the buying and selling went on, the buyer lifting and punching and thumping each cheese and sometimes testing it as one does a watermelon, by cutting out a long sliver to try it. After some haggling about the price, the buyer slapped the palm of the seller, and the seller slapped his in return, and it was a bargain. At ten-thirty the Weigh House bell began to ring. The porters in their white suits and colored hats picked up the trays and shuffled off with them to the Weigh House where they would be weighed and stamped. Jean and Jan were so interested that, of course, they had to get right in the midst of the bargaining and were several times almost run over by the porters. At last they took refuge behind a very fat traffic policeman and were safe for the rest of the morning, only dashing out at intervals to get a view of the jousting match when the Weigh House bells rang the hour.

By noon they were ready to start their homeward voyage in the little boat. It had begun to drizzle now but they found it very cozy inside the cabin. Jean was careful to sit near the window where she could look out at the red and white, or blue and green windmills that seemed to pass them in a long procession. Everywhere the lush, green meadows were spotted with black and white cows or great patchwork quilts of tulip fields.

Jan's mother told them about the canals in winter when she was a girl and everyone still wore quaint old Dutch costumes. She told of the villages half hidden in snow along the dikes, of the great icicles hanging from the windmill arms, of the frozen canals covered with vivid costumes, the peasants wearing sheepskin coats and woolen mufflers, the gentry dressed in rich furs and velvets. In those days there were not many trains or tramways and no automobiles, so that people traveled by boat in summer and by sleigh or skates in

Weigh House, the Cheese Market of Alkmaar.

winter. Everybody, even grandmothers and toddlers, skated in those days, and the babies were pushed along in their little chair sledges.

She described fat, old men in baggy trousers and fur caps whose long pipes rested on their round stomachs, buxom matrons with market baskets, rosy milkmaids with pails of milk hanging from a wooden yoke, children going to school, the whole world swinging along on skates. There were cheap wooden skates tied on with straps, shining steel skates, and even skates of gleaming silver, all of them turned up in long points in front. She told of skating excursions to near-by towns, skating picnics with lunches of hot chocolate and buns and sausage, romantic moonlight parties when sometimes the chaperon got left behind! The first day that the ice was hard was always a school holiday, called Skating Day, and everyone went out on skates. Gaily painted sleighs flew along the dikes or over the frozen canals, drawn by horses a-tinkle with bells. Plump swains pushed their much befurred lady-loves around in chair sledges, and there were the tiny sleds on which the children coasted. Jean could almost see the gay picture.

"But now," continued Jan's mother, "of course all the townspeople wear conventional city clothes; automobiles and trains carry people about, and electric power mills are gradually taking over the windmill's work, so that the little world of Holland has by degrees lost much of its color and gaiety. Only the tulips, the brightly painted houses, and the occasional brilliant costumes in out-of-the way villages are still as they used to be when I was a girl. In twenty years there will be many more changes. Perhaps by that time the

Zuider Zee will be drained and turned into pasture land and fields of hyacinths, and our towns will be building skyscrapers."

"Oh! I hope not," cried Jean, "I wish it might have stayed as it used to be, but at least there always have been and always will be tulips in Holland," and she gazed out of the window over the striped carpet of yellow, red, and purple tulip fields.

"You mustn't be too sentimental about tulips belonging to Holland," laughed Jan, "for at one time there were not any here. During the Crusades the first bulbs were brought back from Persia, but they did not grow here before that time. Since then, fortunes have been made and lost in tulips, and men have died to save a single rare bulb."

"Oh," cried Jean, jumping up and almost spilling her cup of tea in her excitement, "I am going to find a history of Holland tomorrow and read all about it. I want to know how tulips came to Holland and how the sea was turned into gardens, and how the Spaniards besieged Haarlem. I want to read about the ships from the Orient that brought rich cargoes of spices down the Zuider Zee," here she gesticulated excitedly with a sweet cake, "how Cape Horn was named for the Dutch village of Hoorn because her discoverer came from there, and how —"

"And how roast goose with spiced prunes will taste for dinner," laughed Jan's mother. "Here we are at our house again, and tomorrow I will give you the very book you want."

After dinner that night Jean and Jan leaned from the window of the high beamed living room, looking down at their own shadows reflected in the waters of the canal.

"One year more of school in England and then I am going to Columbia University. You may want to know all about Holland, but I want to see where the Pilgrim fathers who sailed from Holland landed on Plymouth Rock. I want to know New York, which was the New Amsterdam of my great-great-grandfathers. I want to follow Hendrik Hudson up the wide river named for him." Jan beamed down at Jean. "If you work very hard and learn how to keep your wooden shoes on, I'll come and dance with you every time I can escape from college."

"Let's practice right now," said Jean and dashed off to find her wooden shoes.

CHAPTER 14:

ENGLISH PRIMROSES

U p and down, up and down paraded Jean, like a wooden soldier. She must rehearse this thoroughly, so that when she gets home she can show John just how it is done. He had been a British soldier in a play which their dramatic club had given at one time, but his marching had been all wrong. She would show him! Her legs were stiff at the knees, and her feet marked time as she stopped to right-about-face at the end of the hotel room. Her bright, red jacket was belted tightly about her middle with a trunk strap. Balanced precariously on her head and leaning dangerously forward over her nose, was her mother's Russian fur muff turned into a high, black soldier's hat. Held rigidly against her left arm was a broom, which made an excellent gun. So absorbed was she in her stiff-legged rehearsal and the equilibrium of her hat meanwhile, that she did not hear a timid knock on her door nor even the louder one later. Suddenly it opened a crack and Maggie thrust her head in, a wisp of hair falling over one eye, a broad grin displaying a row of uneven teeth.

Jean came instantly to attention. "Halt! Who goes there?" she boomed in deep tones, remembering the play.

"Please, Miss, s'only me come to tidy up, Miss," giggled Maggie, dropping a curtsy. Then seeing Jean's disappointment, "But h'I'll be h'anything you s'y, Miss."

"An enemy of the King," whispered Jean.

"H'a h'enemy of the King," said Maggie, dropping another embarrassed curtsy.

"Then die, villain!" roared Jean, advancing on the now startled Maggie with the victim's own broom. This was too much for Maggie, and she retreated behind the door, only emerging to help Jean gather up the rolling muff and balance it on her head again as a magnificent shako.

"Now watch this carefully, Maggie," cautioned Jean. "The wardrobe is the sentry box." She backed stiffly into it, just catching her hat in time to keep it from being knocked off.

"But that hain't the w'y they stands, Miss," said Maggie critically, hands on her hips and her head on one side. "Tike another look."

When Jean's mother returned a few moments later, only the skirts and ankles of Jean and Maggie were visible, as they hung far out of the hotel window watching the guards at Windsor Castle.

"Wot did I s'y, Miss," argued Maggie, pointing at the sentry standing stiffly in front of his box.

Jean's mother did not hesitate. She clutched them both firmly by their belts and pulled them in. Maggie, overcome at being discovered conversing so intimately with Jean, pushed back the unruly lock of hair and made another embarrassed curtsy.

"No 'arm h'intended, Mum," she said, backing precipitately out of the door with her mop pail and the rescued broom.

Jean and her mother collapsed on the bed. "O Mums, isn't she just too wonderful!" chuckled Jean. "H'I can 'ardly control my 'ysterics, when h'I 'ear 'er talk," and off she went into peals of helpless laughter.

"So this is the way you sketch Windsor Tower, is it?" asked her mother. "After all those expensive art lessons in Paris!"

"Oh, but I did that, too. Then I went down to try to sketch one of the guards in his sentry box, but he would not stay still long enough. He looked just like a red and black toy soldier and worked exactly as if he were wound up to march. When he ran down again, he backed into the sentry box. I had to practice it so I could show John how it ought to be done, when I get home!"

"Will you never grow up!" sighed her mother. "I was hoping you would have everything packed and ready. It's almost time for the boat to leave."

When the bags were packed Jean and her mother took a last look at the gray towers and castle of Windsor, at the wide, green stretches and leafy shade of The Long Walk. The day before they had watched the King review the Royal Guards in the Windsor fields. It had been so exciting to see the soldiers on their black horses, their silver helmets and breastplates gleaming in the sunlight, their horsehair plumes streaming in the wind, ride out to meet the King as he advanced on horseback and saluted. The trumpets blared, the horse band played, the people cheered, the fields and forests shone green behind the brilliant uniforms. Jean decided it must be great fun to be a king.

They had visited Eton, too, and Jean had wondered how American schoolboys would feel if they had to wear Eton suits and top hats every day. She was relieved when she saw some of the students in shorts and caps, going out to row.

They had seen the Queen's Dollhouse in Windsor Castle and the endless number of State Apartments. By the time Jean had walked through about forty rooms and thought that she could not bear to see another portrait or tapestry, she was not quite so sure that it would be fun to be a king.

They had wanted to stay on in Windsor, but there was so much more of England to see that they could not linger too long in one place.

In an hour they were on the boat. Jean, who had vaguely supposed that the Thames would be as wide as the Hudson River and the boat about the size of a Hudson excursion steamer, was amused and delighted to find that she and her mother were almost the only passengers on a small, white river boat in a narrow, meandering stream.

They explored the little cabin, tried the awning-covered seats in the front of the boat, and finally settled down on a bench in the high stern from which they might watch the passing scene. Jean thought this a most lovely way to travel. It was like the boat trip in Holland but very different, too, for instead of dikes and windmills and low-lying fields, they sometimes glided along between mossy banks so close together that the branches almost met overhead, like a cool, green tunnel. Sometimes they came out into wider reaches, where water lilies floated in the still shallows, or boats were tied up along the banks. Occasionally they passed young people pushing their narrow punts with long poles. Jean noticed that the girls were all fair-haired and rosy-cheeked, with sturdy young figures beneath their simple sport frocks, and that the youths were tall and rangy and pushed their long poles with easy grace, swinging back and forth rhythmically.

Pushing boats along the shallows near the river bank was different from any other means of water locomotion that Jean had ever seen. She had rowed a boat and paddled a canoe and even learned to navigate a gondola, but here one merely stood in the stern of a narrow punt with square ends and pushed it along the river bed with a pole.

They went through one lock after another. Her mother told her that they would pass twenty or thirty before reaching Oxford, in order to climb up the steep incline of the river. Jean liked to see the boat slip into the lock and have the water gates close behind them. Then she watched the lock slowly fill with water while the boat lifted and lifted. When it was on a level with the stream above, the upper gates opened and they floated out a step higher in the river. At each lock there was a lock house, and when the captain of the boat, a picturesque figure in blue broadcloth, signaled, a member of the lock-house family would rush out, man, woman, or child, to close the lower gates and let in the water from above. Jean noticed that some small boats like punts were carried around without going to the trouble of filling the lock.

At tea time several children came to the edge of the boat with flat wicker baskets lined with strawberry leaves which were filled with huge strawberries, each one bright scarlet with a perfect green crown and stem. Jean's mother bought three baskets, one for the captain with whom they had already made friends. He had invited them to join him at tea on deck, served by the mate. Jean had heard of ambrosia and nectar, but she was sure that tea out of heavy white cups, a plate of golden sponge cake, and three baskets of strawberries consumed on a boat winding through fairyland, must be infinitely superior.

She threw bits of her cake to a stately swan that sailed along beside them and behind whom trailed three fluffy cygnets.

"That swan must be fully a hundred years old," commented the captain.

"How can you possibly tell?" asked Jean.

"Do you see that hump on her beak? You tell the age of swans as you do the age of trees, by rings. Each ring around the hump on a swan's beak means five years of life. They often live to be a hundred fifty years old. They never mate but once and if the mate dies, the swan is single for the rest of its life, always faithful to its first love."

"How romantic!" breathed Jean.

"There is a severe law against killing a swan on the Thames, as most of them belong to the Crown. The others belong either to the Vintners or the Dyers."

"The Vintners or the Dyers?" questioned Jean, puzzled.

The captain explained. "Each year three swan masters, dressed in blue, pleated coats, white trousers, red socks, and a blue cap trimmed with swan feathers, come up the Thames in an ancient barge, just as they did in Elizabeth's time. One swan master represents the king, another the guild of Vintners, another the Dyers. They list the swans belonging to each order, identifying them by the nicks in their beaks. They catch the cygnets and mark them to match their mothers. The swans were originally intended to follow the royal barges as they floated up and down the Thames, as far back as the time of Henry VIII. They are still fed and protected and add much to the beauty and interest of the river."

Jean had been listening entranced to this tale of the swans, throwing her cake bit by bit to the one following the boat. Now that the cake was gone, swan and cygnets turned haughtily away and floated back again to the shore.

Jean and her mother exclaimed over the beautiful roses at every lock house, and the captain told them that each year a prize was given to the lock house which had the most beautiful garden, and that it was always a difficult question to decide. He told them who owned the ancient manors with wide lawns that sloped down to the river, and said that only on the Thames trip could one really see the English gardens. In all other parts of England they were shut in behind stone walls and high hedges.

Jean had never even imagined that such green hedges existed as those which sloped to the river, nor such clambering masses of roses. She loved the wide lawns of the vine-covered manors, the great, spreading trees, the charming informality of these English gardens. There were no straight walks or stiff borders of tulips or carefully planned terraces, no elaborate statues or fountains, only rose-covered walls, meandering paths, broad lawns under great trees, and in the garden beds such a riot of flowers as only Nature could have planted. If she ever had a garden of her own, it would be a green and peaceful English one.

They passed a ruined abbey, half smothered in vines and a gray castle where once the kings of England had sought escape from their kingly duties. Here and there a picturesque village of half-timbered houses (with a lofty church tower rising in the square) gazed serenely down at its own quaint reflection in the water. Sometimes evening bells rang out over the quiet, sheep-flecked meadows. Jean repeated softly:

"The curfew tolls the knell of parting day,
The lowing herd winds slowly o'er the lea,
The plowman homeward plods his weary way,
And leaves the world to darkness and to me."

"Thomas Gray is buried not far from here," commented the captain, "in the very churchyard where his elegy was written."

The boat stopped at a picture-book village and Jean and her mother soon found rooms in a sixteenth-century inn. After a dinner of boiled mutton, boiled potatoes (Jean called them hard-boiled potatoes because she could scarcely spear them with her fork), boiled cabbage, and boiled suet pudding, all entirely unadorned, they started off on rented bicycles to explore the countryside in the long twilight.

They rode down country lanes between green hedges, past thatched cottages nestling under great trees, past old stone manor houses just visible over gray walls covered with climbing roses. They watched the sunset from a low hill, leaning against the crumbling walls of an ancient ruin, and then they rode back again to the village through the quiet dusk.

At the inn each took a candle from the table at the foot of the stairs and climbed up steps which were worn by many feet, walked down a dim corridor where their own flickering shadows seemed the ghosts of ancient pilgrims, to a gabled attic room with two huge beds.

There was still light enough at ten o'clock for Jean to lean out of the window and sketch a quaint dormer across the way, with lead-paned casement windows and mellow, russet tiles.

Jean left her candle burning when they had gone to bed, and it cast eerie shadows on the rough plaster walls, the hand-hewn oaken beams, and the great, carved wardrobe. Soon she was asleep and dreaming of Greenwood Forest and Canterbury Pilgrims and Knights and Ladies of King Arthur long before the candle finally flickered out.

In the morning, after tea in bed, they rode off again on their bicycles for an hour, before joining the captain once more on his little steamer. For another day they meandered along the river, through narrow locks, along quiet reaches dappled with lights and shadows, under a green canopy of leaves, and out again into wider stretches where puffy, white, summer clouds were reflected in the blue depths. There were more glimpses of stately mansions and wide lawns, one that Jean especially loved, with rooks flying around queer chimney pots, a crumbling garden wall covered with a cloud of pink ramblers, and a cool, shadowed inlet where a little punt, with crimson cushions, was tied up waiting for a passenger.

"I wish it were waiting for me," sighed Jean. "What could be lovelier than to float all day in this quiet river. Or just to lie on my back in the bottom of the punt looking up at the tree tops and dreaming. O Mums, can't we have a house in England some time?"

They stopped here and there in the villages, taking

on passengers or letting them off. There seemed to be more people traveling today. They passed Henley, where the Royal Regatta was to be held in a few days, and saw a quaint Victorian houseboat filled with a gay party of young people. It looked like a floating pavilion with white lacework railings around the double decks. Sculls skimmed along to the rhythmic stroke of the broad-shouldered boys, and smaller boats loitered here and there. Everywhere were gay voices and flying pennants.

"Twenty years ago there were dozens of those lovely houseboats," said Jean's mother. "Now they are almost all gone."

"O Mums! If I could only go to the races," cried Jean. "I'd give anything to watch from that adorable houseboat."

Toward evening they slowly drew near Oxford. Jean thought of a poem she had once read, beginning:

"I saw the spires of Oxford
As I was passing by,
The gray spires of Oxford
Against a pearl-gray sky."

A pearl-gray sky, with soft undertones of rose and violet and turquoise blue melting into the gray background, made a perfect setting for the spire after spire that rose in silhouette from among the steep roofs of the old town.

Waiting for them at the hotel was a huge pile of forwarded mail and Jean read the one from Jane, saying she was still in southern France and was heartbroken that she would miss Jean's visit to England. There was also one from John, with Napoleon Bonaparte's footprint in black ink.

"The black hand," explained John. "A dire threat because you don't write oftener." Jean giggled over that. And there was a fat Round Robin which it took more than an hour for her to read. She dropped off to sleep thinking about Jean and Company, Limited, while her mother was still reading her pile of letters.

When she rolled over and opened one eye the next morning, her mother, already fully dressed, was just coming in the door. "O Jean! Jean! What do you think has happened? One of my letters last night was from an American friend who married an Englishman and has lived over here for many years. Several months ago I wrote to her London address to see if I could find her in England, but as I never heard from her I thought she must have gone away. And now look! look!" she cried, waving an envelope covered with stamps and forwarding addresses. "Here is the letter that has been following me all over Europe. And, Jean, she lives right here near Oxford. I have already telephoned to her and she is coming this afternoon to take us to her home for a visit. She has a daughter named Joan, just your age, and a houseboat at Henley and everything!"

By this time Jean had hopped out of bed and was waltzing her mother around and around the room. It was hard to tell which was the more excited and happy. "Best of all a letter from your father says—but I'm not going to tell you what it says. Surprises are so much more fun!" And she gave Jean an extra whirl, just for good measure.

"While we are by ourselves, there is just one place I must take you to, the garden of St. John's College. It's the most heavenly spot in the world. When we get there, I'll tell you why."

They wandered through the streets of old Oxford, stopping now and then to browse in a secondhand bookshop or look through the gates of some college or other, for Oxford has dozens of colleges. Or they admired a tower silhouetted against the sky, or the picture made by the steep-roofed houses with vine-covered dormers and quaint doorways.

Through a lovely tower archway they entered St. John's garden. At this hour of the day there was no one around but an old gardener pottering about with his trowel. Emerald lawns stretched off in the distance, with stone benches in the purple shadows of spreading boughs. A tumbled-down wall was almost hidden with its weight of climbing vines and roses, and against it were borders of variegated flowers, all Jean's favorites: larkspur, stock, primroses, and mignonette. Jean asked the gardener if she might have just one English violet from the border.

"W'ite a jiffy," answered the old man, "and I'll bring ye a noseg'y."

They wandered from one path to another and finally sat down at the gnarled root of an old and mighty tree. Jean's mother smiled at Jean and the smile was the brighter because her eyes were shining with tears. "To me this is the loveliest spot in the world, because it was here that your father first told me he loved me. He was a student at Oxford, and I was traveling with my mother. Ever since that time we have wanted to come here together, and now here I am with you, which is the next best thing, and

THEY ADMIRED A TOWER SILHOUETTED AGAINST THE SKY.

we'll be seeing your father soon—perhaps—" Jean put her finger on her mother's lips.

"Please don't tell me," she begged. "That will be the last surprise of the trip and the best of all!"

But here they were interrupted by the gardener who brought Jean the daintiest, old-fashioned bouquet of violets and primroses and sweet alyssum. "For the young miss," he said, bending double with his battered hat in his hand. "I 'opes they'll please 'er."

Back at the hotel they had roast beef and Yorkshire pudding and gooseberry tart, which is a deep pie with only an upper crust. Jean felt just as if she had stepped into a Dickens book for lunch. There were the rough-plastered walls and hand-hewn beams and a great stone fireplace that must once have had a spit turning before it. At the next table sat Mr. Micawber, Jean was sure. There was handsome Mr. Darnay with him, and Uriah Heep carving the cold cuts. Old Peggotty passed by the door with a scrubbing pail, and wasn't that Oliver Twist over there with little Dorrit? Of course, they were all dressed up in present-day English clothes, but one could easily see through the disguises. Even Tiny Tim, the cripple, was carried in by old Scrooge, who set him down before a steaming plate of beef and kidney pie. Jean expected at any moment to hear him say, "God bless us every one," even if it was not Christmas.

Shortly after lunch Jean's mother's friend appeared, a lovely woman in gray English tweeds with a gray felt hat and a Liberty scarf—a most stunning person. Her liveried chauffeur stowed away the baggage, or luggage, as they call it in England, and off they all went through the green countryside.

Jean's mother was so busy renewing her old acquaintance that she scarcely noticed where they were going, but suddenly Jean clutched her arm. "O Mums, look, look! It's the very house we loved most of all. Imagine staying here! There is the old wall covered with roses and the rooks flying around the chimney pots and that lovely, lovely garden. It's just too good to be true."

As they drove in, a fair-haired girl ran over from the tennis courts to greet them. "What fun!" she cried. "Mater said she knew your mother long ago, and now we shall be great friends, too."

The minute Jean was shown the charming guest room with a high poster bed draped in chintz, and flowery curtains blowing in the wind, she rushed to the small-paned casement window to look out. Yes, sure enough, there at the end of the garden path were the crimson cushions of the little punt. They had been waiting for her, after all!

The maid came to call her for tea which was spread beneath a sheltering tree. The great silver urn, the delicate pink luster teacups, the thin bread and butter with crisp watercress to fold between the slices, the dark fruit cake full of nuts and currants and all kinds of surprises, and great crimson strawberries to be eaten from the stem made an enchanting picture against the green background. Joan arrived with three or four boys and girls who had been playing tennis. Her father appeared in a leather coat and tweed breeches, rosy from a brisk walk with his dogs, and her older brother, Jeffrey, rode up on horseback, threw his reins to the stable boy, and joined them.

What a happy life, thought Jean, far too enchanted to do anything but nibble fruit cake, and wish she might never have to leave here as long as she lived.

After tea the young people all gathered around Jean and asked what she would like to do. She loved their musical voices, their clean-clipped way of speaking, and their delightful English slang. She did hope she could remember it all until she got home and could try it out on some of her friends. They suggested tennis or a walk over the meadows to the near-by village or a bicycle ride to the ruined abbey. But Jean kept her eyes steadfastly on the crimson cushions at the end of the garden path.

"I have never been punting," she said shyly. "May we do that first of all?"

Joan and a tall boy in white flannels raced her to the river and off they went, Jean sitting on one of the crimson cushions that she knew had always been waiting for her. Now they pushed along close to the shrubby bank where little wild things scurried away through the leaves. Now they drifted into wider reaches rippling in the fresh breeze; now they paused to listen to a skylark, a tiny speck suspended in the heavens, or watched a kingfisher making blue scallops along the banks. They pulled water lilies, great waxen-petaled ones with golden hearts, and piled them in the bottom of the punt. The shadows were long when they turned homeward and walked up the flower-bordered path, Jean with her arms full of water lilies.

There were guests for dinner and everyone dressed. Jean put on her favorite evening dress, a crisp, flowered organdy with frills at the shoulders, and Joan was good to look at in green voile with pink roses tucked in at the girdle.

The white damask and crystal and silver shone softly in the candlelight, and Jean thought she had never seen anything so lovely as the old Lowestoft china with the family crest. At first she was overwhelmed by the stiff formality of the dinner. So crisp and clear and precise were the words which she heard all about her that she was almost afraid to speak, lest her own speech should sound careless or clumsy in comparison. She was especially awed by the solemnity of the long-faced footmen, but she tried to cheer herself up by comparing them with the only other English footmen with whom she was acquainted, the fish and frog ones in *Alice of Wonderland.*

The thought made her chuckle and Joan's brother, Jeffrey, who sat beside her looked at her curiously. "Oh, I say, do tell us the joke."

But Jean only smiled mysteriously. "I was just thinking," she murmured.

"Very well, then, tell us about America. I'd jolly well like to stop off there some time and see the Indians and buffaloes and all that sort of thing. I suppose it's frightfully dangerous traveling in the more barbarous states."

Jean's eyes twinkled. She decided that if Jeffrey really wanted thrills, he should have them. "The last time I was scalped by an Indian," she began, "we were living in a log cabin on the prairies of Nebraska. Just as we were starting out on a grizzly bear hunt, armed to the teeth, we were attacked by a band of Indians..."

But here Tom, who had been to America, burst into shouts of laughter in which Jean joined in spite of herself. Jeff looked aggrieved. Jean put her hand quickly on his arm.

"I didn't really mean to do it," she said, "but I used to make up blood-curdling stories to tell to the girls in boarding school in France, and I just couldn't help trying them on you. To tell the truth," she added confidentially, "I've never even seen a buffalo or a grizzly bear except in the Zoo, and the only Indians I know anything about were in the Indian village at the Chicago Fair. And I have never in my life been in a log cabin. We are really quite civilized in America, you know."

Jeff guffawed. "I say, you are ripping."

Jean, startled, looked quickly down at her dress, then blushed as she realized that this was just some of Jeff's English slang.

The next morning Jean and Jeff and Joan and her father all went riding, cantering across wide meadows starred with flowers, the dogs streaming along behind. There was a great woolly sheep dog, galloping along like a young bison, a splendid airedale, and a comical little black Scottie who leaped over the high grass in scallops and sat down to rest with his pink tongue hanging out, at every excuse. Coming home in the heat of the day, they rode more slowly through leafy paths beside the river, while the dogs snuffed delightedly along the bank. After lunch the other boys and girls arrived on bicycles and they all played tennis till tea time. Jean found that her game was very rusty, but it was fun, nevertheless.

That evening there was another surprise in store for her. They drove into Oxford again, to Magdalen College.

(Jean never could get used to pronouncing it Maudlin. It just didn't sound respectable, she thought.) Here in Magdalen Forest they sat on an improvised grandstand and saw *Midsummer Night's Dream*. Jean remembered when she had seen it before, in the forest of Klessheim, near Salzburg. But this was even more thrilling. Titania was the daughter of a well-known English actor; Oberon, a young English lord. Jeffrey and Joan knew most of the other characters, too. One tree was so big that Puck could creep out almost to the end of an overhanging branch and tickle the long ears of Bottom with a straw. From behind another enormous trunk stepped Titania's fairy band. Jean thought this was one play that should never be produced on an indoor stage, but only with great trees and flower-strewn grass for a setting. When Jeff and Joan rushed away afterwards to speak to the actors, Jean sat still and dreamed of fairies and wandering players in an enchanted forest.

Where would she find a forest like this in America, or a green garden like Joan's, or water lilies in a dappled stream or rooks cawing about vine-covered chimneys? Sometime she must live in England!

After everyone was in bed that night, she stole once more through the garden drenched with moonlight, down to the murmuring river, and sat at the foot of an old tree. She jumped when she heard footsteps on the path. There was Jeff come to bring in the cushions from the punt.

"Oh, I say, whatever are you doing here?" he exclaimed, as Jean rose suddenly.

"Just dreaming and wishing I could stay in England forever," she laughed.

"How about going out in the punt?" asked Jeff.

This was almost as romantic as being serenaded in a Venetian gondola, thought Jean, except that Jeff himself was not a bit romantic, just very matter-of-fact and very sporting. Perhaps she liked them better that way after all.

"A penny for your thoughts," smiled Jeffrey, leaning on his pole.

"They are much too silly to talk about," answered Jean. "I was only thinking of fairies in an enchanted forest and roses climbing over an old wall and rooks cawing—and bells at evening."

"Just fancy," said Jeff seriously. Then he stopped poling and sat down. "Do you really think of things like that?"

"Only in my most romantic moments," laughed Jean. "What do you think about on moonlight nights on the river?"

Jeff was puzzled. "Why, dash it all, I suppose about cricket scores and the puppies having distemper and what sort of cake we had for tea—and all that bally rot."

Jean sighed. Why couldn't Jeff be more romantic? But he was nice, anyway, even if he did laugh at her when she almost tipped over the punt to pick a primrose gleaming palely in the moonlight on the bank.

When they said good night at the boat house, Jeff said, "That was topping. Shall we go out again tomorrow night?" Jean ran happily up the path wondering why she liked this tall, blond, unromantic boy so much. Perhaps away back she had English blood in her veins and understood the things he did not say.

The next day they went to the Royal Regatta, watching it from the very houseboat that Jean had seen as they came up the Thames. She could not tell afterwards which she loved most, the houseboat itself, gallant with pennants, the exciting race, the cheering, colorful crowd, or the perfect setting of blue river, leafy trees, and quaint, old town. It did not even matter who won. She only knew it was one more happy day to store away in her memory.

That evening they went out on the river again, with the same crimson cushions in the punt, silver moonlight, and dusky fragrance of the roses. Even though Jeff talked only about tennis and the best places in London for cold cuts, and bally old Eton, had she not seen him that day with a primrose in his buttonhole? Had he not borrowed her pocket edition of *Midsummer Night's Dream* and read it for an hour in the shade of the old oak, and had he not tenderly fed the sick puppy himself?

Jean and Joan spent long hours walking together over the fields, riding through the forest lanes, playing tennis, and having tea with the young people at the neighboring manors, and sometimes driving up to Oxford or down to Windsor. For two long, English weeks they were together. Sometimes Jeff came, too, but more often it was not until evening on the river that Jean saw him. And then, whether they talked about fairy forests or mutton chops it did not much matter, for the river was so beautiful and it was such fun just punting.

The morning they left, Joan and Jeff stood beside the car saying goodbye. "I do wish you were stopping on forever," cried Joan.

"Don't forget about Jean and Company, Limited," answered Jean. "But I'm going to call it Jean and

Company, Unlimited, from now on. The world is just full of Jeans."

"I'd jolly well like to see those Indians and buffaloes in America," Jeff called. "Expect me the next vac!"

But nobody, not even her mother, knew that there was a primrose pressed between the thirty-ninth and fortieth pages of the pocket edition of *Midsummer Night's Dream.*

CHAPTER 15:

BLUEBERRIES AND GERANIUMS IN ICELAND

J ean was much too excited to think of sleeping. She and her mother were sitting bundled up in warm clothes out on deck.

"Tonight I'm not going to bed at all. I've always wanted to sit up all night, and here is my chance. Please say yes." Jean hugged her mother's arm entreatingly, pointing to the blood-red sun almost resting on the horizon and the strange rose-colored sky and sea all about them. It was near midnight, but the sun still shone. "Just think of seeing Eskimos and igloos and kayaks and polar bears tomorrow," sighed Jean dreamily. "It sounds too good to be true!"

Her mother laughed. "I'm afraid you're getting just a little bit mixed, my dear. You're thinking of Greenland, not Iceland. Iceland is one of the most civilized countries in the world. It was originally settled by Norsemen or Vikings who migrated there for political freedom, and was an independent country a thousand years earlier than America. The sagas were written in almost the same language which the Icelanders speak today, and they were producing great literature and poetry while the rest of Europe was lost in the Dark Ages. Even now more books are published in relation to its population than in any other country in the world."

Jean groaned. "O Mums, you sound like a guidebook, and just when I was feeling so primitive, too. I *did* want to go fishing in an ice hole and wear a fur coat with the fur inside and eat blubber sitting on a cake of ice. I think it's mean to call it Iceland, which sounds awfully exciting, and then have it so disappointing. If you insist on talking like a guidebook, I suppose I'll have to act like a tourist," and she pushed her hat up until it was sitting on the top of her head, produced a pair of large, amber spectacles from her purse, and tried to look intelligent.

"As this is an educational trip, I'll continue to be a guidebook in spite of you," retorted her mother. "The Norsemen who discovered the island saw it first in winter, covered with snow and ice, and so named it Iceland, and, of course, the mountain peaks, are hidden always with glaciers, even in summer. But as a matter of fact, it is not as cold in winter as New York City, and the harbor in which we shall land never freezes over. The Gulf Stream flows around the island so that it is as warm as countries a thousand miles to the south. It is only when the northern harbors and fjords become jammed with icebergs that it is terribly cold. There are very few national costumes left, except on the farms, and —"

Jean interrupted sadly, taking off her glasses, "But, Mums, you'll be telling me next that they all have Rolls-Royces, and live in prefabricated houses, and buy their clothes in London and Paris. I thought this would be the most exciting adventure of all and now look at it." She yawned. "Just a perfectly stupid, uninteresting country. It will be such a come down after Venice and

Prague and Sweden and, and—" but here her voice trailed off and she was nodding. Her mother smiled as she tucked the steamer rug more closely about her.

It was two o'clock before she awakened again to find her mother shaking her gently. The sky and sea were bathed in gold, the sun a great, golden ball, and resting against the turquoise streaks of the northern sky were the black cliffs of Iceland and the blue-white mountain peaks shadowed in purple. Jean rushed to the rail, fairly speechless with excitement as she pointed now at a little fishing boat with a sail of pure gold, now at the changing colors in the water, now at the blue-black, jagged cliffs of the shore.

Her mother smiled mischievously. "It seems to me that I vaguely remember your saying something about Iceland being stupid and uninteresting."

But Jean had nothing to answer. She was awed by the strange light of the midnight sun and the wild and startling beauty of this lonely land. "I should think the people would all be poets," she breathed, "and I'm sure I should rather be a Viking than an Eskimo. Besides, I don't think I should like blubber very much, after all."

But Jean's mother was not listening. She was straining her eyes through the golden mist as if she were looking for something infinitely more important than Iceland. Off in the distance was a little harbor and along its shore a line of low buildings. "Reykjavik," said one of the sailors in passing. Jean looked at her mother in surprise as she suddenly pulled off her crimson scarf and started waving it madly.

"But, Mums," she said, "you don't know a soul in Iceland. Do be careful! You almost dropped your purse."

As they drew into the harbor, a pink glow spread over the white mountain peaks and the sky became streaked with red and gold. Now Jean saw with astonishment that her mother was laughing and crying together.

"There he is, there he is," she cried, hugging Jean in her excitement. "I was so afraid to tell you for fear he wouldn't be here."

Then it was Jean's turn almost to fall overboard with joy. After all those long months in Russia, here was her father at last. It seemed hours to Jean before the boat was finally docked. "Think of meeting you in Iceland of all places," she gasped, as she straightened her hat after an enormous hug.

"But why not Iceland," he laughed. "Your mother and I have always wanted to come here together, and it is on our way home. I sailed from Bergen a day or two before you sailed from Leith. And here we all are." He gathered them both in another huge embrace.

"How's that for your polar bear?" asked Jean's mother.

"And here I am blubbering, after all," smiled Jean through tears of happiness.

"My wife and daughter," said Jean's father now to a broad-shouldered, fair-haired man who was waiting politely in the background. "This is my friend, Jon Jonsson, whom I met on the boat. I first discovered that he spoke English and then that I had known him at Oxford."

"I have insisted that you stay with us in Iceland," said their new-found friend to Jean's mother. "My daughter is just a little younger than yours and is learning to speak English. I myself have studied the folk legends of Iceland and will be most happy to tell you what I know. Here is my car."

Jean was so content to be leaning once more against her father's shoulder and so drowsy from staying awake most of the night, that she went fast asleep on the drive home. She scarcely knew when her new friend picked her up and carried her into a room, laying her down gently on a wide bed where she was soon fast asleep.

When she wakened, she thought she must be smothering. On top of her was a billowy white mountain with which she battled sleepily for a few minutes. Even when she sat up, she could scarcely see over it. But now she realized that it was a huge eiderdown puff, and she rolled it off on the floor as she ran to the window. All about her was a neat and compact little city with buildings of wood and stucco and, oh horrors! corrugated iron. Some of them were gray and brown but others were painted in bright colors. She noticed with astonishment that many of the most imposing houses had corrugated iron roofs. Everywhere were automobiles and motor trucks, and men and women dressed in the latest continental clothes. There were even telephone poles and a movie house, and what was that dreadful smell! Oh, yes, fish drying on the fishing wharves! That reminded her of Norway. Beyond the little city she could see the snow-capped mountains and to one side a smoking plain. She remembered that her mother had told her that Iceland was almost completely made up of volcanoes and lava deposits, and that in one terrible eruption not long ago many people and cattle had been killed.

"O Daddy, Daddy," she called in a frightened voice. "Look, look at all that smoke. Do you think the volcano is exploding again?"

Her father came in and patted her shoulder laughingly. "Erupting," he said. "What a Jean you are. That is only the steam from some of those boiling springs with which the island is covered. You would be surprised at how many things the Icelanders use them for—hot bathing pools, the family washing, and heat for their houses. Yesterday I watched a woman dig a hole in the ground near one of them and put in her bread to bake. Do you know that you have slept all day long? Come along now. It's almost time for dinner."

Sure enough, it was late afternoon. Jean jumped quickly into her luxurious bathtub, and while she was dressing, she noticed that her room was furnished with articles from all over the world. She recognized hand-woven towels from Sweden, a painted chest from Bavaria, and chairs from England. As she powdered her nose, she decided that Mr. Jon Jonsson must be a great traveler.

And so he was. While they ate broiled salmon and roast lamb and Icelandic custard and sipped delicate wine, Jon Jonsson told them how he had gotten all these things. He owned, like many other Icelanders, great fishing industries and went several times a year to Norway, Sweden, and Denmark, where he sold tremendous quantities of dried and salted fish, thousands and thousands of barrels every year. He had studied at the universities of Copenhagen and Oxford and had some business interests in France and Germany. Jean's father had already discovered that his library was filled with books not only in the Icelandic language, but in English, German, Danish, and French as well. He spoke about this to his friend.

"In Iceland that is not unusual. Most educated people speak and read several languages. And there are very few who are not educated," he added proudly. "In the long winter evenings we must have something to do, so we read and study and—play chess." He smiled at Jean. "Do you play chess, little namesake?"

"Not very well," she replied shyly.

"Come, I will teach you."

All evening they sat playing chess or looking out over the sea and mountains in the changing light of the midnight sun. Jon Jonsson told her that his name meant Jon, son of Jon, and that for hundreds and hundreds of years in his family there had always been a Jon, son of Jon. Jean laughed and told him that she was meant to be John, too, after her father, but that her mother made a mistake and it had to be Jean instead. How Jon Jonsson did laugh at that. She told him, too, about Jean and Company, Unlimited, and all the Jeans that she had discovered in other countries and the Johns, too. There was Jan (Janesika's brother) in Prague and Hans in Switzerland and Jan in Holland and now Jon, son of Jon, in Iceland. "I know a John at home, too," she added, blushing a little. She changed the subject quickly. "What do we do tomorrow?"

"Tomorrow you will all be rested," he answered. "I will send you in my car to visit Thingvellir and Gullfoss and the Great Geysir."

"Oh, dear! Are there automobile roads everywhere?" Jean sighed.

Jon Jonsson smiled. "Such as they are, but perhaps you would not call them roads. You shall tell me when you get back."

Bright and early they started off the next morning. At least it seemed bright and early to Jean, but it had in reality been light all night. She had had coffee and pancakes before she got up, her breakfast tray almost lost in the folds of the eiderdown puff. There had been another breakfast of porridge and eggs later, and then Jean saw the chauffeur putting in a great basket full of more food for the journey.

"I'll be busy around Reykjavik for two or three days," said their host, "so keep the car and chauffeur as long as you like."

It was such fun to be together again that Jean and her mother and father would have thought that even Reykjavik with its ugly houses, corrugated roofs, and fishy odors was beautiful. But they soon left these behind and came out into the open country, untouched by the hand of man. The roads, too, were quite untouched by the hand of man, thought Jean. In the three days that they were out, the car bumped along over waves of lava, plowed through grassy meadows, climbed sheer cliffs, forded rivers, and crept through muddy bogs. Sometimes walking was preferable, and once or twice they transferred to ponies for side trips up the mountain or into deep ravines.

They visited Thingvellir, the great cleft in the rock where Parliament had been held every year for almost one thousand years, and where representatives came from all over Iceland. Upon this high rock, the laws of the Icelandic Free State were read from the year 927 on. In the year 1000 it was here that the question of the future religion of Iceland was settled, and Snorri, the priest, called upon the chiefs to give up their pagan religion.

They saw the valley where for hundreds of years the young Vikings had wrestled in the oldest form of sport in the world aside from the ancient Greek games, called the Royal Glima, which the guide described. Each man wore straps about his waist and thighs, and the game consisted of throwing each other about by these straps, a feat of agility rather than weight.

They visited Gullfoss, the golden fall, so-called because it shone golden in the sunlight, and they clambered out on the rocks to take a picture. The water fell more than 150 feet with a terrific, roaring noise and was almost hidden by a mist of spray.

"O Daddy," cried Jean in his ear, clutching his arm and pointing. There, sure enough, was the complete circle of a rainbow in the golden spray.

They went farther and saw the site of the once famous Great Geysir from which all the other geysers in the world are named, but which had been comparatively inactive since the great earthquake in 1896. Nevertheless Jean and her father threw cakes of soap into one of the smaller geysers and were rewarded by a bubbling and fizzing and finally a great spout of boiling water.

They drove to the foot of Mount Hekla, a mighty snow-capped mountain, the one which many years ago erupted and overwhelmed the island. They rode halfway up on pony back, and Jean decided she would like some time to climb to its top and look into the crater, though now she shivered a little at the thought.

The guide told them also of the famous forest where almost the only trees on the island grew. "Big ones," he said with a large gesture.

"How lovely," cried Jean, thinking of the giant redwoods at home that towered several hundred feet into the air. "Can an automobile drive through one of the tree trunks?"

"Oh, no," laughed the guide. "When I ride my pony, I can look right over the tops of them, but as they are almost the only trees in Iceland, we think them very grand and beautiful." Jean decided she had better not ask any more questions.

Tired after three days of sight-seeing, racked by the dreadful roads, and stiff from two nights on hard beds in the farmhouse inns, they were happy to get back to their kind host.

"You must give me one more day in Reykjavik," he said, "and then we shall start for the farm where my wife and daughter are eagerly waiting for us."

"Do we go by automobile?" asked Jean politely, though with inward misgivings.

"There are roads for a part of the way," answered her host, "but they are not nearly so good as those you have just been over. How would you like to go by pony back?"

Jean jumped for joy. "O Mums, do let's go by pony! We have our riding clothes and it will be such fun." So it was decided.

"I'll telephone my wife when to expect us," said Jon Jonsson.

"Do you mean to say that you have telephones on the farm, where there are not even roads?" asked Jean incredulously. But she believed it when she herself had spoken a few words over it to Gudrun, the girl whom she was to visit. "What do you think Gudrun said?" she asked her mother afterwards. "She promised to pick a bowl of blueberries for me and put a pot of geraniums in my window."

"That is a great compliment," said her mother, "because there are practically no fruits or flowers in Iceland, except for a very short season."

That evening Jon Jonsson read to them two of the well-known sagas, the story of Burnt Njal, and the Saga of Grettir the Strong. The next day he took them to the museum to see parts of Viking ships, ancient battleaxes and spears, chain armor and gold and silver ornaments worn by the Vikings themselves. Jean could almost imagine that she was sailing with Lief, son of Eric, on his Viking ship, to discover America, more than four hundred years before Columbus even thought of it. Jon Jonsson told her there was a legend that Columbus had visited Iceland to learn all he could of those early voyages before starting out himself.

He took them to visit the modern museum of sculpture where they saw magnificent statues by Einar Jonsson, called the poet sculptor, so full is his work of imagination and strength and beauty. Jean liked best of all the statue of Thorfinn Karlsefni, who first actually tried to colonize America in 1007. There he stood, with the strength of a Viking chieftain and the vision of a prophet, the man who dared to imagine the future of America.

Jon Jonsson took them into the public library and showed them books in many languages, from treasured,

THERE HE STOOD, WITH THE STRENGTH OF A VIKING
CHIEFTAIN.

ancient manuscripts which were brought out of a safe for them to see, to the most recent publications of many countries. As they came out, he bought from a small boy on the street corner what Jean supposed to be a newspaper, but it proved to be a paper filled with a number of recent poems.

"You see Icelanders still write sagas," he said, "and the Icelandic of the present day is so like that in the sagas that our children read them more easily than yours read Shakespeare."

That evening they played chess again. "Tomorrow at nine we shall start," said their host.

Jean was ready and waiting before eight, in her riding habit, but it was nearly eleven before they really got off. She was beginning to learn that no one in Iceland ever hurried or did anything on time, nor was anyone ever upset by this fact.

There were four of them to ride and there were eight ponies. Such plump and jolly ponies as they were, bigger than Shetland ponies, but with thick coats and shaggy manes and tails. The groom brought two ponies up to Jean, a white one with a cross saddle, the other a black one with a splendid sidesaddle, generously upholstered like an armchair, with a hand rail all around one side and the back.

"Which will you have?" asked Jon Jonsson.

But Jean was already in the cross saddle. Off they all went, the black pony catching up to them as soon as her heavy saddle had been taken off and her pack put on instead. Jean's pony sped along at an easy gait, half trot, half canter, and she was most reluctant to change mounts when they stopped at the end of the hour. Jon Jonsson explained that they changed horses every hour on a long trip. When there was much heavy baggage, they took pack horses, too. But today the extra ponies carried only light saddlebags, a picnic lunch, and a pack of canned goods, special delicacies which Jon Jonsson had brought to his family from the continent.

They raced along over green pastures, picked their way slowly through wavy stretches of lava rock, climbed almost perpendicular mountain sides, forded rivers. Still the vigorous little ponies never lost their feet nor their heads. In the late afternoon they stopped beside a hot spring where Jon Jonsson produced a dozen carefully packed eggs which he put in a saucepan and set in the boiling water of a spring.

"How do you like your eggs?" he asked Jean, whose eyes were almost popping out of her head. "Will three minutes do?" And there were soft-boiled eggs for tea along with the delicious lamb sandwiches which were left from lunch, and a big cup of milk for each.

They rode on again, looking down on great plains of pock-marked lava, the craters of geysers and volcanoes. "It looks just like the moon through a telescope," said Jean.

"Yes," explained Jon Jonsson, "Iceland is covered with volcanoes ready to erupt and geysers ready to spout. Sometimes it boils over in one place and sometimes in another. Seven eighths of the island is made up of volcanic lava and icy glaciers, and is entirely uninhabitable. There are only 100,000 people in all of Iceland, fewer than in one of your big cities of America. On this trip you will see but a handful of farms scattered through occasional fertile valleys. There is one now, away off there, and that is where we shall spend the night."

They rested their horses and looked about them. From where they stood they could see snow-capped mountains, rivers, geysers, waterfalls, ominous-looking steaming plains, and away beneath them an emerald green meadow dotted with sheep and cattle. They saw the sun low on one horizon and the moon just coming up on the other. The sky was a glory of rose and gold. As they watched, the shadows grew longer and longer, and the clefts in the mountains turned from blue to purple.

"This is the loveliest hour of the day," said Jon Jonsson. "Do you wonder that Icelanders are poets?"

Suddenly, as they sat there, clouds began rolling up from the horizon. Jon Jonsson leaped off his horse and pulled out of the saddlebags slickers and sou'westers for each of the party. "We must hurry," he said, and off they started. Down it came, a soaking, beating rain that blinded them and almost blotted out the road. But the surefooted ponies picked their way carefully, and in an hour, tired and drenched, the whole party was toasting by the farmhouse fire.

Jean could stay awake only long enough to take a drink of hot milk and eat some crisp, brown pancakes. Then she was off to sleep, buried snugly beneath an eiderdown puff buttoned into a fresh linen case.

She awoke the next morning feeling very stiff after her first day's ride. While she was moving her legs cautiously to see if they still worked, the rosy-cheeked farmer's wife, with golden braids of hair to her knees, brought her coffee and more pancakes. She found she had been occupying the bed of the farmer's daughter, who had slept on the floor instead. She tried to thank her, using the Icelandic words that Jon Jonsson had taught her, "Bestu thakkir." When Jean's father came to pay his hosts for the night's lodging, they would take nothing. Instead there was much hand-shaking all around and more "Bestu thakkirs," and Jean decided these were the most hospitable people that she had ever known.

Jon Jonsson explained that travelers so seldom passed this way that the farmer rarely saw anyone and always welcomed a visitor and his family for the news they brought of the outside world.

"This especially has been a great occasion for them," he said, "having three Americans under their roof, probably the only ones they have ever seen. I always bring them a few books to last till I come again, and that makes them happy, too."

They rode on in the brilliant sunshine, the air so clear that they could see great distances. After crossing another mountain, they came again to greener country, and at noon Jon Jonsson stopped at the crest of a jagged cliff.

"All this that you see before you now is mine," said he. "Yonder is my farm," pointing to a dozen low gables in the distance. "The fields near the house are the hay fields, which we cut for winter food, and these other fields are for grazing. If the season is dry, we must change the pastures often so that the cattle may be well nourished. Look!"

He took out his field glass for Jean to look. She saw the hay makers at work, the men swinging along with scythes and the girls following with rakes. She turned the glass and saw snow-white sheep and spotted cattle in the next field and beyond a herd of shaggy ponies. Jon Jonsson made a hollow of his hands and gave a great halloo-oo.

"The war cry of the Vikings," he explained winking at Jean. "Now look again."

There at the farmhouse door, in the round frame of the field glass, she saw a woman with a white headdress shading her eyes, and a young girl running toward them.

"Come on," cried their host, and off they went, clattering down the mountain, Jon Jonsson waving and hallooing, and Gudrun, still tiny in the distance, waving her arms and running toward them. Jon Jonsson galloped on ahead. As he came up to Gudrun, he swung down suddenly and caught her up to the saddle before him. He waited for the others to overtake them.

"Behold the Queen of the Eskimos," he said laughing. "Now for the royal feast of blueberries and cream!"

As Gudrun jumped from her horse, Jean saw her quaint Icelandic country dress with a tight bodice and full skirt, bordered with a vine of silver. Her long, blond braids fell straight over her shoulders from under a flat, little, black skull cap with a long tassel. Her mother was even more lovely, with gold borders on her dress and a headdress that looked like a plain gold crown with a long, white veil draped over a peak in the center of it. She welcomed them hospitably and took them to their rooms.

Jean noticed that from her high window sill she could step out onto the level of the green grass, and that more green grass grew on the roofs. There was even a lamb balanced precariously on his wobbly legs on the sloping roof, crying piteously for its mother. The lower half of the rooms was beneath the level of the ground. The roofs themselves sloped directly up from the meadow. That was why the gables that looked so small from the outside opened up into such spacious rooms.

There was a big living room, still called in Icelandic "bathroom," because in Viking days the main room always had a great bath in the center where the chiefs entertained their friends as in Roman times. When the water did not come from a hot spring, it was heated by stones which were warmed in wood fires and thrown in. Iceland supposedly at one time had many forests, but due to the love of the Norsemen for hot baths, these were all sacrificed.

There was a spinning room where wool from the farm was still spun and woven into fabrics, the dairy where butter and cheese were made and the cream separated, and any number of sleeping rooms with wide beds covered with mountainous puffs, "like so many cream puffs," thought Jean. But best of all, she loved the great kitchen, fragrant with the delicious odor of fresh bread and pancakes. For supper, in addition to blueberries, a luxury which lasts only a short season, there was skyr, a smoothly beaten curded milk eaten with sugar and thick yellow cream, fresh trout from the brook, and delicious roast beef. Vegetables and fresh fruits are almost unknown in Iceland because of the very short season of summer sunshine. But Jon Jonsson had brought canned fruits and vegetables which were a great delicacy to them, especially on the farm.

Gudrun and Jean were a little shy at first, but before long Gudrun was speaking to Jean in quaint English, showing her the precious potted geranium that she had nursed through the long, winter months, and her pet lamb. After supper they went out in the fields and helped rake hay, while the sun still shone low on the horizon.

Finally it became dusky in spite of the pink glow in the sky, and Jean knew that it must be growing very late. She was sleepy, too, after the long ride. She and Gudrun chose their favorite ponies that were loaded with hay for the loft, and, scrambling up on their backs, perched there like two elves peeping out of moving haystacks.

Jean lay down for just a minute while Gudrun led the ponies away to be unloaded. When she came back again, Jean was sound asleep. She dreamed she was riding a rocking horse and eating blueberries

and cream, while she looked through the telescope at a potted geranium. Soon the rocking beneath her became the ocean, and she was standing with Lief, son of Eric the Red, on the prow of a Viking ship sailing to America, and the potted geranium turned into the Statue of Liberty waving the Stars and Stripes. Suddenly something woke her and she sat up while Gudrun, smiling roguishly, hid the straw with which she had been tickling her.

As they went in at the door of the house, Jean heard the telephone ringing, and presently Jon Jonsson came back to say he had heard from Reykjavik that there was a passing cruise ship sailing for America the next week.

"I knew the Statue of Liberty had something to do with it," cried Jean as she told them of her dream. "But I'm glad the boat is not coming any sooner, so that we can ride horseback and rake hay and pick blueberries for a whole week."

CHAPTER 16:

JEAN DISCOVERS AMERICA

Jean was miserable. Here she was almost home again in America, and she knew that she really ought to be the happiest girl in the world. She had her father and mother with her again, after two years of seeing them only occasionally. She would soon be joyfully greeted by Aunt Sally and Grandmother, Peggy and Betsy Jane. But what if they had changed or what if they thought that she had? Then there was John. Before she left America, she had been sure that John was quite perfect, freckles, red hair, and all, and she had been thrilled by his letters. But since then she had met so many other boys: the dark-eyed, handsome brother of Giovanna, the nice German boys in Switzerland, Paul on the boat, Jan in Holland, and Jeff in England. She often opened her pocket edition of *Midsummer Night's Dream*, just to be sure that the primrose was still safely pressed between its leaves.

At home in America again, she would probably have to go to stupid dances and the movies, which she hated, learn to play bridge, and do everything that American girls and boys did. But would she ever hear again the singing boats in Venice or waltz on skates or go punting in the moonlight to come home with her arms full of water lilies, or eat ices while the tinkling chimes in the tower played old folk songs? Would she ever again be able to sit quietly in a dim cathedral or dream romantically in a castle tower? Her friends would not understand, of course. She remembered with a little shiver how they had all thought that Rosemary was conceited when she came home after a summer abroad and could talk of nothing but what she had seen in Europe.

Then there was the marvelous European food. How could she ever live without it? Hors d'œuvres in France, roast goose with apricots in Holland, delicate pancakes made of elderberry flowers in Austria, sponge cake and strawberries in England, hot chocolate and ambrosial cakes in Italy. She could not believe now that she had ever ordered just plain roast beef and mashed potatoes on the boat coming over. In the light of later gastronomic discoveries, roast beef and mashed potatoes sounded so unpoetic.

There was school, too. School would be so difficult. She would probably have to drop back a grade, lose all her friends, and go to college a year later than the others.

"Oh, dear, oh, dear, oh, dear," she wailed to herself. "I'm afraid I'm not in the least patriotic. I don't want to go back to America a bit," and two large tears began to trickle slowly down the sides of her nose.

At that moment her father, who had been supposedly dozing in the steamer chair beside her, yawned, stretched, and glanced at her face for the fraction of a second. Then he studied the sky and announced in a matter-of-fact tone, "Looks like rain."

Jean laughed a little, but the laugh got all mixed up with a sob. "O Daddy, I'm so glad you've waked up. I'm miserable."

"Miserable, hey, after two wonderful years in Europe, and all New York waiting on the dock to say 'welcome home'? I know," nodding his head wisely, "it was that pâté de foie gras for lunch," and he pinched her chin affectionately.

Jean gave a long and heartfelt sigh. "I don't know if even you will understand, Daddy. A man seldom does. Perhaps I'm silly and romantic and all that, but these two years have been so marvelous, just like reading the most thrilling fairy tale in the world, with beautiful illustrations on every page. And now I've got to go back again to living in an ugly old country," her voice caught in a little sob, "where people think you are putting on airs if you talk about music or painting or wear foreign clothes or speak other languages or are the least tiny bit different. I am not the same girl who left America two years ago. I've grown up and I've seen life and, please don't laugh at me, Daddy—but I am a woman of the world now. I know such a lot more than I used to."

Her father whistled, a soft, long-drawn-out kind of whistle, but he did not laugh. He did not even smile; he looked very serious. "Tell me all about it," he said, and Jean poured out her misgivings. She wished that she were still a little girl so that she could climb up on his lap and tell him her troubles as she used to. Instead she slipped her hand into his under the steamer rug, and that made it easier.

"H'm, I see. I brought you up to be a good little American, and now that you've seen Europe, it's all off. I can remember once when I felt exactly as you do, that everything poetic and romantic and picturesque and really beautiful was on the other side of the Atlantic. I am glad you feel that way, a little bit, at least, because there are many people in this world who feel that nothing at all exists outside of America. If they do by any chance go to Europe, they pursue American beefsteaks and coffee and bathtubs from Copenhagen to Constantinople, and never have time to look for anything else. You have had the great advantage of traveling and seeing beautiful things and making friends, at the very most impressionable time of your life. You have also learned how to use your eyes and ears as you never used to. Perhaps now you'll know how to use them better in your own country." He paused. "I'll make a bargain with you. I promise to show you something new or beautiful or interesting in America every day, something that you never knew was there before. I began looking for these things when I was about your age and I've been finding them ever since."

"O Daddy, you are so good to me! But I know you can't possibly make me think that any view is half as lovely as that from the hilltop in Prague, or any houses as picturesque as the little ones in Sweden, or any music as marvelous as what I heard in Salzburg, or anybody as nice as—" but here she stopped and blushed just the tiniest bit.

"Well, is it a bargain? Shall we try it?" asked her father. "I'll bet you anything you say, but be sure it's something beautiful and romantic," he teased.

"Will you really?" cried Jean. "Just wait till I think of a good one. There are so many things I want. There's a pale pink coral necklace in Venice, and an embroidered peasant apron in Prague, and a pair of square-toed green shoes in Salzburg, and a little carved wooden Madonna in Rothenburg, and a first edition of—"

"Oh, come now," protested her father, "how about the Golden Fleece or the Russian crown jewels?"

"But you promised," said Jean, "and you've never broken a promise to me yet."

"Very well," and her father struggled up out of his steamer chair to make a profound bow, with his hand on his heart, sweeping an imaginary plumed hat to the deck. "I am yours to command."

Jean thought hard, a deep frown between her eyes, her chin in her hand. "Oh, I know," she cried at last, "I want to see the Army and Navy football game more than anything else in the whole world."

At this her noble knight burst into a loud roar of laughter. "There's my little sporting American again. Now let me ask you, did you ever see anything quite so exciting in Europe as a grand old American football game? I score one point already. Come on, I'll beat you a rousing game of deck tennis," and off they went arm in arm.

Her father paused a moment to look speculatively at the sky. "I guess we'll be having fair weather from now on," he murmured.

"I'm sure we will," said Jean, and squeezed his arm very tight. Talking things over had certainly helped.

A few days later they stood side by side leaning over the rail, as they came up the river again to New York. Once more they had passed Fort Wadsworth, Ellis Island, the Battery, the Aquarium. It was the most beautiful hour of the day, just at sunset, and the towers of the great city were bathed in gold. The sky behind them was opalescent, shimmering. Twinkling lights shone here and there in the tall buildings.

"Why, Daddy, this is like the light in Venice at sunset. I never saw New York look this way before."

Her father laughed. "Another score for me. I told you that you had been learning to use your eyes and would see things that you had never known were here, just because you saw them every day. I can show you a view across Central Park at night, where the lights look like those on the hilltop at Prague. In New York you'll see the architecture of Italy and France and England. It's been there before, but you never noticed it. You'll see Europe all around you now, because you know how to look for it."

The great ship was moving slowly up the river, as stately and serene as the evening. Noisy little tugs came rushing out, chugging and tooting. They pushed and pulled while the sailors threw out heavy ropes as thick as Jean's arm, which were caught by dockhands and wrapped around windlasses on the pier. As the giant ship slowly edged her way into the slip, they could see tiny figures at the far end of the dock, waving and shouting.

"There's Aunt Sally," cried her mother, almost falling overboard with excitement, "and Grandmother, bless her heart."

But Jean was still searching the crowd. There was not a bit of red hair in the whole lot and not a bark among all the laughing and cheering. Well, perhaps they had forgotten about her. After all, two years was a long time, and of course now there were Jan and Jeff, too, so that it really did not matter. At least, not very much.

Just when she had finally decided that she did not care about American boys, anyway, there came the faint familiar sound of barking. Her heart jumped up into her throat, almost choking her. She craned her neck to see and there, away up on the roof of the pier was a gleam of shining copper, John's hair, of course, and Napoleon Bonaparte bouncing about, rushing to the edge of the roof as if to jump over and then dashing back again to John, or what must be John. The red hair was there, and the figure was vaguely familiar, but it had stretched; goodness, how it had stretched! It was considerably taller and thinner than it had been two years before, the hair was smooth, and the suit and necktie were exactly right. Jean could not believe that this was the tousle-headed, freckle-faced, knicker-bockered John to whom she had said goodbye such a short time ago. Why, he was really handsome now.

Her heart did a funny little flipflop, and she had to say, "Silly," to herself very sternly several times.

Soon they were sitting about on trunks and suitcases, waiting for the customs officers to examine their baggage. Grandmother and Aunt Sally had almost hugged Jean to pieces, and now Napoleon was trying to knock her off the same steamer trunk that had made her waver about going to Europe in the first place. John was standing by, making only occasional desultory remarks, but beaming from ear to ear.

Back at the apartment was old Lucinda, her face shining for joy, with all Jean's favorite dishes for supper: Virginia ham, and candied sweet potatoes and huckleberry pie. Jean squeezed her father's hand under the table.

"O Daddy, this tastes a thousand times better than anything I ever had in Europe."

"Another point for me. I have kept up my record pretty well so far, haven't I?"

The next day John and Napoleon arrived in the middle of the unpacking, and Napoleon went off to the corner again with his pet riding boot to chew on. But this time Jean and John did not even notice him.

"Well, what about those Giovannas and Jovankas and Janesikas, that you wrote me about? However do you pronounce their names! Were they all as nice as you thought they would be?" inquired John politely.

"Oh, yes, they were all charming. You know we have a club of Jeans, Jean and Company, Limited. Only we found so many Jeans that I decided we ought to call it Jean and Company, Unlimited. We have a Round Robin letter that we all write in, and send photographs

JEAN DISCOVERS THE REAL AMERICA.

and everything. It's so exciting. I'll show it to you the next time it comes."

There was a pause. John went to the window and looked out. Then, "What about the Johns? Don't tell me you have a John club, too, and hear from them all once a week."

"Silly," laughed Jean, "but I did meet some other Johns. There was Hans in Switzerland and Jan in Holland, and Jon Jonsson in Iceland. And did I write you about Jani in Budapest?" She paused, and added shyly, "There were some that weren't Johns, too."

"Well, bring them all on, and I'll challenge each and every one to mortal combat," declared John sternly, rolling up his sleeves. "And Napoleon will bite 'em! I've taught him to bite all undesirable aliens. I should have sent him with you in the first place, so that he could have bitten them sooner!"

Jean giggled. Then she suddenly remembered Napoleon. "O Napoleon Bonaparte, what *are* you doing?" she squealed, rescuing her boot. "Look, he's chewed the strap off entirely." But she did not scold him. She hugged him, instead. "I'm so glad to see you again, you can eat the whole boot if you want to."

Inwardly she marked up another point for her father. Jan was too fat and Jeff, well, even Jeff did not have red hair and freckles.

School was not half so difficult as she had expected. What she had missed in geometry and Latin, she had made up for in French and German and history and geography. Her English courses she had kept up by reading, anyway, and the first chapters of her book had been credited toward English composition. By substituting various subjects and working extra hard, she would be able to graduate with her class.

Peggy and Betsy Jane greeted her with open arms, and listened eagerly to her European adventures. In return, she felt it tactful to draw them out about their Christmas holidays at Lake Placid and their summer conquests on the Cape. Perhaps their experiences were not *quite* so interesting as hers, but it was fun to compare notes, anyway.

She found that nobody minded in the least if she did not play bridge. "You'd probably play a terrible game if you did," declared Peggy reassuringly, "and it's much cleverer of you to say you don't play at all. People hate amateurs." Peggy considered herself most professional.

Much to her surprise, she found that some of the new movies were quite fascinating, especially those that showed parts of the world where she had been. She even liked going to dances if she went with John, because he was so tall and led so perfectly. He taught her the newest dances in no time at all and thought it was great fun when she showed him how they waltzed in Europe. They almost cleared the ballroom floor as they whirled violently down the room, the couples scattering in alarm, then perching in safe vantage points on chairs and window sills to applaud. America was not half bad, she decided.

Her father was as good as his word. Every day he found for her something as interesting and beautiful as what she had seen in Europe. One day it was St. Patrick's Cathedral against the late afternoon sky. Another day it was the Cloisters, that miniature museum full of treasures, and one evening the lights of the city from the top of the Empire State Building. He took her to hear the Vienna Boy Choir, to eat in a Swedish restaurant with its groaning smörgåsbord, to see a new building with an Italian Renaissance façade, to stand spellbound before a Rembrandt in the Metropolitan. They wandered into shops full of Swedish and Russian handicrafts, German toys, Czechoslovakian glass, Danish silver, and Italian jewelry.

On Saturdays she went shopping with her mother, and they made a game of hunting for European styles. They found Tyrolean peaked hats and dirndl dresses, embroidered frocks from Dalmatia, evening cloaks like the medieval robes in the murals at Venice, Norwegian sweaters and mittens, English sport tweeds, blouses from Czechoslovakia, and of course lovely lingerie from Paris.

But she now began to see something else, too. She enjoyed all these familiar European things, and it was fun to eat Italian spaghetti, hear German opera, see exhibitions of modern French paintings, and plant Holland bulbs in the window boxes. But there was something else, something much more important. She was not quite sure yet what it was. The things that she was beginning to enjoy most of all were things that she had not seen anywhere else in the world, like the Radio City building, the old Van Cortland mansion, the New York skyline, paintings of snowy New England landscapes, murals of workmen straining at great machines, factory smoke in the sunset light, fields of asters and goldenrod, tall-spired, white country churches. These were real American things for real Americans.

All the other countries had brought their treasures, their talents and personalities, their racial traits and their rich traditions and backgrounds, and America had absorbed them all. But out of this great melting pot had grown other things that were magnificently American, young and strong and vital, and beautiful, too. She would never stop loving European things and would look forward eagerly to returning as often as she could, but now she would begin to use her eyes and ears for discovering America.

That night she slipped up behind her father, covering his eyes with her hands. "Guess who," she whispered in sepulchral tones.

"Julius Caesar," he guessed obediently.

She shook her head.

"Greta Garbo."

"No."

"Shakespeare."

"No, sir-ee."

This time he concentrated terrifically. "Alice in Wonderland."

"No, a thousand times no. I'm Christopher Columbus and I've just discovered America." She plumped herself down on his lap, long legs and all. "It's all your doing, and I haven't earned that football game, because you have kept your promise and shown me something thrilling every day since I came home. But please may I go, anyway? And do you suppose," pinching his nose very gently, "that you could possibly get an extra ticket for John?"

GLOSSARY

aber ja, but yes.

ach, ja, Oh, yes.

Alkmaar, community in northern Netherlands.

alles, all.

allons, (French) let's go! go on! you don't say?

Arpad, Magyar chieftain who led his people into the present Hungary.

Attilla, the Hun, king of the Huns, who plundered and demanded increased tribute from the people of Central Europe in the fifth century.

auch, also.

Augean stables, (Greek mythology) a king of Ellis whose stables contained an enormous amount of oxen, and remained uncleaned for many years. Hercules cleaned it in a day by diverting through it the rivers Alpheus and Peneus.

aurora borealis (northern lights), a luminous display across the sky at night supposedly caused by the upper atmosphere.

baroque, a style of architecture.

Bergen, a city and seaport of southwestern Norway.

bestu thakkirs, thank you.

bonjour, good morning.

Budapest, city, capital of Hungary.

Burgomeister, head of village.

Byzantine, a style of architecture developed by the Byzantine Empire.

campanile, a bell tower, especially one built separate from a church.

chalet, a herdsman's hut or cabin in the Swiss mountains.

compagnie, company.

crèche, (French) a representation of the stable at Bethlehem with the Infant Jesus, surrounded by Virgin Mary, St. Joseph, the oxen and asses, and adoring shepherds and Magi.

Crêpes Suzette, French pancake.

croissants, crescent-shaped rolls.

delft, a color, reddish-blue.

dolce, a sweet dessert.

Dalmatia, a region of Croatia.

déjeuner, lunch.

Diocletian, Roman Emperor, 284 to 305 A.D.

dirndl, (German) a dress with a tight bodice and a full skirt.

Doge, chief magistrate in the former republics of Venice and Genoa.

Dominican, a religious order of Roman Catholic preachers.

doucement, gently, calmly.

Dubrovnik, city in Croatia, formerly called Ragusa.

Festspielhaus, a festival play-house.

far la nanna, bambin, go to sleep, baby.

Franciscan, friars following the rule of St. Francis.

fiesta, a religious festival.

Frau, (German) a woman, especially a married woman; Mrs.

Friesland, province in northern Netherlands.

Giudecca, a Venetian island.

Glockenspiel, a series of graduated bells arranged on a rod; now, a series of graduated,
narrow metal plates arranged on a frame so as to produce bell-like tones when struck by a mallet.

goulash, a ragout of beef or veal flavored with paprika and vegetables.

Hardangerfjord, an inlet, southwestern Norway.

Hammerfest, northernmost city in Europe, on West Kval Island.

Hellbrunn, clear water.

Herr, (German) title of respect equivalent to English Mr.

hors d'oeuvre, a relish or appetizer, served usually at the beginning of the meal.

Huss, Jan, Bohemian religious reformer.

Ich bin, I am.

kaas, cheese.

kermis, a fair.

Krippe, (German) a representation of the stable at Bethlehem with the Infant Jesus, surrounded by Virgin Mary, St. Joseph, the oxen and asses, and adoring shepherds and Magi.

le jour de paix est arrivé, the day of peace has come.

Leyden (Leiden), city, Netherlands.

Lilla Mormor, little grandmother.

Lofoten Islands, two island groups in Norwegian Sea, northwest Norway,

loggia, a roofed, open gallery.

Lowestoft ware, a soft china made at Lowestoft, England, from 1757 to 1802.

mademoiselle, (French) an unmarried woman; Miss.

Magyars, one of a dominant people of Hungary,

ma pauvre mère, (French) my poor mother.

Marken, a small island in the Zuider Zee,
 Netherlands.

meine alte Mutter, (German) my old mother.

Mezőkövesd, town of northeastern Hungary, famous
 for its traditional costumes and fine embroideries.

mia madre, (Italian) my mother.

mustachio, a mustache.

Odin, Norse name for god Woden, chief Germanic
 god.

Oslo, formerly Kristiana, capital of Norway.

parler français, speak French,

pâté, a pie, patty, or pastry, also a delicately seasoned
 meat paste.

pâté de foie gras, patty or paste of fattened goose
 liver and truffles.

patois, dialect.

piazza, an open square.

pour les chères petites, for the dear little children.

prawn, edible shellfish.

pronto, quick, quickly, promptly.

Provençal, of or pertaining to Provence, France.

Provence, province in southeastern France.

pumpernickel, variety of bread made in northern
 Europe from unbolted rye flour.

Pyramus and Thisbe, (classic legend) a youth and
 maiden of Babylon.

Ragusa, Former name of Dubrovnik, a city in
 Croatia.

Rathaus, a town hall.

Reykjavik, town on coast, southwestern Iceland.

Rialto, famous bridge of Venice, a marble arch over Grand Canal.

Richard Coeur de Lion, former king of England and duke of Aquitaine and Normandy.

Salzburg, city in western Austria.

Sarajevo, city in Bosnia.

schnapps, a strong Holland gin.

Schuh-plattler, a Swiss dance.

Šibenik, seaport in Croatia.

sie sind die Kinder von, they are the children from.

siesta, a short sleep or rest, especially at midday.

Signor, a lord or gentleman, especially an Italian of distinction or rank.

Signorina, Miss.

Skagerak, arm of North Sea, south of Norway.

Skål (Skoal), an exclamation pledging health in drinking; a salutation or toast by crying "Skål!"

skyr, sour, curdled milk, also, a dish prepared from curds.

smörgåsbord, in Sweden, hors d'oeuvres.

Société de St. Jean, Society of St. John.

Spalato, Italian name for Split, Croatia.

stock-jaerre, a two-seated carriage.

Tack för maten, Thanks for the meal.

Tannenbaum, fir tree.

Tante, aunt.

Thor, Norse god of thunder, hence, of might and war.

Titania, (Shakespeare's *A Midsummer Night's Dream*) queen of fairies, wife of Oberon, king of fairies.

Tromsø, city and seaport, northern Norway.

Trondheim, seaport of Norway.

Tu vas bien, chérie? Are you all right, my dear?

un point, one point.

Vasa, Gustavus, ancient hero of Dalarna.

Versailles, former royal palace outside Paris; site of the Peace Conference following the First World War.

Viva l' Italia, Long live Italy.

voilà, there.

von, from.

wellsweep, a hand, water-raising device over a well used to raise or lower a bucket.

Wenceslaus, king and patron saint of Bohemia.

Whitsuntide, the week beginning with Whitsunday, i.e. the Christian Feast of Pentecost, especially the first three days.

Zagreb, capital city of Croatia.

Zeeland, province in southern Netherlands.

Zuider Zee, shallow inlet, formerly a lake which was connected with the North Sea by a great flood in the thirteenth century. A vast project was begun in 1920 to drain the Zuider Zee.

CPSIA information can be obtained
at www.ICGtesting.com
Printed in the USA
BVHW040347011021
617866BV00015B/1217

9 781950 843503